CRIME SCENE
JERUSALEM

CRIME SCENE JERUSALEM

ALTON GANSKY

COOK COMMUNICATIONS MINISTRIES
Colorado Springs, Colorado • Paris, Ontario
KINGSWAY COMMUNICATIONS LTD
Eastbourne, England

RiverOak® is an imprint of
Cook Communications Ministries, Colorado Springs, CO 80918
Cook Communications, Paris, Ontario
Kingsway Communications, Eastbourne, England

CRIME SCENE JERUSALEM
© 2007 Alton Gansky

Published in association with the literary agency of Spencerhill Associates, Ltd., PO Box 374, Chatham, NY 12037.

This story is a work of fiction. All characters and events are the product of the author's imagination. Any resemblance to any person, living or dead, is coincidental.

This novel deals with a twenty-first-century man caught in first-century Jerusalem. From time to time a first-century character quotes something he/she heard from the lips of Jesus. Since the story takes place in a time long before the canonization of the New Testament and modern translations, I faced a problem in how best to make such quotations and words that would become Scripture and still maintain the proper milieu. I chose to render the original languages into English myself using various sources that are listed in the bibliography. The quotations that appear in the text are "allusions" as would have been spoken by Aramaic-speaking Jews in first-century Palestine. Footnotes that state "Based on …" are my renderings of the biblical text.
—A. G.

Cover Design: BMB Design Inc.

First printing, 2007
Printed in the United States of America

1 2 3 4 5 6 7 8 9 10

ISBN 978-1-58919-096-2

LCCN: 2006932332

To the newest member of the family, the precious
"Cloe-bear." May the world learn to smile as often as
you do.

—Alton Gansky

Acknowledgments

I would like to extend my thanks and appreciation to Lt. David Cavanaugh, San Diego Police Department, and forensic specialist Jennifer C. Sanders for their kind help and insights. The tour through the Forensic Science Section was as memorable as it was enlightening. The Chinese lunch we had wasn't bad either.

Thanks also go to the great people at Cook Communications—editors, production, and, of course, the publishers.

My agent, Karen Solem, also deserves praise for putting up with my phone calls, e-mails, and odd questions. She has been and remains a source of wisdom for me.

Not to thank my wife, Becky, for her support, encouragement, and willingness to read the rough draft without complaint would be a crime.

—Alton Gansky

E-mail

To: Maxwell Odom < withheld >
From: Alton Gansky < alton@altongansky.com >

Well, here it is, Max: your story just as you told it to me. Will anyone believe it? I don't know, but I do know that I feel privileged to have been selected to help tell your story. Your account moved me and gave me much to think about. I hope you like it. I changed none of the facts or events that you experienced. I just tried to make it flow a little better.

Now it's time to launch this into the world. Maybe it will make a difference.

I still have a few questions, but I'll send them to you under separate cover.

Stay well, friend, and if you make any more strange trips like this one, please let me know. I want to hear every word of it.

Blessings,
Alton "Al" Gansky

chapter
1

He was young, no more than twenty-two or twenty-three. Age had yet to weather his olive skin, or dim the luster in his eyes. He walked with a bounce in his step, and pearl white teeth beamed when he smiled. He also talked nonstop. I wanted to remind him that he lived in one of the most troubled areas of the world; that terrorists walked his streets and planted bombs on school buses. If that wasn't enough to create a permanent dent in his enthusiasm, I considered informing him that he was shackled to a low-paying, dead-end job.

I kept my mouth shut. It was no fault of his that I was depressed. That was the problem with perky people—they annoyed those of us who prefer to be dismal.

"You will enjoy your stay here in the Jerusalem International Hotel, Mr. Odom." His words were muddied with accent. "We have the best of everything. You must try our restaurant. Our cook is the best in the city. You will thank me for recommending him to you."

I grunted, certain that he wanted a tip more than a thank-you.

He asked, "Where have you come from? Have you traveled far? Is this your first time in Jerusalem?"

We paused at the elevator doors and I thought it best to answer before he could spring another question.

"San Diego. Yes, it is far. Yes, this is my first time in Jerusalem."

"This is a wonderful city. You must take in all the sights. There is so much to see." He punched the white button on the wall next to the bronze elevator doors, then punched it again as if he could annoy the elevator into arriving sooner.

"I won't be here that long."

"No time to see Jerusalem?" He seemed crestfallen and looked at me as if I had begun to drool on myself.

I spoke before he could protest more. "The city has stood for centuries without my attention. I'm certain it will survive if I ignore the tourist traps."

My eyes burned and felt dry as autumn leaves. Hours in a Boeing 747-400 had exacted their toll: San Diego to New York and then on to Tel Aviv. From there a car carried me to Jerusalem. My back ached from sitting, and I longed for a healthy dose of quiet and the kind of distance from others only a hermit could appreciate.

"So you have come for business?"

Nodding, I looked back at the lobby with its rose-hued marble floors and artistic wrought-iron furnishings fleshed out with thick cushions dressed in durable gold-colored fabric. Several of the walls were made of limestone block, stacked in the same fashion as ancient buildings. Windows with black anodized aluminum frames stood in contrast with the block walls, the blending of contemporary with pseudo-ancient architecture. I had been in scores of hotels and the Jerusalem International rivaled the best of them.

A chime announced the arrival of the elevator and the exuberant bellhop pushed the luggage cart into the empty car. My baggage was minimal: a large suitcase with wheels, a carry-on bag, a computer bag with my laptop, and a black nylon bag that held my hanging clothes—two suits.

"This San Diego, it is in California, no?"

"It is in California, yes. Southern California."

He looked serious. "I shall go there someday. I wish to travel the world. I have seen pictures of your city. Very pretty."

"Not the part I see." He tilted his head to the side. I didn't offer to explain. "I assume the rest of my luggage has arrived?"

Another blinding smile. "Yes, Mr. Odom. I delivered them to your room only an hour ago."

"Good. That's good." I leaned against the back wall of the elevator and let it support my weight. The word *nap* was rapidly gaining importance in my life, and if the elevator didn't arrive soon the young bellhop would have to carry me to my room.

I got a break. The elevator made it to the twenty-third floor without a single stop. The last thing I wanted was some tourist lady reeking of perfume to join us.

I stole a glance at the bellhop. He bounced on the balls of his feet and I wondered how prevalent the use of methamphetamine was in Jerusalem. He had the antsy actions of someone familiar with speed.

15

Even thousands of miles from home I can't stop being a cop. It was time to focus on other things—if I could.

The doors parted and we made our way down a thickly carpeted corridor. Expensive-looking, bronze-trimmed sconces splashed yellow light on the beige walls.

"You will enjoy your room. It overlooks the Old City."

"I'm certain I will."

My room was at the end of the hall. A swipe of the electronic key card I had been given when I checked in disengaged the lock. I poured into the room like water pours into a glass. Mr. Happy followed, propping open the door with a small rubber wedge he removed from his pocket.

With practiced skill, he off-loaded my luggage, setting the suitcase on a short wood table designed to hold such things. The garment bag he hung in the closet and my laptop case he set on a cherry table that served as a desk.

The room set me back on my heels. My hosts had spared no cost. Soft white plaster walls surrounded me. Pseudo-stone Ottoman archways graced the doorway between the living room and the bedroom. The suite was furnished with a sofa and a wide coffee table with a glass sheet over a woven Persian tapestry. Everything about the room glinted with the sheen of expense— everything but the small black television that rested in an arched niche. Apparently the American fascination with large-screen TVs hadn't made it to this part of the world. On the exterior wall were arched windows framed in the same anodized aluminum I saw in the lobby. Beyond the window was the monochromatic Old City of Jerusalem.

The suite was far more than I expected. Originally, the meeting planner had arranged for me to stay in a different, less opulent hotel but something had gone wrong with the arrangements.

When I tried to check in, they said they had no record of my reservation and were booked solid. A call to the meeting planner set things in motion. Either he upgraded my room as an unspoken apology or this was the only room left in the city. Either way, I was the beneficiary.

Beneath one of the two windows was a pair of cardboard boxes, a UPS sticker affixed to each. My packages had arrived and I could see no dents or tears to indicate rough treatment. That was a relief.

"I will help you with those," the bellhop said and shouldered past me.

"No, that's all right."

He hunkered down and lifted one of the boxes to the wide coffee table.

"It is no problem. It is my pleasure to help." He removed a penknife from his pocket and cut the tape that held the box lid secure.

"I said I would take care of it."

He ignored me. No doubt visions of a large tip danced in his brain. He pulled the box open.

I quick-stepped forward and seized his arm, spinning him. "I said leave it alone." I gave the arm a sharp tug.

His skin paled and his eyes widened. Genuine fear draped his face. I let go and unclenched my teeth.

"I'm ... I'm sorry, Mr. Odom," he said and took a step back. He rubbed his arm and I felt two inches tall.

"No, I'm the one who is sorry. I'm not feeling well," I lied. "I'm afraid all the traveling has stolen my manners." I removed my wallet, opened it, and extracted a twenty. He would have no trouble converting the currency.

He didn't move.

17

"Please." I wiggled it, encouraging him to take my guilt offering. "You've been a big help. The hotel is lucky to have a man like you."

The compliment made him smile. He took the cash with a small bow.

I felt relief. The last thing I needed was an assault-and-battery charge on a hotel employee while a guest in a foreign city. If he made issue of it, I could be out on my ear with no place to stay, or worse, a place to stay in the local jail. I could see the newspaper headlines: AMERICAN CRIMINOLOGIST ATTACKS LOCAL HOTEL EMPLOYEE. I apologized again.

He bounced from the room with the same energy he entered. The door closed behind him. I stood drained, wallet still in hand. My eyes moved from the door to a full-length mirror that hung on one of the walls. The shell of a man looked back. He held the same wallet and wore the same gray dress pants, white polo shirt, and stood about the same height—except the man in the mirror hunched slightly like a man who had just finished carrying a bag of concrete mix on each shoulder. His hair revealed the same color brown and receding hairline, but looked less combed than it should. He also appeared twenty pounds lighter and fifty years frailer. I found no pleasure looking at the reflection. Why were mirrors so doggedly truthful?

I walked to the desk and tossed my billfold onto its smooth, unmarred surface. The wallet fell open and an American Express card escaped and the flap over the photo section flopped back. It contained only one picture, the image of three happy people. I was one of them, looking like my reflection should look.

The sight of the photo opened a drain in my feet, and my soul poured out. I reached forward to close the billfold but had to pause over the old image. My fingers lowered to the surface and I touched the photo as if uncertain of its reality.

It was real. I closed the wallet. I was sick of reality.

I turned my back on the desk and wallet and moved through the arched opening to the sleeping area. A king-size bed dressed in a thick crimson spread reigned over the room. Several chairs were situated around the expansive space, and a small, round table stood like a sentry in the corner. Another small television rested on a delicate iron stand.

I stripped off my shirt, kicked off my shoes, and shed the rest of my clothing. A minute later, hot water stung my skin as I stood in the shower. I let the water flood down my back and cascade over my head, and I fought back tears that threatened to add to the flow.

Twenty minutes later, washed, dried, and under control, I crawled onto the plush bed and closed my eyes. Lying on my back, arms stretched to the side like a diver in a swan dive, I wished for sleep. I wouldn't be needed for another two hours. I would need to be my best then and a nap would make me all the better. The problem with sleep is the more you wait for it, the more reluctant it is to arrive.

I tried to empty my mind but my thoughts, like bees in a bottle, were impossible to control. Still I refused to give in. I wasn't moving from the bed. A mist of memory swirled in my brain....

✝✝✝

"Because I told you to. That ends the matter."

Bruce Yates sat behind a metal desk that had endured at least fifteen years of work. At one time it was a handsome piece of furniture, but it had endured too many hours of service. Its surface was scarred and stained by a thousand coffee cups. Bruce Yates didn't look any better. Two years from retirement, he wore the

19

mantle of a man with thirty years of police experience—thirty hard years. He had been my supervisor for most of my career. As the director of the Forensics Science Section of the San Diego Police Department, he piloted a busy ship.

"I'm fine. I don't need a leave of absence," I said. I crossed my arms as if the motion would add the needed exclamation point. I was doing my best to be intimidating.

Yates doesn't intimidate. Decades of trading blows with politicians, lawyers, criminals, and more had left him with a thick emotional callus.

"You're not fine, Max. You're a mess, and you've stretched my patience to the failure point. I've cut you some slack, maybe too much slack."

"I'm one of the best investigators you have—check that—I *am* the best investigator you have, not to mention the most unique." My position did not fit the norm of the forensics unit. Most employees in this section were forensic specialists—people who gathered evidence from a scene—or forensic scientists—the folks who did the higher science. None were cops. None except me. I had trained and worked in a city where homicide detectives often served as forensic specialists. When the department hired me on, they dropped me in homicide. Before long I had worked myself into a hybrid of two sections. I was a one-of-a-kind in this department.

"I won't argue that, but it changes nothing. You're skating on thin ice. That's bad enough, but I'm on the ice with you. I don't plan to get wet."

My jaw tightened.

He raised a finger. "Be very careful what you say next. It only takes a pen stroke for me to make your leave permanent."

"You're being unfair."

"And you sound like a child. Unfair? I've been more than

fair. I've received six complaints about you interfering with the investigation."

"They're moving too slow."

"The detectives and investigators are moving at the same speed you do when you work a case."

"This is different," I protested. Protesting was easier than facing the fact that he was right.

"It's different for you. It *should* be different." He paused and let his tone settle. "I can't pretend to understand what you're going through, but you can't continue to poke your nose into the process. I've run interference for you, but I can guarantee that if you do not rein yourself in, the next call I receive will be from the Old Man himself. Then things will be way out of my control."

"No one is going to bring the chief into this."

"Detective Hernandez has already threatened to do so. I did him a solid favor a couple o' months ago so he owes me. I had to call in that chip to keep your fanny out of the fire."

"All I'm trying to do is lend my experience to the case."

"No you're not. You're seeking revenge." He paused. "Not that I can blame you."

"It's not about revenge, Bruce." It was a hollow protest. That's exactly what it was about.

The tension in the room congealed. I stood my ground, determined not to budge, but I knew it to be a lost cause. Bruce cut through it with soft words. "Max. We can argue all day but when all is said and done, you're taking a leave of absence. I think you need it; more importantly, the department shrink thinks you need it."

"And if I refuse to take leave?"

"Then you'll be packing your stuff in cardboard boxes. It's not like I have any choice in the matter, Max. Suck it up and take the leave."

21

I could no longer hold my arms crossed. There were only two of us in the room, and I was the only one pretending things were about to change. The vacuum inside me expanded and I felt ready to implode.

"Bruce … I … never mind."

"You what?" He leaned back in his chair, and it protested with a piercing screech.

"I don't want to just sit around for two weeks. I … I don't want to be alone in the house." Hearing my words stunned me. My gut had been screaming that truth but my mouth had refused to give the feeling freedom. "I need something to do, something else to focus on. Give me a case and I'll stay out of everyone's way. And I won't go near the investigation. I promise."

Bruce studied me, pursed his lips, then looked at the ceiling. "No can do, Max, but I might be able to do something else for you. How do you feel about travel?"

"You know I travel. I do at least one conference a year on scientific investigations. I did the FBI Academy last year and taught a symposium to JAG investigators."

"I'm talking about a few more miles than those trips. I have a request from the Israeli police for someone to speak to their forensic department on evidentiary protocol."

"I thought they had a top-notch department," I said.

"They do. After the tsunami of December 2004, they sent a team to locate and identify seven Israelis who died when the wave struck. They identified all seven—out of three hundred thousand dead. They know what they're doing."

"So why ask outsiders for help?"

"Not help, Max. Knowledge. They're one of the best because they bring in the best to improve what they do. Truth is we might learn a few things from them. You want the gig?"

"When would I leave?"

"Two days."

"Why so quick? This thing must have been in the works for months."

Bruce nodded. "It has been. Steve Lessing was going but he's out with appendicitis. He's not going anywhere for a while."

"All the more reason to keep me around," I said. "Steve does the work of two men. Without him, you're going to be severely shorthanded."

Bruce raised his hands to his face and rubbed as if scrubbing off dirt. He rose, leaned over the desk. "Okay, here it is, Max. You can go on leave or you can take this out-of-country trip. Truth is, I'm gonna catch it as it is just for offering the trip to you. Still, I'm willing to take a little executive slapping to help you get back on the road to normalcy."

"I'm telling you, I am normal."

Bruce slammed his hand down on the old desk and the sound of it shook the pictures on the wall.

"No, you are not. I say so, the shrink says so, and everyone in the department says so. No one can be normal so soon after the event. Go home or take the trip. Decide now, because you're leaving my office in the next thirty seconds."

I pushed him too far. I've seen Bruce angry before, but this was several notches above anything I thought him capable of. I assumed he was acting for my benefit. It was a good act.

"I'll take the trip."

chapter
2

Sleep must have found me. A jarring *bliiiing-riiiing* yanked me from slumber, pulling me through miles of hazy consciousness until I bolted upright in the bed. I don't recall sitting up or draping my legs over the edge of the mattress, but nonetheless, that was what I was doing.

The phone sounded again with its odd ring-ring pattern. My heart tumbled like a stone down a hill. Not fully awake, I snapped up the receiver.

"Yeah ... I mean, hello."

"Mr. Odom, this is the front desk. Your driver is here to pick you up."

"Driver?" I blinked and tried to corral my thoughts. "Oh yes, of course. I've been expecting him." I looked at the alarm clock at the side of the bed. The driver was ten minutes early. That was good for me. "Please tell him I'll be down in ten minutes."

I hung up and took several deep breaths. A vile film coated the inside of my mouth and I smacked my lips a few times. That would have to be dealt with.

Seven minutes later I was dressed, the post-nap film had been evicted from my mouth, my hair was combed, and I was ready to go.

Almost ready.

I fast-stepped to the living room of the suite and saw one open cardboard box—the box opened by the bellhop before my civility slipped a cog—and one sealed container. It took only a few moments to extract the contents I had shipped from the United States. I lumbered to the door with a pair of aluminum-clad cases in hand and exited. A minute later I was in the elevator headed to the lobby. This time it made four stops before disgorging its contents of six people into the wide hall off the lobby. I let the others exit first, then lugged my cases with me into the bustling community of tourists who chatted loudly about all they had seen. Through the expansive lobby windows, I could see three tour buses, a line of taxis, and a stream of cars on the street.

Weary but excited tourists made the lobby a beehive, and I had to move slowly through the coagulation of humanity. Finally, I pressed through to the concierge, a man with droopy brown eyes, gave my name, and told him I was looking for my driver. He nodded and pointed toward one of the windows just to the left of the door.

25

"The tall man. The one standing at the window. He gave his name as Yoshua ben Joseph."

I thanked the man and started to the front of the lobby. I felt like a salmon swimming upstream. Reluctantly, the gibbering mass of travelers parted before me and I forced my way to within a few feet of the driver.

He had his back to me but I could tell that he was tall, slim, and well proportioned. His hair was a shade lighter than coal and trimmed close to the scalp. He wore a black pullover, collarless shirt, khaki pants, and plain white sneakers. He seemed untroubled by the noise, the hubbub, or the rapidly filling lobby.

"Mr. ben Joseph? Yoshua ben Joseph?"

He turned and smiled. The grin seemed genuine, as if he had been looking forward to this moment. I judged him to be in his midthirties. His skin was a shade darker than the bellhop and his eyes were chocolate brown. He wore no beard and no yarmulke. I had done my homework. I knew Orthodox Jews wore the skullcap at all times while the less-strict groups wore them only at prayer time.

"I am Yoshua ben Joseph."

I set my cases down and held out my right hand. "I'm Maxwell Odom. I was told that you were my driver."

He looked at my hand for a moment, then took it in his and shook firmly. His was a strong hand with long fingers.

"Shall we go?" He motioned toward the door.

Looking the way he directed, I saw several cars that could be his. "I suppose we should."

With a turn he started toward the doors leaving me to carry the cases alone. *There goes your tip, pal.*

Ten steps and fifteen "excuse-me-pleases" later, I reached the entrance doors. So many people were filing in and out that the automatic doors were stuck open. I prepared myself to exchange the bedlam of the lobby for the chaos of the street and crossed the threshold—

Wrong. All wrong.

I stood as still as if I had not only looked into the face of Medusa but kissed her full on the mouth. The parts of my body that moved were my knees, which shook like leaves in a tornado. My stomach plunged, my heart stuttered, and my lungs went on strike.

Everything was wrong.

"A stroke," I muttered. "I've had a stroke."

In front of me—right where the busy asphalt street bore the weight of buses and automobiles—was a dirt street that hosted the foot traffic of men and women. The only vehicles I saw were wood carts pulled by donkeys. Some were towed by men.

A chicken ran across my path.

I wanted to rub my eyes but my emotional paralysis prevented it. Instead, I blinked, and blinked again. Then I closed my eyes for long seconds. Once I opened them again, I saw the same scene I had tried to shut out.

Things began to sway. No, that wasn't correct. It was me that was swaying. My knees felt hollow, my spine morphed into Jell-O. Darkness edged in from the periphery of my eyes. In a moment I would be down. Passing out seemed a good idea.

Something touched my shoulder. A hand.

"Take a deep breath." Yoshua stood next to me. His eyes expressed concern, but the hint of grin on his face made me think he was enjoying this.

"But ... Where? ... How?"

"Breathe," he said. "Good, now again."

Air flooded my lungs as I forced myself to inhale. My heart slowed to a rate I'd expect if I had just reached the summit of Mt. Everest. I felt certain that it was about to shatter my sternum and shoot out of my chest.

27

"Aside. Move aside." A new voice. I cranked my head in the direction of the sound and saw—it couldn't be.

"I said, move aside."

A pair of men approached. Still stunned, I stood my ground. The sight of them contributed to my confusion. They wore crested metal helmets, short armor made of leather strips reinforced with bronze. Each held a javelin that was two feet taller than its owner. The man closest to us lowered his javelin and swung it in a horizontal arch. It struck me on the chest. It would have hurt more, maybe even broke the skin, if Yoshua hadn't yanked me back.

They walked on. The man who hit me said something and the other laughed. As they walked down the dusty street, men and women parted before them like water before the bow of a great ship.

"Those were ..." I began. "Why are those men dressed like Roman soldiers?"

"Hard to say. My guess is, it's because they are Roman soldiers."

I set my cases down and rubbed the spot of impact. I checked for blood. There was none. The man wanted to inflict pain but not injury. He was good at it.

As I watched them walk away, stunned confusion changed to anger. "I'm not going to let him get away with that." My cop attitude kicked in.

"Yes you are," Yoshua said. "Even without the javelin, sword, and dagger, he's more than a match for you. Besides, you'd have to fight him, his friend, and those two over there." He pointed. I looked and saw two more soldiers, their red capes fluttering in the hot air.

I bent over, placed my hands on my legs, and inhaled deeply. I had never lost my mind before, so I was uncertain what to do. This seemed as good an action as any.

The air was thick with heat, dust, animal smells, and laced with the aroma of cooking food. The overpowering smells turned my stomach.

Bleaup.

The sound was loud and close. I jumped back and raised my head in time to see a wall of hairy hide walk by. It took a second for me to realize I was gazing at the broadside of a camel.

Bleaup.

Apparently an unhealthy camel. The sound that came from the front end of the beast paled to that which erupted from the rear. I took several steps back.

"I did not need to see that," I complained. "I've got to get out of here ... get back."

I turned and looked for the glass entrance doors to the hotel. Instead of seeing a twenty-four-story stone, steel, and glass structure, I saw a two-story mud and stone building. It had only one wood plank door, and one window with no glazing, just a square hole in the wall with a cracked wood lattice.

"Come with me," Yoshua said. It sounded like an order.

"Where's the hotel? Where are the cars, the buses ...?"

"Come with me."

I faced Yoshua. "Come with you, where?"

"You need to sit down."

"Ya think? I need more than a chair; I need a hospital and a psychiatrist. This can't be real."

"Don't forget your cases." He turned and started to walk away.

I considered staying put until I felt a tug on my pants leg. I swiveled around and gasped. A bent man with white eyes and no pupils stood behind me with his hand held out. His beard was matted and he smelled vile. "Alms? Alms? HaShem will bless those who give alms to the poor."

Standing next to him was a boy of eight or nine years. "Alms for my father?"

"I ... I ..." I had lost the ability to speak and I was making a fool of myself proving it.

Suddenly, Yoshua was beside me again. He pulled aside his cloak and opened a small leather pouch. From it, he removed a coin and handed it to the cataract man.

"May the God of our fathers bless you," the old man said.

"And you," Yoshua said. The boy and beggar walked toward the next person on the street.

The boy gave me the once-over. "Sir, your clothing is strange—"

The beggar groped for the boy and found his shoulder. "Come, come, do not return kindness with questions."

"This will go much better if you stay with me." Yoshua picked up my cases and handed them to me. I took them. A second later I was following him down the street.

"How come you're dressed differently?" When I met him just a few minutes before, he had on a collarless shirt, slacks, and sneakers; now he wore an outer robelike garment over a tunic that reached to the knee, a leather belt, and sandals. I glanced down at my own clothes, which were the same as I had put on in the hotel room. I suddenly felt very conspicuous.

"This is how we dress here."

"Here? Where is here?"

"Jerusalem, Max. We're still in Jerusalem." He kept walking, taking long strides. I had to hustle to keep up, dodging people in the street who looked at me as if I had just stepped off a spaceship—if they knew what a spaceship was.

"This isn't Jerusalem, pal. I saw Jerusalem from the air. I did some homework before coming here and I saw pictures of

Jerusalem. This isn't it. This is … is … the set for a movie. Is that it? Somehow, someway, we ended up on the set of a movie."

"See any cameras?"

No, smart guy, I don't see any cameras. "Okay, then. I've had a psychotic break. I've gone around the bend, lost my mind, slipped a cog, derailed, gone nuts—"

"Your mind is fine," he stated, "although your actions indicate otherwise."

"What should my actions be? One moment I'm walking from a modern hotel and the next I'm being smacked in the chest with a javelin by a guy in a metal helmet, approached by a blind beggar, and backpedaling from a camel with a nasty habit."

"Here, sit down." He stopped in front of a stone building and pointed to a table and two benches located under a striped cloth awning. Several other tables and benches filled the space. Only one of them had occupants, two men who reclined on the benches and chatted.

"What is this place?"

Yoshua smiled. "Fast food." He walked through the maze of tables and was met by a short man with a stringy salt-and-pepper beard. The man nodded and disappeared through a doorway. Yoshua returned, sat on one of the benches, swung his legs up, and lowered himself to its surface, propping himself up on his left elbow.

I sat, setting my cases next to me.

"Feel better?" Yoshua asked.

"No. And why are you lying down?"

"It is the way we eat here. People recline at table, not sit."

"I'm not reclining anywhere. Take me back."

"Back where?"

I buried my face in my hands. A moment later I raised my

31

head and said, "Back to the hotel—the real hotel—the one with glass windows, a concierge, chipper bellhops, and twenty-four floors."

"No."

"This isn't happening. It can't be. If I walk far enough down that street, I'll be back where all this began. It has to be that simple."

Yoshua smiled. "If you walk far enough down that street, you'll be in the Hinnom Valley. It's the city's trash dump."

Anger threatened to take over my confusion. I started to say something else when the man I saw Yoshua speaking to stepped to the table and set down a wood platter with food and two metal cups. He stepped away and returned a moment later with a clay pitcher and what looked like a hiker's water bag.

Yoshua sat up and pointed at the food. "Salted fish, dried fish, grapes, figs, and bread. Eat. It will make you feel better."

"I doubt it."

He shook his head. "There are those in the world who can only feel content when unhappy. You, Maxwell Odom, are their poster child." He took the engorged bag from the table and poured a deep red fluid into the cups. He then took the jug and poured water.

"Drink up."

"What is it?" I drew the cup close and sniffed it.

"Water and wine. It's good for you. Besides, the wine will help calm your nerves."

"You water down the wine?"

"No, we wine the water. The alcohol helps purify it."

32

There were things floating in the water, particles from the fermenting I assumed. I pushed the cup away and looked at my guide. He had closed his eyes and tilted his head back. He held his hands shoulder high.

"Blessed art thou, Jehovah our God, King of the world, who causes to come forth bread from the earth." He opened his eyes, lowered his hands, then reclined on the bench again. A moment later he reached forward, and took a piece of dark-brown fish and nibbled it.

"Why are you doing this to me?" I asked.

He studied me for a moment. "There's something I want you to see. More accurately, there are some things I want you to examine."

"Examine."

"That's what you do, isn't it? Examine evidence, details, recon-struct events?"

"You want me to do forensic work? You gotta be kidding. Here? In this place—wherever or whatever this place is?"

"I told you, this place is Jerusalem. You've been asking the wrong question. Our 'where' hasn't changed, but our 'when' has. This is Jerusalem all right. First-century Jerusalem."

I shook my head. "Not a chance. No such thing as time travel."

"Yet here you sit."

I replied, "I'm more inclined to believe that a blood vessel has ruptured in my brain and I'm lying on the bed in my hotel room dreaming all this."

"Well then, you won't mind looking at a few places in your dreamworld. What have you got to lose?" He pushed the platter toward me. "Here, at least eat some imaginary grapes. I still think you should try the fantasy fish. I don't want you to insult our host."

"Make fun of me all you want, but I'm not playing along." I turned my attention to the street. A dog, a mere fur-lined skeleton, trotted down the street, its head held low and skirting any close contact with anything on two legs. I noticed something else: Many people walked with their heads down. I knew enough history to

33

know that this was an occupied land—the real first-century Israel, not this ... wherever I was.

Women, dirt-brown robes reaching their ankles, strolled the street. Some carried pails of water, others examined produce in road-side markets. Still others had young children in tow. A cloth covered their heads. I could see very little difference between the clothing of men and women, except that the cloth used for the women seemed more delicate. I saw a few women whose robes were embroidered at the hem.

Occasionally a woman walked by who didn't fit the mold. One such woman wore no head cover; her hair hung to the shoulders and her garments seemed far more delicate and expensive. I guessed she was the wife of some Roman big shot. Whoever created this set had gone to a lot of work. I had to ask myself: *Why?*

I cut my eyes to Yoshua. He was watching me and I could see a patina of pleasure on his face. He was enjoying this. Not gloating. Not amused at my confusion. He didn't seem that coldhearted. To me he looked like a man who had just drawn his fourth ace from the deck.

I started to say something snide when a booming voice rolled across the narrow street. Heads turned. Mine, too. Directly across from us, standing between two vendors, stood a tall man with a long gray beard. The beard hadn't seen a pair of scissors in years, if ever. Unlike the other men I had seen, his clothing bore no trace of dirt, not even dust from the street. His outer garment was a pale white, and a head cloth with two wide blue stripes draped the side of his face and hung to his shoulders. A string of tassels lined the garment. At the end of his full-length robe dangled four tassels, similar to what Yoshua wore, one from each corner. The hooded man's tassels, however, were larger and brighter.

Helping him stick out like a polar bear in Texas was a small box tied to his forehead by a leather strap. He wore another such

34

box on the back of his left hand; the leather straps binding it to his flesh ran up the full length of his arm.

"Shema Yisrael Yahweh elohaynu Yahweh echad.[1] Hear, O Israel, the Lord is our God, the Lord is one. Blessed is he who says the Shema." He looked at those in the street. A few stopped, many continued on their way.

He raised his voice another ten decibels. "I thank you, Lord, that there remain among us those who have not bowed the knee to false gods; people like me who hold you in their hearts. I thank you that I have been selected to be your servant. Deliver us, O Lord, from those who hold our bonds, and those who have deserted you to associate with the pagans who hold not your name as precious...."

"Oh, brother," I mumbled. I looked at Yoshua who stared at the braying man across the street. "That guy is full of himself."

"He is a Pharisee." Yoshua kept his gaze fixed on the man, the glower on his face a billboard of his displeasure at what he saw.

"A Pharisee?"

"A member of a powerful group of religious laymen."

"You don't seem pleased to see him," I prodded.

"Pretenders," Yoshua said. "Their words sound full of faith but they are full of illusion."

"Now, now, it isn't nice to rain on someone else's parade." If I was going to be stuck in this illusion, I might as well have fun at Yoshua's expense. After all, he started it with that "imaginary grapes" and "fantasy fish" crack.

He turned his attention to me. There was no anger in his eyes, no expression of annoyance, but I did pick up a hint of hurt. "They trouble the people. They add religious burdens that weigh down the hearts of the people. They are the keepers of rules."

"We all need rules. Rules keep things in check, moving smoothly."

Yoshua's expression changed. "Do you believe that?" Something in his eyes made me think he knew more about me than he was letting on.

"There are times when rules should be bent," I admitted. I returned my gaze to the loud man. I had no desire to keep eye contact with the man reclined across the table from me.

"He doesn't look like the others. What is that thing on his forehead?"

"A phylactery. In Aramaic we call it a tefflin. It's a small box with a tiny piece of parchment inside. On the parchment is a verse of Scripture. He has another phylactery on his left hand."

"Seems an odd practice," I said.

"It has a purpose." Yoshua turned his face skyward then said, "And it shall be to you a sign on your hand, and for a memorial between your eyes, so that the law of Jehovah is in your mouth, for by a strong hand has Jehovah brought you out from Egypt."[2] He looked at me. "Do you understand?"

"Yeah. You're saying that the guy is taking some Bible verse literally and is wearing Scripture to remind him of something."

"Of God's provision and of his Word."

"But you think this guy is a pretender. He seems religious enough to me."

"He is a performer. His prayer should be done in private, not done for show."

Something occurred to me. "Why is he speaking English?"

"He's not. His prayer is in Hebrew."

"No way. I don't speak Hebrew. I know English when I hear it."

"Do you know Greek, Latin, Aramaic when you hear it?" He reached for the fish.

"I'd probably recognize it, but that guy isn't talking in any of those languages. It's English all right."

"There are many languages spoken here." He bit off a piece of dried fish. "The Jews you see speak Aramaic. It's a language similar to Hebrew. Hebrew is our religious language. The Romans speak Latin and business is conducted in Greek."

"Four languages. And everyone speaks all four?"

"Many do. They have at least a working knowledge of most of them. The Jewish men learn Hebrew as boys in the synagogue, girls learn it at home. All Jews speak Aramaic."

"The beggar spoke English," I insisted.

Yoshua shook his head. "Aramaic. The Pharisee is using his Hebrew because the Scriptures are in Hebrew."

"I'm telling you I don't know those languages. There's no way I would understand them. I'm hearing English."

Yoshua shrugged and pointed at the Pharisee. Something had changed.

"Elohay baka ba tachtiy...." Al-eebowshaah Al-ya`altsuw 'oy-abay liy Gam kaal-qoweykaa lo' yeeboshuw Yeeboshuw habowgadiym reeyqaam ..."[3]

"What ...?"

"... Your ways, O Jehovah, cause me to know, your paths teach me. Cause me to walk in your truth, and teach me, for you are the God of my salvation. Near you I have waited all the day. Remember your mercies, O Jehovah, and your kindnesses are from the ages."[4]

"Did you do that?" It was as if someone had flipped a language switch and the Pharisee changed midsentence.

"Is there a problem?"

"You know what I mean. That guy is with you, isn't he? He's in on all this. A hired actor."

"I thought you said this was all a dream or the result of a stroke. Now it's an elaborate stage play?"

"I mentioned that this was a fancy set, like a movie set."

37

He smiled. "That's right. You did."

"I'll figure this out, you know—unless I'm right about the stroke. In that case, I'm bleeding into my brain and all of this will disappear when I die."

"You are a morbid man, Max Odom."

"I'm practical. It's the way I was trained. I'm a man of facts."

Yoshua laughed. "As long as the facts suit your needs."

"You don't know me," I shot back. "You know nothing about me. You think you've sized me up in the few minutes we've been together?"

"Max," Yoshua began in soft tones, "you'd be surprised at what I know."

I turned from him. I'd had all of the man I could take. The Pharisee rattled on.

"How long is he going to be doing that?"

Yoshua pushed up from the bench. "Longer than I care to hear. Come on, it's time for you to get to work."

"Work? What do you mean, work?"

He didn't answer. Instead, he rose and started down the street. I was tempted to stay put.

I didn't.

chapter 3

Again I worked my way through the crowded, narrow street, five paces behind Yoshua. He moved at a steady speed, not fast, but quick enough to leave me behind if I didn't keep shoe leather to hard pack. The cases seemed to grow heavier every few steps. I am in pretty good condition for a middle-aged man, but the shock of what I was experiencing was sapping my energy as if I were running up a hill—and we were moving uphill.

I wanted to call out to him to slow down, to wait until I caught up, but I reeled in the urge. It didn't matter, I told myself. None of this was real. I was hiking through my imagination, strolling through a dream or the creation of a damaged brain. In any case, it would all end soon and I would I either awaken or succumb to whatever medical condition dropped me in this place that could not exist.

The last thought worried me. Was I dying? Was this the fabrication of a brain damaged by the mounting pressure of blood against gray matter? Maybe I had fallen in the shower and everything since had been the work of an overactive subconscious.

Maybe.

If so, then my presence would be missed. I was due to deliver a lecture on advances in field forensics, and if I didn't show, someone would check my room. After all, I was dealing with scientists, military police, and cops. That's the way our kind think. Right? I had to be right. Perhaps I was already resting in a Jerusalem hospital while doctors worked to make right whatever had gone wrong.

Perhaps.

It had to be something like that, I reasoned with myself. Time travel is impossible, and what Yoshua suggested meant that I had gone backward in time to the first century.

But it was all so real.

I could see people walking, hear them talking. Dogs barked. Camels yapped. Goats bleated. As we moved from the narrow market area, Yoshua turned up a street narrower than the one we had been on. Houses, some only the size of shipping containers, lined both sides of the lane. Like the other buildings I had seen, these were made of mud brick, although some had been cobbled together with uncut stone. Each building had only one or two windows and those were covered with a lattice of thin wood.

Each house had a courtyard circumscribed by a stone wall. Each enclosure had a fire pit and what looked to me like a clay oven. In some of the courtyards, animals rested in the afternoon sun. Women, old and young, worked at sewing or cooking. Children played. A wind from the west pushed smoke from the fires into the cerulean sky. It was then I noticed that most of the courtyards were situated on the east side of the houses. Better to make use of the prevailing winds, I told myself.

All the houses stood with their single door open. Since there were so few windows, I could see very little of what lay inside. It was like peering into a cave rather than a home. To my eye, it looked like the lowest form of poverty. Cramped houses, no plumbing, no comforts. Yet the people didn't seem to notice. If I were back in San Diego, the city council would long ago have declared the area blighted, claimed eminent domain, and put up another strip mall.

I jogged a few steps until I caught up with Yoshua. When I came alongside, he gave me a glance and a smile.

"Who are these people?" I asked.

"Which people?"

"All these people." I raised the kit in my right hand and tried to point to one of the homes.

"They're just the people of Jerusalem."

"They live in such squalor."

Yoshua stopped abruptly. "Squalor? You think this is squalor?"

"Of course it is. They have nothing."

He looked sad. "You think wealth is measured by what one has in life?"

"Yeah, that seems pretty straightforward. Don't you think?"

"I think wealth is measured by *who* one has in their life, not *what*." He looked at the small houses. "It's true, there are bigger homes, grander homes, but this is not squalor. People have lived like this for centuries, most happily.

41

"Here, houses are not showpieces. The house is where one sleeps and stores provision. The courtyard is where they live. They are a community; neighbors who gather to share meals and conversation. In your time, people use houses to keep others out."

"You're a romantic. I see only poor people."

"Odd, I see only people."

He started walking again.

This path, like the previous, was uphill.

"Where are we going?" I asked.

"The upper city."

"The what?"

"Just stay with me."

I tried, but unencumbered with a pair of field kits, he moved faster. I had the feeling that walking was his preferred means of travel.

The buildings changed as we made our way up the grade. The community we had left reminded me of a pile of boxes, as if a gigantic UPS truck had lost its load. Here, instead of buildings of mud brick, timber, and uncut stone were houses erected with hand-cut stone dressed with plaster. They were larger, too—five to ten times larger. Instead of flat roofs, many of the homes had tiles. I knew enough history to recognize a Roman influence on the architecture. Some of the buildings boasted marble, and unlike the lower city where each home had a small courtyard, these mansions rested behind courtyards filled with gardens and pools. They also had furniture, something I had not seen in the poorer homes.

42

"I don't think we're in Kansas anymore, Toto," I quipped. "I bet this is the section of town the chamber of commerce likes to show off."

Yoshua paused and looked around. "This is where the rich live." His words bore no animosity. He seemed a man making a casual observation.

Everything I saw confirmed his simple statement. The roads were wider and cleaner, and fewer animals roamed the streets. I gazed at a small group of men gathered into a tight circle and debating something. They wore the same Jewish clothing I had seen earlier, except their garb was cleaner and clearly made from better material. I also saw more women moving about, also dressed in finer apparel. Roman women with their flowing, gossamer dresses and short, uncovered hair, stood out like a searchlight in the midst of candles.

"What are we doing here?"

"This way," he replied.

"That doesn't answer my question."

"It will."

We moved east and I grew weary of walking without knowing why and where I was going, but the situation held me captive. At the moment, I was a puppy on the end of fate's leash. I could scamper around all I wanted and tug against the restraint, but in the end I'd still be tethered.

I had spent some time with the police chaplain—to be accurate, he spent time with me. I hadn't called him, but he came by and perched on my sofa for a solid hour. At one point in the conversation he said, "Life is like riding a raft down a wide river. Most of the time it's smooth sailing, but every once in a while the white waters come up on us. In those cases, the best we can do is hold on tight until we're on the other side."

43

I thought it a stupid metaphor then, and my opinion hasn't changed. Nonetheless, I felt like I was on that dumb raft again, and Yoshua was the only one with oars.

I fell behind Yoshua as we continued. The streets, although wide, were filling with people and that swimming upstream feeling came over me again. I was jostled and jostled back in return. No one seemed to mind—except me.

"How many people live here?" I asked Yoshua.

"About twenty-five thousand."

"It seems a lot more than that."

He slowed until we were again shoulder to shoulder. "You see the wall, don't you?"

I shot a glance at the towering gray friction-fitted stone wall. "It's a little hard to miss."

"It encircles the city. Even so, it is only three and a half miles long. Jerusalem sits on a single square mile."

"And twenty-five thousand people fit inside the walls?" That seemed beyond belief.

"Normally, it is enough, but this is the season of holy days. The population is many times the norm. Jews have come from all over the world to be here. Some stay in the city; many others stay outside the walls."

"Kind of like New Orleans during Mardi Gras."

"No, it is nothing like Mardi Gras."

The words came with barbs. I decided not to press the point.

After another hundred steps we came to a stop in front of a wide limestone block home. It was two stories tall, the second story taking up only half the area of the first floor. The rest of the second floor was balcony. Several latticed windows punctured the front wall, which was recessed behind an arch colonnade. A set of exterior wood stairs led to the second level.

Yoshua moved to the stairs and started up. I followed.

"Shouldn't we check in with the owner?" He didn't answer. Instead, he trotted up the last few steps and pushed open a thick

44

panel door. I followed but at a slower pace. "Do you know what B and E is? It means breaking and entering."

Against my better judgment, I traced Yoshua's steps and entered the upper structure.

"What do you see?"

"What do I see? Is this some kind of test?" I set my kits down.

"It began here." He gazed forward. I detected sadness in his words. "Nothing has been moved."

I worked my hands, clenching and releasing, trying to work out the finger cramps brought on by my field kits. I said nothing. I didn't move. In truth, I didn't know what was being asked of me.

"What do you see?" Yoshua repeated. "Use your God-given skills."

"My skills come from hard work and study."

Yoshua didn't seem in the mood to argue. He stood statue still and I got the feeling he could outwait a slab of granite.

"Okay, I'll play along, but you're not going to like my bill."

I took a deep breath and focused on the room. It was a single space, the only walls being those that defined the exterior. Two windows, each with a wood lattice like those I had seen on other homes, let in enough light for me to see and cast stripes of shadow on the floor and furnishings.

I followed a well-practiced pattern. The first thing I did was look down at my feet, then the rest of the floor. Many investigations are bungled by careless people, and sometimes cops, who walk on evidence. Preserving a scene remained the first order of the day.

The floor was covered in flat but uneven wood planks roughly a foot wide. The wood was unpolished but sanded smooth. I saw nothing on the floor to make me think a violent crime had taken place. No blood. Always a good sign.

45

Certain that I wasn't crushing evidence under my size elevens, I moved toward the center of the room. A long hewed-timber table dominated the center of the space.

Benches with cushions surrounded the table, branching away like spokes from a rectangular hub. The pillows were simple linen and devoid of decoration. Unlike bed pillows, these were flat. I thought of Yoshua reclining at the table in the market eatery.

On the table rested several copper plates and earthenware bowls, as well as three pitchers. On the plates rested the leg bones of some animal that had become dinner. Several pieces of flat bread were visible.

"I thought you said nothing has been moved."

"I did." Yoshua held his place by the entry door.

"I see serving platters and enough couches for a dozen or more people, but there are no plates for the guests."

"Plates?"

"You know, dinnerware ... plates to put your food on. There are no forks or knives."

"Ah. Such things aren't used here. Food is served on platters set in the middle of the table."

"How do you get your food?" I pressed.

"With your hands, of course. Bread is used to sop up the juices."

"You mean everyone just reaches in and grabs whatever they want?" My mother was certainly rolling over in her grave.

"It's a little more civilized than that."

46

"I'll bet."

Keeping my hands to myself, I stepped between two of the couches and leaned over one of the earthenware pitchers. I couldn't see inside. I thought of returning to my kits and making use of one of the flashlights—alternate light sources as we call them in the business. Instead, I lowered my nose to the opening and took a sniff.

"Wine." It smelled sweeter than any wine I had experienced.

I stepped back from the table and looked around the room again. Something was in the corner. Checking my steps, I made my way to the objects. A large hammered metal basin, another but larger pitcher, and a long white linen towel rested on the floor. At the end of the towel, I could see dark stains.

Returning to my kits, I donned a pair of latex gloves and retrieved a high-intensity penlight. Squatting, I shone the light on the dark spots of the towel enabling me to get a better look. It didn't take years of training to recognize dirt when I saw it. I picked up the bowl. It felt heavy. Under the light, I could see a residue of dirt at the bottom.

"Well, the bowl is dry, which means that it wasn't used recently. That's consistent with the bread on the table, which is about as stale as bread can get." I stood. "I don't see any signs of a violent crime here, pal, although there is plenty of evidence of a felonious assault on a defenseless dinner."

"Do you make light of everything?" Yoshua asked.

"Pretty much. Especially in situations that make no sense. What am I supposed to see here? Where are we?"

"Most people call it the upper room."

"The upper room, eh … *the* upper room? The one where Jesus held the Last Supper? That upper room?"

"Yes. You've heard of it?"

"Of course I've heard of it." I looked around. Could this really be the place?

"How did you hear of it?"

"My parents made me go to Sunday school when I was a kid."

47

"They were faithful people?"

I shrugged. "Faithful enough to drop me off in the parking lot every Sunday morning and pick me up after they had gone to their favorite restaurant for breakfast."

Yoshua frowned. "What did they teach you in Sunday school?"

"About the Last Supper?" My mind backpedaled four decades until I could see old Mrs. Roberts. Looking back, I realized I couldn't recall her first name. Maybe I never knew it. I smiled as her image floated to the forefront of my mind. I remember thinking she was old, but I doubt she had reached thirty-five. I was older now than she was then. At the tender age of nine, everyone over twenty looks old. "I recall a picture she held up. It was a print of Leonardo da Vinci's painting. The one he painted on the walls of some monastery."

"Santa Maria delle Grazie in Milan, Italy."

"If you say so." I looked around the room. "This looks nothing like the painting."

Yoshua chortled. "That painting was done almost fifteen hundred years after the fact. There's nothing Jewish about it. The furniture, the room, almost everything is Italian."

"I suppose you have a point there."

"Who are you?" The voice startled me. It was new and about an octave higher than Yoshua's. I snapped my head to the doorway. There stood a serious-looking young man.

"We're friends," Yoshua said. "Don't be afraid."

The young man's eyes darted from Yoshua to me and back again. Not more than five foot six in stature, he was thin, with a scraggly beard that was more peach fuzz than hair. I doubted that he had seen eighteen years of life yet. He stood on the threshold, his body at a slight angle, one shoulder still outside. He looked ready to bolt.

"I don't know you." He stared at me as if he suspected me of picking his pockets.

I said nothing. His sudden appearance had taken me aback. Again I wondered if this place had laws about breaking and entering.

"I am Yoshua, a friend of the Master's."

The young man glared at my guide. His eyes moistened and I expected a trickle of tears.

"You know the Rabbi?"

Yoshua nodded. "This man is named Maxwell son of Odom."

"Max is fine."

He looked me up and down. "Your clothing ... are you Greek?"

"He is a foreigner, Mark," Yoshua said before I could speak.

The man Yoshua had called Mark took a step back. "How do you know my name?"

"Your bravery is well known and spoken of by many."

He seemed to soften. "I am not brave." As if to disprove his own point, he pushed by Yoshua and went to the table. "Are you here to rent the room?" He began to gather the stale bread, stacking it neatly on a platter.

"No," Yoshua said. "I wanted Max to see this place."

"I should have cleaned it earlier ... I left the bread out ... It's been ... As you know there's been trouble in the city."

"Yes, I know." Yoshua stepped to my side and spoke softly. "To Jews, bread is considered a gift from God. One does not waste it or leave it to go bad. He's embarrassed."

I didn't care about bread. I saw something that caught my attention. "Mark ... it is Mark, right?"

He didn't turn. "Yes."

"I'm a little out of place here, Mark, so forgive me if I step on

49

some obscure custom, but I need to ask you about those marks on your neck."

Without turning, he raised and touched four angry-looking scratches.

I looked to Yoshua. He picked up on my unspoken question and gave me a nod. I approached in measured steps. "May I see?"

He straightened but didn't turn, and he made no motion toward the door or toward me. For that, I was grateful.

With a gentle touch I pulled back the robe and the undergarment he wore. Four blazing red marks reached from below and behind his left ear to the top of his shoulder. They were scratch marks, thin gouges made by a human hand. I had seen thousands in my career, usually delivered by a woman fending off an attacker. I had a feeling that it wasn't a woman who gave these to him. They looked too deep and wide.

I looked at the rest of his neck then asked him to turn. It surprised me that he did so on the first request. Yoshua had called him a brave man, but he looked like a teenager who had just had all the life hollowed out of him with a very dull spoon.

"May I look at your arms?"

Yoshua joined me as Mark raised his hands and held them out. I pushed back the sleeves of the robe. On the outside of his left arm were another set of abrasions. I saw something else: deep blue bruises covered both forearms.

"Where I come from, Mark, these are called defensive wounds. You've been fighting."

He nodded.

"I assume you earned the scratches the same way."

He turned back to the table and resumed cleaning. I frowned. A second later I noticed Yoshua staring at me. "What?"

Once again he nodded at Mark.

"This is nuts," I mumbled. "Mark, who were you fighting with?"

He didn't answer.

"Did you start the fight?"

"No. It was not a true fight."

"Those bruises tell me that you were fending off an attack by a least one person."

"There was more than one. Many more. Only two or three came close to me."

"You were in a fistfight with three people?" That didn't seem right. If he had been throwing punches, I would have seen scraped and swollen knuckles. His hands were fine. I shared that fact with him.

"I did not strike anyone. They came after me."

"Who came after you, Mark?"

He faced me again. At first his face was filled with fury and his eyes blazed in anger, but it lasted only a second or two. The bitter cold of utter brokenness replaced the heat of anger. He slumped to one of the couches, his head down as if counting the nails in the floorboards.

"I tried to follow … I wanted to help … to be there for him." He shook his head. Then his shoulders began to quake. "There were so many. More than I could count. At first, I followed at a distance. I was afraid to get any closer.... I … I …"

I moved the padded bench opposite Mark and sat down. "Tell it from the beginning, son. Take your time." I started to make a snide remark about my having centuries worth of time, but my professionalism put on the brakes. I held my tongue and waited for the crushed young man to tell his story. I knew how to wait. I waited to hear stories of rape, murder, assault, and everything else imaginable. I could wait for this tale.

51

"The Rabbi and his disciples celebrated Passover in this room. He had made arrangements with my father."

"Your father owns this house?"

"Yes. He is a man of means. He rents this upper chamber during the holy days. The Rabbi had made arrangements. Some of his disciples came to my father and said, 'The Teacher says, "Where is my guest-chamber that I may eat the Passover meal with my disciples?"'[1] They came to him while he was ... carrying a pitcher of water."[2]

That cocked my head to the side. Yoshua picked up on my confusion. "In this society, women normally carry the water. A man with a water pitcher stands out."

"My mother had gone to market," Mark explained. "I have no sisters."

"No shame in a man doing what needs to be done," I said. Mark looked up, puzzled. "Never mind. Go on with your story."

"We prepared the Passover meal for the Rabbi then left to attend our family celebration."

"How well do you know this Rabbi?"

"Everyone knows of him, but my family knows him well. We were honored to have him under our roof. I had hoped to be his disciple one day."

"Then what happened?"

"We celebrated our Passover meal. Not long after we finished, I heard the Rabbi leave with his disciples. Many were whispering among themselves. They seemed upset."

"About what?"

"I don't know. I went to bed. But in the late night someone began banging on our door. I thought they would knock it down. I covered myself in my bed linen and answered the door. My father joined me a moment later. Outside was a large crowd. A huge crowd." He stood and began to pace. "They stood there staring at us; they had torches, and I saw that some carried clubs."

"The crowd was at your door?"

"No. They stood some distance off, but I could see them well enough. Only three men stood at the door. I could see the anger on their faces, the hatred in their eyes." Tears trickled down his cheeks.

"What did they say?"

"'Where is he?' they demanded. 'Who?' my father asked. 'You know who.'

"I heard the sound of people on the stairs. A group of men were making their way down from this room. They were temple guards.

"My father said, 'He has gone. He is no longer here.' The men were not satisfied. They threatened to search the house, but someone stopped them. He said, 'I know where he is.'"

Mark stopped speaking and I studied him for a moment. He was a cracked eggshell on the verge of splitting open. I gave him a few moments before asking, "Who said he knew where the Rabbi was?"

"It was ... one of his disciples. I have seen him with the Rabbi many times. It was Judas Iscariot who spoke. He told the men to follow him."

Judas was a name I recognized easily enough. There's a reason mothers don't name their children Judas. Hearing the name of the traitor had put the exclamation point on a thought I had sequestered in the dungeon of my mind. Yoshua wanted me to track Jesus. As illusions go, this was a doozy.

53

"How could Judas know where Jesus had gone? Clearly he hadn't left with them."

"The same way *I* knew were the Rabbi had gone. He went

there often when he came to Jerusalem." Mark raised his head. "I closed the door. I had never seen such a large group before. There were Roman guards, temple police, men from the chief priests."

"Do not be ashamed of your fear," Yoshua said softly. He took a seat next to Mark. "We all have felt fear."

Mark began to shake his head. "My cowardice made me hesitate. I waited too long ... too long. My father and I argued. I wanted to warn the Rabbi, but my father feared for my life. He ordered me to bed. I went."

"But you didn't stay, did you?" I said. "You got those bruises and scratches because you fought with some of the men."

"I ..." He looked up as if confessing a grievous sin. "I waited for a time, then I could wait no longer. I wrapped my bed linen around me and ran from the house to the garden." He lowered his head again. A tear fell to the floor and was absorbed immediately, swallowed as deeply as Mark's remorse threatened to ingest him.

He continued, "I waited too long. The mob had already taken him. I followed, trying to be invisible in the night, but I couldn't even do that. I must have made too much noise. They were headed back into the city. Some men at the back turned and chased me. I ran, but one of the men caught me from behind. He tried to grab me but missed."

"Is that where the scratches on your neck came from?" I pointed to his wounds.

"Yes. I fell but got up quickly. The man began to strike me. I raised my arms to defend myself but he was too strong. He reached for one of my arms but caught only the linen I was wearing. I wrestled free of it and ran ... and ran. I can still hear him and some of the others laughing at my nakedness ... I can still hear ..."[3] He raised his hands to his face. Sobs came in convulsive waves.

54

I have never been good at these moments. More times than I can count I have had to face a distraught parent or spouse or child so overcome that logic and reason were drowned in hot, raw emotion. I had developed a pat response: "I promise that the department will do everything in its power to get to the bottom of this." Then I would direct them to the detective in charge of the case. They were useless words; plaster meant to cover the calloused soul I had developed.

Yoshua was the most articulate. He put an arm around Mark and let him weep.

chapter
4

I stopped and set my field cases down.

"I'm done, finis, kaput." I positioned one of the cases so that it rested flat on a level piece of ground. Then I sat on it.

Yoshua halted and turned. He was ten paces ahead of me. I was sucking air by the barrelful, but he seemed unfazed by the brisk walk. He had maintained that separation since we passed through the gate in the thick stone wall that surrounded Jerusalem. He called the opening The Fountain Gate.

"Are they heavy?" He motioned to my field kits.

"They're heavy enough. They're not designed to be carried on long hikes, especially by an out of shape guy in his late forties."

My fingers were stiff from lugging the boxy kits. I had been at this business for eighteen years and had never carried a field kit more than fifty yards. Since leaving the strange second-floor room in the southwestern part of the city, I had carted these things through the upper city, lower city, and out the southeastern wall. Yoshua led me down the steep embankment at the base of the wall until we reached a dry riverbed; he then marched us north.

He nodded in a manner that said nothing, approached me, and then sat down on the ground crossing his long legs in front of him. He picked up a twig and studied it as if a message had been carved in its side.

The sun was sliding toward the horizon, and the spring night conjured up a light breeze that caressed my warm skin and set leaves to dancing on the branches of trees. It felt good, but not good enough to change my mood. "I'm staying here."

Yoshua continued to eye the twig. "How long will you need to rest?"

"You're not hearing me. I'm not going any farther. This whole thing is ridiculous. I've played along up to now, but my patience has reached its end."

"That happens a lot, doesn't it, Max?"

"What? Me losing my patience? Yeah, it does. Not that it's any of your business." I felt a twinge of guilt at my rudeness then gave myself a slap across the mind. You can't offend an illusion.

I pulled my left shoe off and emptied a small amount of dirt on the ground. It wasn't enough to make a decent anthill, but it felt like half a hillside on my insole. "I keep telling myself that this is a hyper-real dream and that I'll wake any moment."

Yoshua raised his eyes to meet mine. "And if it isn't?"

"Then I've suffered a psychotic break. Bad dreams I can deem the result of simple neurosis, but this ..." I moved my hand in a

57

sweeping arc indicating the valley we just walked through and the hillside upon which we sat. "This is the result of a mind that has come loose from its moorings, unable to distinguish between reality and fiction. That's the difference you know."

"Difference?"

"Between neurosis and psychosis." I shifted my weight. The field kit made a lousy chair. "I had a psych instructor in college who said everyone was neurotic in some way. Some smoke cigarettes, some drink too much, some avoid crowds, others seek attention, others overeat, but the really interesting people were psychotics because they don't know if you are real or not."

"Seems a cold thing to say." He tossed the twig.

"Perhaps, but it got a good laugh."

I gazed across the valley. Makeshift tents dotted the slopes. We had passed many of the shelters on our journey to this point. Fire pits sat in front of many of the tents. Some of the shelters were occupied, others stood empty, their owners conducting some kind of business in the city, I supposed.

"Who are those people?" I asked. "The ones in the tents."

"Pilgrims. Some have traveled a great distance."[1]

"Pilgrims? Oh, you mean for Passover."

Yoshua nodded.

"When we were in the second-floor dining room, you led me to believe Passover had been several days ago. Why are these folks still here?"

"The Feast of Weeks is ahead. Some have stayed for it."

"Feast of Weeks?"

"Feast of Weeks, Feast of Harvest, the Day of First Fruit, Shavuot ... Pentecost."

"I recognize Pentecost." Then I admitted I didn't know what it meant.

"It's the Greek word for the Feast of Weeks. It means 'fifty.' The Feast of Weeks begins after a week of weeks—forty-nine days after the first Sabbath of Passover. The feast begins the day after that— the fiftieth day. It's a festival of thanksgiving. In the future it will become a celebration of the day God gave the Law to Moshe— Moses."

"How can you know what's going to happen? ... Never mind. You were with me in the twenty-first century. This whole time thing is giving me a headache."

I returned my gaze to the valley. "They camp out there for weeks?"

"Those that can, do. Those who live in nearby towns travel back to Jerusalem when necessary. Those from some distance away, stay."

I shifted my gaze farther across the valley again. We sat on the eastern side of the Kidron Valley. Across the way I could see the thick stone walls of Jerusalem, each stone carefully situated, held in place by gravity and friction. No mortar in those walls. From our elevated vantage I could see a wide, rectangular structure. A massive stone courtyard surrounded it. The structure stood proud amidst the other buildings of the city. Sunlight glinted off portions of the exterior. I knew enough history to know I was looking upon the great temple of Jerusalem.

"It seems out of place," I said.

"What does?"

"The temple." I pointed to the distant building. "When I flew in, I could see a different building standing there. The Dome of the Rock. It was hard to miss."

Yoshua looked sad as he nodded his head. "There have been two temples. I suppose we could say three. What you're looking at is the result of Herod the Great's work. The first temple was built by King Solomon a thousand years before this time, three thousand before yours. It was glorious in every way; covered inside and out with gold, made of stone and cedar, all crafted by the most skilled workmen. It took seven years to build, and when it was dedicated, the fire of God descended upon it."

"Fire of God, eh? What happened to it?"

"The Babylonians pillaged and burned it six hundred years ago."[2]

"So another temple was built?"

"Fifty years later, exiles who had returned from captivity in Babylon began construction. That temple was only a shadow of what once stood there. Still, it remained for over five hundred years."

"That's the temple I'm looking at today?"

Yoshua shrugged. "In a way. About fifty years ago, Herod the Great began restoring and adding to the second temple.[3] Work continues. It won't be finished for another thirty-five years or so."[4]

"I suppose it's something a nation can be proud of." I rubbed the small of my back. The longer I sat, the less comfortable I felt.

Sadness overshadowed my guide. "Forty years from now, the Romans will destroy it. They will kill thousands in the process. All that will remain is a foundation wall."

"The Wailing Wall," I ventured.

He stood. "It's time to go. The sun will be setting soon." He started up the grade.

"I told you I wasn't going to budge from this spot." I crossed my arms and waited for Yoshua to stop.

He didn't.

"I'll wake up soon," I told myself. Unless, of course, I had had a stroke and all of this was fantasy foisted upon me by a damaged brain. That thought gave me chills. The idea of me lying on a hotel bed, unable to move or to cry out for help lodged ice cubes in my spine.

I watched as Yoshua moved slowly up the hillside.

"You're fooling yourself if you think you can outbluff me," I shouted. "I don't manipulate that easily."

I know he heard me. I had been loud enough to be heard across a football field. Still, he didn't turn; he didn't falter.

"If he thinks I'm just going to follow after him, then he has another think coming." I stood and stretched my back. *Right here. Yes, sir, this is were I am going to stay.*

Yoshua kept walking. I shook my head.

Two minutes later I picked up my kits and started after him.

†T†

I found Yoshua standing at a rough wood gate fixed in a four-foot-high stone wall. He was leaning on the gate and gazing into the distance. The wall was little more than uncut rocks piled one upon another, but it seemed sturdy. Over the wall I could see clusters of trees, some flowering plants, and fresh spring grass. The breeze continued to make music with the leaves.

"I hope I didn't keep you waiting," I snapped. My sour mood had curdled. I waited for the "I told you so," but it never came. He didn't even look at me when I stepped to his side and set my field kits down.

"This is what I wanted you to see." He nodded to the area inside the perimeter wall.

61

I let my eyes trace the objects before me. The stone wall circumscribed an area of two or three acres. Unlike the area outside the enclosure the trees were pruned and the plants were lined in order. Someone had taken great pains to make the space pleasing to the eye. I had to admit it was inviting.

"It's a garden," Yoshua said.

"I figured that. Who does it belong to?"

"Mark's family. They've owned it for several generations."[5]

"Mark? The same young man we met in the upper room?"

"Yes."

I looked the area over again. It was serene. Spring had arrived and flowers had bloomed to meet it. Trees stretched their twisted limbs as if trying to tickle the sky. A large stone device stood near the center of the garden. A rough wheel with a hole cut in the center rested upon a basalt base.

"What kind of trees are these?" I asked.

"Most are olive trees."

"I assume that stone contraption is an olive press." I pointed.

He looked at me and smiled, as if I were a child who just took hold of a difficult concept. "You're right. That's why they call this place Gethsemane. The word means 'olive press.' Olive oil is used for food and as fuel for lamps. It's very important in this culture. Very symbolic."

The name Gethsemane drew vague recollections from my childhood Sunday school class. "This is where Jesus prayed before Judas betrayed him."

"This is where the worst of it began. From the upper room to here, Jesus taught his disciples. There were only eleven then. Judas had left to do what only Judas would do." He took a step back from the gate. "Here's where your work begins. Tell me what you see."

62

I didn't expect to find much. I had a Swiss-cheese understanding of the story of Christ, but I knew enough to understand that he didn't die here. I doubted that there would be much to see, and I started to tell Yoshua so, but I didn't. I am trained to look for the unexpected in unexpected places. My experience wouldn't let me turn my back. Besides, I detected a note of challenge in Yoshua's words, and I love a challenge—even one that comes to me in a dream.

"Shall we go in?" he asked.

"Not yet." I forced my eyes to trace my surroundings. The ground was slightly moist, and new spring grass was pushing its way through the soil. That's when I saw them. "How many people come here?"

"Not many," Yoshua answered. "Why?"

"Look down at your feet. What do you see?"

"The ground. The grass."

"What about the ground and grass?"

"You mean the footprints?"

It was my turn to smile. "Yeah, I mean the footprints. Judging by how the grass is trampled down and the soft earth depressed, I would say we had a small gathering of people here."

I stooped to study the impressions. There were several sizes, but all were large enough to tell me that they belonged to men. None of the impressions had sole marks. I wore modern footwear. I could see the shape of Yoshua's sandals as well as those from my own Bostonian oxfords. Although the sole prints didn't have a manufactured pattern, they were made distinct by cracks and wear marks. It was clear that these were made by sandals.

"Judging by the various sizes and the unique markings, there must have been a half dozen or more men standing here. That's odd isn't it?"

"Odd?"

"If, as you say, Jesus went through the gate and into the garden area, then why did a small group of men stand around outside the perimeter wall?"

63

He closed his eyes and spoke. "Then Jesus came with them to a place called Gethsemane and said to the disciples, 'Sit down while I go off to that place to prayer.' And having taken with him Peter and the two sons of Zebedee, he was afflicted with grief and distress."[6]

"What's that?" I rose and stepped to the wall.

"It's from the Bible. The gospel of Matthew." He stepped closer to me.

I opened one of my cases and removed a flashlight. The light directs a focused beam. There was still some daylight, but the extra illumination would help me direct my gaze and could reveal something I would otherwise miss such as ... I removed a pair of tweezers from my kit and a small paper evidence bag.

"What did you find?" Yoshua said.

I pinched the jaws of the disposable tweezers shut on a single strand of material. "I assume people of this era make their clothing from wool."

"Wool or flax," he agreed.[7]

"Well, this little guy tells me that someone wearing a wool tunic sat on the wall." I placed the white strand in the bag and sealed it, then felt stupid. I was gathering evidence as if I had a trace lab waiting to process it. I doubted such a lab existed in the first century, and when I woke up from this bizarre nightmare, whatever evidence I gathered wouldn't exist. Old habits die hard.

"What can you tell from that?"

"Not much. If I could send it to a crime lab, the technicians could prove that it is wool. If we had the cloak or tunic or whatever it came from, then we might be able to show a match, but that would be stretching things. Right now all I can say is that someone, probably one of the people who left the footprints, sat on this wall and left a little bit of his clothing behind."

I examined the wall some more and found another few strands, which, out of deference to my training, I bagged and stored. I closed my kit.

"I assume you quoted that Bible verse for a reason," I said.

Yoshua nodded. "The biblical record shows that Jesus took only three of his eleven remaining disciples into the garden with him."[8]

"I thought there were twelve ... oh, right. Judas had already taken off." I looked at the ground impressions. There were enough footprints to indicate that a dozen people had been here. If this were a real crime scene, I'd make casts, but it wasn't and I had no intention of carting plaster casts around with me even if my kits contained the ingredients and other things needed to do the job—which they didn't. I felt foolish enough plucking wool fibers from a stone wall.

I stepped to the gate and could see footfalls leading into the enclosed garden. In some places they were clear; over areas of stiffer soil, they disappeared. There were enough impressions for me to believe that a smaller group than those outside the gate had moved through. If Yoshua was right, then there should be four sets of prints. It looked right.

Careful of where my feet landed, I moved through the gate and followed the light impressions. I could hear Yoshua behind me. The footprints came and went. Despite the uneven terrain, I was able to trace them for about fifty or sixty yards to a place under an ancient-looking olive tree.

"They separate," I said. One set of footprints led away from the tree ... and returned. That wasn't quite right either. Before me were enough prints to indicate that three of the four remained near the tree and one of them moved off to the left. I followed the lone tracks. Not fifteen feet away, things changed. Once again I crouched to study the ground.

65

"Found something?"

I didn't look up. "See these impressions?" I pointed at four indentations in the soft soil. Grass was clumped at the distal end of each indentation. "Someone fell here. These two back ones were probably made by the subject's knees; these two a little farther along are from his hands. It looks like he dug the heels of his hands in the ground while trying to break his fall. It was a hard landing. I bet it hurt."

Backtracking a few steps, I noticed that the spacing of the footfalls was different. "Can you see how the stride has changed? He was staggering."

"How can you tell?" Yoshua leaned over the footprints.

"When a man walks, he does so in a heel-to-toe fashion. That means that the heel of the foot lands with greater weight. When a person runs, they tend to push off with their toes and the balls of their feet. But when someone staggers, everything changes. The feet come down flat and slide, they separate and splay as the person struggles to remain upright, and the distance between the steps decreases remarkably. Look how close the last few strides are."

I rose and moved along the trail. "Whatever it was, it came on him quick. One moment, he's walking normally; the next, he staggers and falls facedown, digging his knees and hands into the ground. It couldn't have been pleasant."

A few steps later I added, "Look here, the tracks continue on in the same troubled pattern. He got up." I found similar impressions to the knee and hand indentations a few feet back. "He fell again." I turned to Yoshua. "Got any Bible for that?"

It turns out he did.

"Then he said to them, 'My soul is encircled and overwhelmed with anguish, so much so that I am close to dying. Remain here and watch with me.' And having gone forward a little he fell to his face."[9]

"You got quite a memory, pal."

He shrugged. "Some things are worth memorizing." He studied the ground. "That was from Matthew's gospel. The gospel of Mark says, 'And having gone on ahead a little, he dropped repeatedly to the ground, and was praying that if it were possible, the hour might pass from him.'"[10]

"Sounds like Mark got it right. Hey, is that the same Mark as—"

"Yes, it is. Maybe I should say, 'will be.'"

I moved on. The trail ended abruptly with the same evidence of another fall. "Looks like this is the end of the line." I directed my light to an area of grass that was pressed down. It didn't take much imagination to see that a man had fallen here and remained for some time. The grass was disturbed as if whoever left the impression had been writhing. Of course, there wasn't a clear outline of a human form. There never is, but a couple of decades at looking where bodies had landed after being bludgeoned, shot, stabbed, or otherwise done in had trained my eye to find the little clues.

"I thought Jesus came to the garden to pray," I said.

"He did. Why?"

I removed a premoistened swab and dabbed at one of several brown spots on the grass. The sterile cotton tip gathered some of the material. I studied it. It resembled coagulated blood but not as dense as I would expect. There was one way to find out. I snatched up a small white plastic bottle from my kit.

"What's that?" Yoshua leaned over.

"Phenolphthalein." With one hand, I opened the thin spout. "This is similar to the Kastle-Meyer Color Test. The phenolphthalein turns pink in the presence of blood ... and potatoes and horseradish, but I don't see any of that around here."[11]

The clear drops touched the swab. Pink.

"Blood," I said. "But ..." I wasn't certain how to finish the sentence.

"You seem uncertain."

I returned the plastic bottle to its place and deposited the swab in a sealable plastic tube. "Sometimes a criminal will try to wash away blood to conceal his or her crime but that's close to impossible to do effectively. In those cases I find blood that has been diluted. These spots are blood, but they look a little thin." I shook my head. "The pattern is off as well."

"I see a dozen or so spots spread out on the ground. What's wrong with that?"

I turned my face to Yoshua. Every time he asked a question, I had the feeling he was playing dumb, that he knew more than he was letting on.

"There's a whole science to interpreting blood splatter. If a man is shot in the back and the bullet exits his chest, the resulting blood splatter will be different than if he had been stabbed or bludgeoned with a baseball bat."

"And these stains tell you what?"

I returned my attention to the pattern. "The blood isn't streaked. The ground is an uneven surface, but I would still expect some streaking if this was a scene of violence. This indicates that blood fell straight down and the splatter indicates that the fall was short, as if the man were on his hands and knees. What I can't figure out is why the density, the viscosity of the blood is so thin. I need a lab for that."

Yoshua was smiling.

"What's got you grinning? You're going to quote more Bible aren't you?"

"I won't if you'd rather I didn't."

"Knock yourself out, pal. I plan on waking up soon anyway."

"Being in agony he prayed fervently; and his sweat became like drops of blood, dropping down upon the ground."[12]

"What's that supposed to mean? Does it mean he sweat like he was bleeding or that he actually sweat blood?"

"Can a man sweat blood?"

"No. Of course not … well, there is hematidrosis in which the skin capillaries break near the surface and mix with perspiration. That would explain the thin nature of the blood splatter."

"Wouldn't it also explain the drop pattern?" For a moment I though Yoshua had read my mind.

"Yes, it would, but do you know how rare a condition that is? It's usually associated with extreme physical strain; psychogenic stresses. Even then there have been just a handful of cases in the last century."[13] The spots of blood fixed my attention. Could Jesus have really been in such psychophysical distress to actually sweat blood? "It's the least likely explanation."

"What is the most likely explanation?"

Yoshua was beginning to annoy me. "I don't know."

"Do you know what language the New Testament was written in?"

Where'd that come from? I admitted that I didn't know.

"Greek," he said. "Common Greek to be exact. It's a very precise language often having several descriptive terms where English has only one. The word used for blood in the passage I quoted is *thromboi.*"

"Thromboi? Like thrombosis? A clot of blood?"

69

"That's where the medical term comes from." Yoshua seemed to sadden. "If we rendered the Greek literally, the passage would read, 'And he sweat clots of blood.'"

"He felt that much fear?"

"Maybe he prayed that hard."

That took me aback. I knew psychological aberrations could bring about physical responses but not something like this.

"In college I learned of psychology students blindfolding volunteers then telling them they were about to feel something hot. They then touched them with a piece of ice. The volunteers reacted as if they had been branded with a hot iron and some even raised blisters. That is the power of the mind."

"The students you mentioned were fooled into believing something that wasn't true. Jesus wasn't fooled."

I had nothing to say. My mind was spinning, and my only desire was to wake up from this nightmare. I couldn't process what I was seeing and hearing.

Awkward minutes passed as I looked at the ground that bore evidence of a man who staggered and fell and who, by some mechanism beyond my learning, bled without being injured. How fervently must a man pray to bring on the rare disorder of sweating blood?

"Something else bothers me," I admitted. "How did the blood reach the ground? Jesus would have been dressed, right? Judging by your clothing and what I've seen other men wearing, there isn't much exposed skin for blood and sweat to fall from."

"Have you ever played sports, Max?"

"When I was younger. I liked racquetball."

"Ever sweat through your clothing?"

"Sure, but that's after an hour of extreme physical exertion."

Yoshua cocked his head to the side.

"That must have been some prayer," I remarked and studied the stains again. "I suppose I could be looking at bloody sweat from his face and neck." That disturbed me and I lapsed into silence.

Yoshua cleared his throat. "I'm a little surprised that you haven't mentioned the other footprints." The silence was broken.

"The ones that lead back to the place where the others waited for him. I saw them. I do one thing at a time and do it well, only then do I move on. I was going to get to those, although we already know what they mean. Jesus came here and collapsed then returned to the guys he left behind, then came back. My guess is that he did that at least twice."

"Three times."[14]

"If you already know all this, then what am I doing here? If you believe all the Bible mumbo jumbo, then why ask me for proof? If you're having doubts, then talk to a preacher."

Yoshua paused before speaking. He looked me hard in the eyes.

"I'm not the one with doubts, Max."

chapter
5

Your buddy Mark said that a mob came to his door." I stood, but my eyes remained fixed to the ground.

"Yes, he did." Yoshua stepped to my side.

"We should be able to find evidence for a group that large having been here." With deliberate steps I moved forward in a zigzag fashion, tracing the ground, plants, and surroundings for signs that a crowd had trampled a portion of the garden. It didn't take long.

The sight stunned me. Grass, flowers, and bushes in an area I judged to be a hundred feet wide and twice that long showed signs of trampling. The size of it kept me from making an accurate assessment. I was just guessing.

"How big a mob was this?" I wondered aloud.

Yoshua answered with what I took to be another quote from the Bible. "After he said these things, Jesus went with his disciples across the brook Kidron[1] to a garden, into which he and his disciples entered. Judas, who was betraying him, knew the place, because Jesus frequently met with his disciples there. Judas took the company of soldiers and officers from the chief priests and from the Pharisees there. They came with torches and lamps and weapons."[2]

"One of the gospels again?"

"Yes."

"You could have been an actor with that memory of yours." I thought about what he said. We had crossed the Kidron Valley, we were in the garden, and Mark had told us of the pursuing crowd. "I wonder how big a company of soldiers it was. That's the phrase you used, right? Company of soldiers?"

"It is. The original word was *speira*. It referred to a tenth part of a Roman legion. Sometimes it is called a cohort."

"Now if I only knew how big a Roman legion—"

"Six thousand men."

I stopped. "You're kidding, right? Six thousand men? That would make a company … what … six hundred soldiers? Mark said there were men from the high priest. So there are six hundred soldiers, a bunch of temple guards, and some thugs. Is that your understanding?"

"Yes."

I tried to wrap my brain around that fact. "So there could have been seven hundred men or more. All to arrest one man? Even if they set out to arrest Jesus and the remaining disciples, six hundred plus men is a bit of overkill." I shook my head.

"Something is troubling you, Max. What is it?"

73

"Besides being stuck in a hyper-real nightmare? Lots of things, not the least of which is why someone would dispatch such a massive group of armed men. What were they afraid of?"

"Afraid?"

"A leader doesn't use that level of manpower unless he thinks things might go bad for him. Was he afraid that Jesus had raised up an army, or did something else frighten him?"

Yoshua offered no answers although I felt he had them.

"Wait a minute." Something occurred to me. "Didn't Jesus arrive in Jerusalem with some big fanfare?" Something from my brief stint in Sunday school percolated to the top of my mind. "He rode in on a donkey and the people sang songs or something ... the triumphal entry? Palm Sunday. I remember that. On Palm Sunday the church celebrates Jesus' arrival in Jerusalem before his death. Right?"

"With a memory like that you could be an actor."

"Cute. So they were afraid of the crowds? Of course. That makes sense."

Several hundred men trampling grass in the wee hours of the morning could make quite a mess. Before me was the flattened mat of packed-down grass, clumps of gouged ground, broken plants, and the detritus of human presence. I didn't bother examining the unique markings from the soles of the sandals. It would not have been a useful effort. Six or seven hundred men meant twelve to fourteen hundred sole prints. An investigator could spend days sorting out the mess and then have nothing useful for his efforts. Besides, with darkness settling, I needed to look for evidence I could use.

74

Other objects caught my mind. A dark clump of material rested ten feet in front of me. I approached and stooped for a closer look. Charred linen. I donned a pair of latex gloves, removed a pair of plastic tweezers from my kit, pinched the material, and raised it to my nose. It wasn't pleasant.

"Someone's been playing with fire." I dropped the material and stood. As I surveyed the area, I could see bits of the material scattered over the ground. Much of it had been trampled into the dirt. "Torches. Oil-soaked linen wrapped around a wood handle. They probably used that olive oil you mentioned earlier."

"Mark said they came to his house late in the night. The path across the Kidron can be treacherous, even during the full moon."

"And flashlights are still a few centuries in the future." I backtracked, my eyes glued to the ground. The trampled earth gave way to undamaged terrain. "They stopped here. The mob there, a few people here. My guess is—"

Something on the grass seized my attention. I focused my light on a dark rust-colored spot. Stooping again, I could see a patch of dark material and splatter pattern extending several inches to my right. I ran a moistened swab over the spot and exposed it to phenolphthalein. It turned pink.

"Blood? Like before?" Yoshua joined me.

"Yeah. A fair amount of it. Someone got hurt."

Yoshua said nothing.

I continued. "It's an odd pattern." I pointed at the bulk of the stain. "Some of the blood pooled here, but I can see a spray pattern. Not arterial. Probably force splatter."

"Force splatter?"

"Blood spray from some kind of impact." I rose and looked around. "Usually when someone hits someone else with a club, rock, or other blunt object, they drop it nearby."

75

I wandered to my right, my eyes tracing each foot of ground. A hedge of plants blocked my path. I was about to turn around when something glinted in the moonlight. Pushing back the thin limbs, I saw a flat metal object. I removed it as carefully as I could. The coolness of the metal seeped through my gloves.

In my hands rested a short sword with a slight curve to it. Just two feet in length, it still felt heavier than I would have guessed. One edge of the sword was blunt, the other sharp. The handle was wrapped in leather and the metal blade—I guessed iron—bore the scars of years of use. This was not the fine sword of a nobleman; this was the tool of a workingman.

The most distinctive element of the weapon was the dark reddish brown spot near the tip. I didn't bother to break out the phenolphthalein. In a real-world situation I would, but not here. I knew blood when I saw it.

Yoshua approached. "You found it."

"In the bushes. The weapon is in the vicinity of what I assume to be an attack on someone and would account for the blood splatter. I'd be willing to bet that the blood on this matches the blood on the ground. I'm amazed there's not more blood around."

"How so?" Yoshua asked.

"Someone got physical here. A sword and pooled blood is proof of that. Why isn't there more evidence of violence? One patch of blood indicates one event. If someone launched an attack, there should be much more. Perhaps someone stopped it—"

A rustling froze my words midsyllable. I pivoted toward the sound and listened. At first there was nothing, then I heard the sound of a man moving branches. I took a step back and saw the glow of fire six feet off the ground, its yellow light flickering on a nearby tree.

"Come out," Yoshua ordered. Maybe it was the image of a mob that had been playing on the television screen of my mind that did it, but the sound unsettled me. Yoshua and I were alone in the fading light of the day.

The sound stopped, but the glow remained. I caught a whiff of a familiar smell—the odor from the burned cloth.

"No one will hurt you." Yoshua moved toward the sound and the glowing tree.

"Are you nuts? You don't know who's in there. Stay here in the open."

He rested a hand on my shoulder like a father comforting a child, then turned his attention to the noisemaker. We waited in silence for long moments, and each moment brought a new, frightening thought to mind. Robber? Some of the gang that arrested Jesus? One or more of those Roman soldiers I encountered in the city?

Yoshua spoke again. "You have nothing to fear from us."

There was a rustling, and the glow grew brighter in the dissolving shreds of daylight. It took a second for me to realize that the light was no brighter, just closer. A man emerged, a torch in his hand. He was dressed in the same simple clothing I had seen others wearing in the city. His head was uncovered, revealing dark, shiny hair; his beard was thick and ragged. I guessed him to be in his early thirties, but he walked like a man much older. As he approached, he lowered his eyes but I caught him glancing at the short sword I held. Was he afraid I'd use it on him? I thought I'd let him hold that idea for a while.

Yoshua smiled like he knew the man, but the stranger gave no indication of knowing my guide.

"Who are you?" I asked.

He looked up and I saw his eyes trace my form. He looked puzzled. I assumed he had never seen a man in twenty-first-century dress. Of course, I had never seen anyone in first-century attire before a few hours ago. I figured we were even.

"My name is Malchus, servant of Caiaphas, high priest of our nation."

He said servant, but his body language suggested slave.

"What are you doing here, Malchus?" Yoshua asked.

"I ... I came for that." He pointed at the sword.

"What? The sword?" I asked. I started to tell him it was evidence but caught myself. My instincts were still intact, but my brain reminded me that none of this was real—no matter how real it seemed.

"My master wishes it."

"Why does he want it?" I pressed.

"He does not explain himself to me, sir. He says 'go' and I go. He says 'come' and I come. I do not question the high priest."

"And if I refuse to give—"

Yoshua cut me off. "The sword is special to you, isn't it?"

He looked away. As he did, I noticed something strange about his head: The right side of his scalp was missing a wide swatch of hair, just above the ear. "Yes, it is special, but I do not want it for myself. My master has desire for it. I must take it to him."

"Life is filled with disappointments, pal. You may have to tell your boss—"

"You were here, weren't you, Malchus?" Again with the interruptions. Yoshua never took his eyes off the slave.

The question seemed to embarrass the man ... no, not embarrassed, I realized—it moved him. He nodded. "I was here."

"Tell us what happened, Malchus." Yoshua's words were smooth, soft, unthreatening. "You are among friends."

I wasn't ready to call him friend yet, but I held my tongue.

He turned and walked to the spot Yoshua and I had been studying earlier. He held the torch before him, although there was still pale sunlight left. My instincts unsettled me. I could not believe I was where I appeared to be, but it still bothered me that someone was walking on my crime scene. It took several mental calisthenics to remind myself this was not *my* crime scene. It was all an illusion, some aberration of the brain that I had yet to define.

Malchus studied the ground and stopped at the spot where I had discovered the blood traces. He seemed to deflate before my eyes, and for a moment I thought his knees would buckle and he would do a header into the ground. He didn't.

Questions began to explode in my brain like popcorn kernels in a furnace. He knew right where the blood was located. He had admitted to being here during the events that left the evidence, but he knew the spot better than I expected.

I followed him, the sword still in my hands.

"Was it here?" Yoshua asked.

Malchus nodded and stared at the dark stain on the grass. If he didn't look so healthy, I would've thought he was gazing at his own blood.

The visitor inhaled deeply then looked at Yoshua. I could see tears in his eyes. "Just a few nights ago … I was with … We stood over there." He pointed to the area I had identified as having been trampled by a large crowd. "Many of us. My master sent me around to gather as many people as I could: priests, temple guards, and other servants. We met at the house of my master. There was a cohort of Romans there. My master is well loved by the Romans."

"Why so many?" I asked.

"Because of whom we were to capture. The people loved him and heralded him as a great prophet. My master knew him to be a liar, a breaker of the laws and traditions, a misleader of the people. He had to be stopped."

79

The last sentence sounded rehearsed and lacked conviction. He cut his eyes away when he made the statement, an indication that he was lying—or at least that he had strong doubts about what he was saying.

I could see that his emotions had him off balance. It was a good time to turn the screws a little. "Did you see what happened? Whose blood is that?"

He didn't look at me, nor did he bother answering the questions.

"Take your time," Yoshua said. "What happened next?"

"When we learned that the false teacher and his gang were not at the house, the man led us to this spot."

"What man?" By choice, I delivered my question with a sharper edge than Yoshua might. I knew the importance of being seen as the one in control of the conversation.

He might be a slave, but he didn't intimidate easily. He frowned at me but answered. "The one called Judas. He was one of the Teacher's own. He led us here."

I could have guessed that. One didn't have to be a Bible thumper to know that Judas Iscariot betrayed Jesus.

Malchus continued. "I was at the front of the group. My master wanted me to see everything and report. I saw everything. I saw too much." He sighed, the kind of sigh that begins deep in a person—in the dark caverns of the consciousness.

"Judas led us each step of the way. We came to the garden and I was surprised to see the Teacher standing about where you are. It was just him and ten or eleven others. He stood there like he was expecting us; waiting for our arrival." Malchus paused. "Why didn't he run? There were hundreds of us and only a few of them. He just stood there looking at us. His face ... was so sad."

"You were armed?" I asked.

He shook his head. "Not me, but the soldiers were. So were the temple guards. Others had swords and clubs."

"You expected a fight?"

"Yes. Of course. What man doesn't fight for his freedom; fight to escape death?"

Yoshua asked the next question. "Did he fight?"

"No. Judas walked to him and kissed him. He said, 'Hail, Master.'[3] Jesus allowed it, but I heard him say, 'Judas, you betray the Son of Man with a kiss?'[4] Judas took a step back and turned to us. He seemed to be waiting for something, as if he expected the Teacher to do more....'"

Malchus drew the back of his hand beneath his eyes and sniffed. It was clear that something was eating at him.

"Then?" Yoshua prompted so softly I barely heard it.

"I didn't see him coming. One of the disciples, a big man, screamed like a demon and charged toward us ... toward me. He had something in his hand. I saw it glint in the moonlight."

His words died in his throat. It took a moment for him to continue. "My eyes were fixed on the Teacher. Had the attacker not screamed, I would not have seen it coming. He would have killed me instead of ... the pain ... I've never felt anything like it. I tried to move away, but I was too slow. I saw the blade ..." he pointed at the sword I held, "I saw that blade come down. He was trying to split my skull, but he missed."

Like an actor in a slow-motion movie scene, Malchus raised his right hand to his right ear. "The sword glanced off the side of my head and ... he cut off my ear. I remember the blood. It covered my hand and ran down my arm. The pain ... I screamed." He lowered his hand and studied it. "I could feel the flesh of my ear and scalp dangling in my hand." He shuddered.

So did I.

"Did he attack you again?" I wondered.

"He started to. When I looked up, I expected to see the sword on its way to my head again. Instead, I heard a loud voice and saw

81

the Teacher. I don't remember what he said. My ear ... the pain ... the screams ... I saw him standing between me and the big man with the sword. He stood between his disciples and our men, his arms stretched out as if he could hold both groups in place with a mere gesture. I heard pieces of conversation. He said something about swords and dying by the sword, and his ability to call down legions of angels—twelve legions I think he said.[5] I can't be sure."

"Wait a minute," I said. "Are you telling me that some man cut off your right ear?"

"Yes."

"I know it's nearly dark, but I still see two good ears on the sides of your head and I doubt you have a plastic surgeon in this town."

Malchus looked puzzled, as if I had just started spouting gibberish. He blinked a few times and I imagined his brain trying to translate what he just heard.

"Tell us the rest," Yoshua said.

"I had fallen to my knees ... I couldn't stand. The pain had taken my strength. I kept screaming. I begged for someone to help me. The Teacher kept talking then stopped. I felt his hands on my shoulders and he pulled me to my feet. He tugged at my hand but I didn't want to move it from my head. My ear was in my hand ... my ear ...

"A moment later, I let him guide my hand away. I felt him touch my ear. It felt as if it were on fire. Darkness pressed into my eyes and I felt sick. Then ..."

He raised both hands to his face. I heard him sob. We waited while Malchus struggled to control himself. Seeing this grown man weep troubled me. What he was saying had to be a lie. I knew where he was going with this and there was no way I was buying it. Still, he gave all the physical clues of a man relating a story of personal injury. I had heard hundreds of them, and his behavior was what I expected from someone telling the truth. The emotion was raw and honest, and he gave no sense of acting.

He bent, resting his hands on his knees, and took in several deep inhalations, then straightened. "He ... he took the mass of flesh ... my flesh ... in his own hand, then placed it on the side of my head. I thought he was trying to stop the bleeding, but ... he didn't say anything. The pain stopped. My ear and head felt warm. I looked into his face and saw him smile. We had come to arrest him and he was *smiling* at me. He stepped away and I touched my ear. There was no pain. It felt ... normal. Several people standing nearby gasped and stepped away—"

"No, there's no way." I handed the sword to Yoshua and retrieved my penlight. "Here, hold this." I crossed to Malchus who quickly backpedaled. "Stand still, I'm not going to hurt you." I turned on the light.

"What ... what is that?"

"Think of it as a tiny torch. Stand still. I want to see."

Malchus held his ground, but I could feel him tense when I took his right arm. I directed the light at the man's scalp. The ear looked whole and intact, but I could see subtle differences. To be sure, I examined his left ear then returned to the right. I placed the small light in my mouth so I could use both hands to press the skin.

A faint line ran around the ear from an inch or so above to the jawline. At first I thought it was a scar but then realized I was wrong. The line had no bulk to it like a scar would, no thickening of the skin. Instead, I found a slight color difference in the tone. The flesh around the ear looked newer, younger.

I tweaked his ear. He squealed and slapped my hand away.

"I don't know what I expected to find," I mumbled to myself.

83

"I'm standing in first-century Israel; why shouldn't I meet people with magically reattached ears?"

"Miraculously," Yoshua corrected, "not magically."

"As if there's a difference."

He gave me a sad look then turned his attention to Malchus. He held out the sword. "Take it to your master."

Malchus raised quivering hands and took the weapon. He thanked Yoshua.

"Before you go, Malchus," Yoshua began, "why do you think the Teacher healed you?"

He shook his head. "I don't know. We were his enemies." He paused and his shoulders drooped. "It doesn't matter now."

"Why?" I asked.

"Because he's dead. We killed him."

Malchus the slave turned and walked away, torch in one hand, bloody sword in the other.[6]

chapter
6

Y ou haven't said anything since we left," Yoshua said. He was two paces ahead of me, leading us back down the path that had brought us to the private garden.

"Didn't anyone ever tell you that silence is golden?" I said between puffs. My legs were starting to ache and my fingers protested having to carry the two heavily packed cases. I felt thankful that we were moving downhill, but I didn't fool myself. Jerusalem was on the distant slope of the valley, which meant I'd be walking up the other side of the Kidron. It wasn't an exhausting hike, but one I chafed against. I had no desire to hike down this slope or up the other one. I didn't want to be trekking through the backwater areas of Jerusalem.

"I've heard that's true. Outside voices are easy to shut out. It's the inside voices that bother most people."

The breeze picked up and the deepening night carried a chill with it. The air was not cold, but it seeped into my bones like an arctic frost.

"What's that supposed to mean?"

Yoshua hesitated, allowing me to step to his side. I moved past him and he took two quick strides to pull alongside. "Your mouth is quiet but your brain is not."

"How would you know that? Last time I looked, my skull wasn't transparent."

He chuckled. "Your skull isn't, but your emotions are. You wear them on the outside."

"I do not."

He shrugged. "Have it your way, Max, but there are few things as pathetic as a man who wants attention but won't let anyone give it to him."

I stopped midstep. "Where do you get off talking to me like that? You don't know me. We've been together ... what, a couple of hours."

"Time and knowledge are not always linked."

I couldn't believe my ears. I was one frayed strand from snapping and this guy was tugging on what little reserve of decorum I had.

"You're not my shrink, pal. I doubt you have the training to know what goes on in the mind of a man like me."

"What kind of man are you?"

"Just an average man. Nothing more and some days much less."

"Is that what you believe?"

"Belief is a contrivance to make sense of the world—except the world doesn't make sense. It has no logic, no foundation, therefore no sense."

"Yet you spend your days trying to make sense of it."

"I gave up on that a long time ago. I couldn't make sense of my own world, now you're asking me to make sense of this one. Well, I can't. I don't know how long this aberration will last but it can't end soon enough."

"You find this world worse than yours?"

"I doubt it can be worse. I live in a very violent time. Far worse than this place could ever be."

"You just met a man who had his ear cut off," Yoshua said, his voice as steady as ever. Something else about him that irritated me.

Had I been more rested, had things not been what they were, I might have been able to control myself more and suppress the laughter that exploded from me. But I wasn't rested and things were exactly what they were. "I'm afraid you don't know what violence is. Granted, having someone take a hearty swing at your head with a sword rates up there as a violent act, but where I come from, it's pretty mild."

"You don't believe that."

That was it. Something inside me popped. So far I had tolerated the nonsense that played out before my eyes. I had gone along with the illusion, the madness, the psychotic break, whatever it was that made me think I was two thousand years in the past and half a world away from home.

I dropped my kits and they landed hard. I knew the foam rubber packing would keep things from breaking, but the few remaining brain cells connected to reason made me wince at my actions.

87

"You want to know about my world, Yoshua? You want to know what it's really like? It's worse than you can imagine. Where I live, we've raised the ability of one human to be cruel to another to a new level."

I paced and tried to force down the anger that steeped in me. I thought, *Why bother?* Spouting off made no sense. I prided myself on detachment, logic, and self-control. Each one of those strings gave way.

"You know what I did last month, pal? I went to a house in Hillcrest. A man had murdered his wife. Not just murdered. No, that wasn't good enough for him. He had to go to the next level. He strung her up by the wrists from the ceiling and cut her in half with a chainsaw. You think that blot of blood back in the garden was ugly. It wasn't. It was nothing compared to that crime scene. My job was to make sense of it. Find clues. Put the lowlife away for good. I've been trained to be detached, but how do you stay detached in a room that has blood splatter on every surface and half a corpse hanging from the chandelier?

"Last month, I helped nail the person responsible for the death of a five-day-old baby left next to a Dumpster at San Diego State University. We got the killer. It was the child's mother. She was seventeen. Seventeen! By my accounting, that's two lives wasted."

I moved close to my guide, standing eyeball-to-eyeball. "Every day I work in the stomach-turning reality of life in a civilized society." I poked him in the chest. "You want to know about my world? I live in a time when passion is measured with a rape kit; anger by blood splatter; hatred by the caliber of automatic weapon used. I live in a world where child abuse is no longer shocking and is mentioned on the evening news only if there's time after the discussion of which movie starlet married which rock singer."

Yoshua didn't move. He stood like a tree while I ranted and

poked his chest again. "That's my world, buddy. It's painted in crimson, lit with the fires of bigotry and hatred. It's a me-first world and no one else matters. I live in a world where we have to ask questions like 'What do we do with an eleven-year-old murderer?' and 'Whose responsibility is it to care for drug-dependent babies born to parents too stoned to know when to feed the child?' I live in a world where junior-high girls beat another girl to death because she made a face at them."

I stepped away from him, picked up my kits, and started back down the path. "As far as I'm concerned, you can have that world, and this one too. Your friend Malchus might have been better off if the sword had caught him square on. At least he wouldn't be a slave anymore."

I marched away leaving the growing gloom of the garden behind but carrying my own with me.

†✝†

"Turn left," the voice behind me said. These were his first words since I had slipped a cog on the other slope of the Kidron Valley.

"Why?"

"Because I know where we're going and you don't."

"Maybe I don't want to go with you."

"Suit yourself." Yoshua strolled past. "Be sure you stay within the walls of the city. Robbers often hide along the roads." He paused, then, "For that matter, it isn't all that safe in the city after dark."

The last strains of light were giving way to the night, the sun having finally crept off to the other side of the world. Dusk would soon be darkness cut only by torches, lamps, and the waning moon, which rose like a slow-moving balloon. I had a good sense of direction and found my way back to the same gate we passed through when we first left the city. Once inside, I was lost. The tightly packed streets ebbing and flowing with humanity robbed me of my bearings. Yoshua moved through the masses with ease, occasionally saying some greeting to a passerby. Women looked in my direction but averted their eyes the moment I noticed them.

Three children raced past, one of them bumping me hard. I started to shout at them but thought better of it. Whether this place was real or not, it was not my world and I had enough trouble to deal with.

The white walls of the city closed in on me. The smells of a tightly packed populace and animals; the sound of conversations overlaying conversations filled my ears. My stomach turned and my head began to spin. The weight and confusion of being out of place washed over me like the tide. I had experienced as many nightmares as anyone else, perhaps more, but this one took the cake. My mouth dried, sending what moisture it had to my palms.

I was lost. Not just in the city of ancient Jerusalem, but in the world. Clearly my mind had slipped its moorings and was now free-floating in my uncontrollable emotion.

Eyes of a thousand strangers bore deep into my being, coring my confidence. I shut my eyes. I've always prided myself on my ability to shut off emotions. Emotions were more often useless distractions than helpful allies. They amounted to little more than a man sitting in his car pressing the accelerator and brake at the same time—lots of noise but little movement.

I forced the rising confusion and—I'll just say it—fear back into the dungeon of my subconscious. I could deal with it later. A stiff drink, maybe two or three, had always worked. That's what I needed, the shocking belt of a smooth scotch or the bitter hit of several vodka shots. It always worked in the past.

Someone grabbed my elbow. My eyes snapped open. I expected to see one of the men dressed in soldier garb with one hand on my elbow and the other on his spear. Instead, I saw the concerned face of Yoshua.

He said nothing. His grip was tight but not painful. His was the hand of a man familiar with work. His fingers felt thick on my skin and his wrist didn't budge when I tried to jerk away.

With me in tow, he walked down the street and we moved past buildings vaguely familiar from earlier that day. We were on our way to the upper city. I didn't ask where we were going. It didn't matter. One place was as good or as bad as any other.

Time trickled by in a torrent. I know that sentence makes no sense, but that's how it appeared to me. Everything was so real and came so fast that I couldn't take it in, yet time seemed to drip by— a temporal oxymoron. Still, time and distance passed, and I realized that we had returned to Mark's house. The sun had finally clocked out leaving the waning gibbous moon to work alone in the dark.

Mark and his father arranged for a meal in the upper room. The four of us reclined at table—a task that proved challenging to me—and, after the old man uttered a prayer like the one I heard Yoshua voice earlier, ate fruit, vegetables, bread, and a meat of uncertain origin. I didn't ask. Unlike before at the street restaurant, I ate my share. The walk to the garden and back had fired my appetite.

Once the meal had been set, Mark's father, Hosah,[1] and his mother, Mary, saw to it that the meal had been set to their satisfaction and a young servant girl served us. Despite my hunger, I ate slowly, as did the others. It seemed that a shared meal had great value here. Still, the joy of communal eating that I expected was absent. Something hung over these men, a persistent black cloud

91

that shadowed them. Yoshua seemed most at peace, but Mark and his family seemed poisoned by sadness.

"How was your journey, Brother Yoshua?" Hosah asked. "Did you find what you searched for?" It was an obvious effort to lighten the mood.

"The journey went well," Yoshua asked, breaking off a morsel of bread from a round loaf. "Brother Max is a very observant man."

Brother Max?

"We are honored to have you under our roof, Brother Max," Hosah said, but I thought I detected a glint of distrust in his eyes. Mark gave the same impression. Even Mary, although she never spoke to me directly, shot inquisitive glances my way.

"Um, thank you."

"I hope our humble home serves you."

I smiled. Humble? By contemporary standards it would be considered midsize and simple. It was much larger than the homes I had seen in the lower city. I couldn't think of a response.

Yoshua filled in for my silence. "The garden still looks lovely. HaShem has blessed you."

"Blessed be HaShem, the Most Holy," Hosah replied.

I looked at Yoshua. He smiled. "I'll explain later."

"The garden will never be lovely again." Mark's words were tainted with anger, his eyes fixed on the table.

Hosah gave him a hard look, but it dissolved into an expression of shared regret.

"You say that because of the arrest?" I asked.

"Of course," Mark snapped.

"Watch your words, Son," Hosah ordered. "Brother Max is our guest."

"Yes, Father. I only meant ..."

In the pale, flickering light emitted by ceramic oil lamps on the table, I could see the scratches on Mark's neck that I had examined earlier.

"We met someone there." I sat up. Leaning on one arm was becoming painful.

"Someone?" Hosah said. He looked at Yoshua. So did I. My guide continued to eat without comment.

"A man named Malchus. He had quite a story to tell."

Mark's jaw tightened. Hosah broke eye contact. I had touched a nerve.

"He said he was a servant to—"

"We know who he is, Brother Max. He serves the high priest."

"He serves the Devil himself," Mark huffed.

"John Mark!" his mother snapped loudly. "You will not speak that way in this house."

"Why not, Mother? He is the one responsible for the Teacher's death. The Rabbi would still be with us if not for him. My only regret was that Simon's aim fell short."

"Silence." Hosah's words were iceberg cold. "If you cannot control that youthful tongue of yours, then you will not use it. Do you hear me?"

Mark said nothing.

"Do you understand, boy?"

"Yes, Father. I apologize."

Hosah took a deep breath and I had the feeling that Mark had been a half second away from a resounding backhand.

"Did he say what he was doing in our garden?" Hosah's anger was barely disguised.

93

"He came for the sword," I said, watching their response. Nothing was said. I decided to stoke the flames. "We gave it to him. He left with it."

"It is of no concern to us," Hosah said.

"It belongs to Simon," Mark objected.

"Then let Simon retrieve it."

"At least he was there."

Hosah was on his feet before the last syllable had a chance to echo in the big room. "You mind your words, boy."

Mark started to rise, but his mother sat up and placed a hand on his shoulder freezing him in his place.

"I would enjoy some more wine," Yoshua said as if nothing had transpired. I readied myself for a father-son fight, and Yoshua was asking for more of the sweet wine. Hosah nodded at the servant girl who quickly filled everyone's cup. A second later she stepped back into the shadows.

"John Mark," Yoshua began. "How many people were with the Teacher that night?"

"Just the eleven. The traitor had left."

Yoshua nodded. "How many disciples did the Teacher have when he walked our streets?"

"Too many to count, but about one hundred and twenty faithful followers."

"Yet, only eleven traveled to the garden with him. I wonder why."

"They were the only ones at the Passover meal. Only those went with him."

"How many others were invited?" Yoshua took another bite of bread.

"Invited?" Mark looked puzzled.

"Rabbi Yoshua had private business with the Father. Perhaps he required privacy more than company."

Mark said nothing.

"Brother Mark, do you believe your father would have tarried had the Teacher made an invitation to him?"

Mark shook his head. Even in the dim light I could see water brimming in his eyes. "No, of course not."

"Your mother has been a faithful follower in the women's circle. Your father shares the same faith. You wrong him this evening suggesting otherwise."

"I was not invited yet I went to warn the Master." Mark's words were those of a man trying to hold shifting ground.

"Your courage serves you well, Brother Mark, but your wisdom is still that of a child. You added gray hair to the heads of your parents. They need a faithful son as well as a son of faith. Do you understand?"

He nodded, rose slowly, and embraced his father. If my heart and mind weren't covered in an inch-thick callus, I might have been moved. In an honest, inward moment, I admit the callus thinned some.

They returned to their dining benches, each trying to make as little show as possible while dragging a sleeve beneath his wet eyes.

The eating resumed but the stooped shoulders told me that these were people bearing shiploads of sorrow.

✝✝✝

The moon hung high in the obsidian dome, surrounded by a sequined banner of stars. Living in a major city, I seldom saw stars like this. The spangled darkness reminded me how the Milky Way earned its name.

I was standing at the top of the exterior stairs, ostensibly trying to get a breath of fresh air, but the air wasn't so fresh. It was perfumed with the odors from cooking fires and animals, and a foul stench wafted in from the south.

"Beautiful night," Yoshua said.

"It stinks."

He nodded. "Beyond the south wall is the Valley of Hinnom. The city trash dump is there. It's also the place to drop off dead animals ... and dead criminals."

"Lovely. Do they put that in the tourist brochure?" I remembered him mentioning the place earlier.

"Many years ago, people sacrificed their children to the idol Molech. The Ammonites worshipped him. They would erect a stone statue with arms. A hollow cavity was filled with wood and burned until the statue was hot. Then infants would be set in the arms. They died horribly. Even my people were led into the practice. King Ahaz and King Manasseh committed the same crime.[2] What do you do with a valley like that? The people consider it cursed ground so they turned it into a dump."

"Sort of a practical social statement."

"Exactly."

"You didn't come out here to give me a history lesson, Yoshua."

He smiled. "Ever the detective. I wanted you to know that we will be sleeping here. Mark has brought up sleeping pallets. You'll find yours on the floor near the corner. I suggest you get some sleep."

"I don't want to sleep. I want to wake up."

"Still having trouble believing your eyes?"

"I refuse to believe that any of this is possible."

"Back to thinking about strokes, psychotic breaks, and bad dreams?"

"It makes more sense than time travel."

Yoshua laughed. "There are more things in heaven and earth than are dreamt of in your philosophy."

"More Bible?"

"Shakespeare. *Hamlet,* act 1, scene 5."

"You're kidding, right?"

He turned. "Okay, how's this: 'My thoughts are not like your thoughts, nor are your ways like my ways,' declares the Lord. 'For as the heavens are above the earth, so are my ways above your ways and my thoughts above your thoughts.'[3] The prophet Isaiah."

Yoshua disappeared into the room but I stayed put, letting the ever-cooling night embrace me. The night air was colder than I expected, but it was spring, that time when winter wants to hang on and summer is still too far away to make a difference.

I thought about my chills, the taste of the food I had eaten an hour before; of rough wood beneath my shoes, and the pungent smell that filled the air. It was all so real. Everything had been real, but it couldn't be. People do not travel back in time, at least outside the pages of science fiction books.

Still ...

I thought about the Bible quote, about God's ways not being my ways. If I believed in God, it might have meant something, but I had no use for such myths. I preferred the rational to the irrational, no matter how irrational it seemed.

That last thought made my mind slip. "Great, now I'm confusing myself."

I gave in to the growing weariness, left the night behind, and crossed the threshold into the wide room. A small ceramic oil-burning lamp was positioned near a mat on the floor at the distant corner. Another mat was ten feet away. A human-sized lump lay beneath a wad of bedding. Yoshua had wasted no time settling in for the night.

After I slipped my shoes from my feet, I crawled onto the

97

sack—and that's exactly how it felt: a thin sack of stuffed cloth with coarse blankets to provide warmth. This was going to be a miserable night. With any luck, I would wake up back in my own time—or not wake up at all.

"Good night, Max Odom," Yoshua said. "Don't let the rats bite."

"Good night—rats?"

I thought I heard a snicker.

chapter 7

The moonlight that had poured in through the lone window in the upper room dissolved into darkness and I drifted into sleep shortly after. It seemed that I had just fallen into the sweet, silent arms of slumber when a bare foot nudged me in the back. I rolled over and blinked against the stronger light of the sun. I had been sleeping for hours, but it felt no more than a handful of minutes.

"It's time to rise, Max." Yoshua towered over me. "The sun has been up for an hour."

"A whole hour? Sloth, thy name is Max."

My morning dose of sarcasm didn't faze him. "How did you sleep?"

"I kept dreaming of rats."

"At least you had company."

Now who's being sarcastic?

Noise from the street below told me that Jerusalemites started their day early. I slipped from the tangle of blankets, glad to be free of their coarseness and subtle smell. Standing, I surveyed my clothing. I hadn't bothered to undress. Something about sleeping in a strange bed, in a strange town, and in a strange millennium made me reluctant to disrobe. My shirt and pants sported more wrinkles than a raisin.

"There is fruit on the table, and bread. You should eat. We leave soon."

"We leave for where?"

"For the next stop on your journey."

I poured water into a ceramic cup. It was discolored. I sniffed. It had a slightly sweet smell. I took a tentative taste then realized that wine had been mixed with the water. Of course. A sensible action in a world with no concept of sanitation.

"And that would be ..."

"Ready yourself. I must speak to Hosah before we leave and offer our thanks for his kindness."

"Ask if he has a road map back to the twenty-first century."

Yoshua didn't reply. He walked from the room and down the stairs like a man whose tunic had just gathered fifty pounds of lead. Something was on his mind.

I brushed myself off and ran my tongue over the morning goo that covered my teeth. Ridding myself of that unpleasantness was reason enough to eat. At the table I saw bread, fruit, and several small loafs of something else. I raised one of the palm-sized pastries to my nose. Figs. Someone had made fig cakes. I took a bite. The taste came across stronger than I expected but it was good. My stomach rumbled to life. Now, if I could only find a coffeemaker.

I finished my quick meal, rubbed more sleep from my eyes, stretched my complaining back, picked up my kits, then went to the top of the stairs and slipped on my shoes. In the courtyard below I saw Yoshua waiting; his face turned toward the distant wall of the city. There was no telling where his mind was. He stood alone. No Hosah, no Mark, no servant, no one.

I waited for him to move, to pace, to turn and look for me. He didn't. He was a man frozen in place.

I negotiated the stairs and moved to Yoshua. I tried to be noisy about it but he never turned.

"Where is everyone?"

"Which everyone?" he replied.

"Mark, his mom and dad, the servant girl. Who else would I be talking about?"

"They are about their day's business. It's time we began ours." He began with those irritating long strides. Just once, I'd like him to offer to carry one of the kits.

The streets were filled with people. Women walked alone or in small clumps of humanity, their long robes dancing around their moving feet. Most walked with heads down or turned to one another. They chatted but not loudly. The robes varied. Some seemed coarse and frayed, others looked fresh from the tailor. Different classes, different bank accounts. Some women—young women—wore veils across their faces.

"Hey, Yoshua." I trotted to his side. "How come some of these women cover their faces but others don't?"

101

"The women with the veils are virgins."

I hadn't expected that. "How would you know? … Never mind."

"They are unmarried. The veil shows their modesty."

"That wouldn't go well where I live."

"Very little here would."

I stepped around a goat and veered away from an approaching bag of bones that I was pretty sure had at one time been a dog.

"Tell me where we're going," I insisted.

"Out of the city."

"Helpful as that is, could you be more specific?"

We passed beneath the stone arches that supported the aqueduct. The structure impressed me; an amazing feat of planning and construction.

"We are going to the Water Gate in the southeast wall. It's on the other side of the lower city, then to a place where the Hinnom meets the Kidron."

His words were blunt, and he didn't look at me when he spoke.

"Okay, what's the problem?" I asked.

"Problem?"

I sighed. "Look, if I did something wrong, then tell me. Just bear in mind that I didn't ask for this nightmare. So what'd I do? Mess up some custom? Slept on the wrong side of the bed? Ate too much? Ate too little."

"No."

"Then why so moody, pal? I feel like I should be apologizing."

He finally looked at me. "You did nothing wrong." He lengthened his stride and I wished I had spent more time on the treadmill. Thankfully it was downhill. I tried not to think about the journey back up.

102

I attempted to pass the time with conversation. Between puffs, I said, "Yesterday you said you'd explain about that word." I struggled to recall it. "I think it was HaShem."

"It's Hebrew and means The Name. Jews in this age and the centuries to follow feel the name of God is so sacred that they will not speak it except in the reading of the Torah and prayer."

"So they refer to the big guy in the sky as The Name."

Yoshua cut me a stern look. "The Creator deserves more respect than any person or people can give. Reverence for the name of God goes back many centuries. They honor their Creator by respecting his name … not by calling him the big guy in the sky."

I had hit a nerve. Part of me felt good about it. The victim here was me, not Yoshua. He moved in this culture like it was his home. Maybe it was. Me, on the other hand, well, I wouldn't know how to find a loaf of bread in this place. As much as it galled me, and no matter how convinced I was that this was all the result of some decaying part of my brain, I needed someone like Yoshua.

Words came to me; words meant to sting, but I locked them in the dungeon of my thoughts. Yoshua gave all the signs of a man with too much on his mind; too much weight on his shoulders.

We passed through a valley that ran through the city. Yoshua called it the Tyropoeon Valley. We then entered the wide pass in the wall that circumscribed the city. The word gate doesn't do the structure justice. It was more of a building than a simple opening in the wall. As we passed through, I could see several open rooms, each filled with people. Some argued in front of a man I assumed to be some kind of judge, others carried on business. Yoshua moved us through the crowded structure. I did see two large, thick wood doors, one at the opening to the structure, the other at the exit. The doors could be slid to close access to any-one outside trying to get in or anyone inside trying to get out. I hoped Yoshua knew their schedule.

103

Pressing past packs of people, we were soon outside the city. Every minute we walked, the fewer people I saw. In the distance I could see smoke.

"That's the valley you were telling me about last night, right?"

Yoshua nodded.

"The place where they burn dead animals and garbage."

Another nod. Yoshua just wasn't going to be chatty.

I gave it another try. "Tell me we're not going there."

"We're not going there."

Did he mean that?

"I'm serious."

"So am I. We're not going that far. Stay with me."

"As if I have a choice."

We were no longer just walking. We were hiking and my kits grew heavier in my hands. I wished I had left them behind. Scrub brush was everywhere, but a thin path enabled us to move forward. I missed a step and my foot slid a few inches in a direction I didn't want to go. Dirt filled my shoe.

"Hang on a sec," I said, setting my kits down and using one of them as a seat. I removed my shoe and emptied a pickup-truck load of dirt back to the ground where it belonged. A few seconds later I was back on my feet, my shoe empty of its unwanted cargo.

I was also alone.

Yoshua had left me.

Standing on my toes, I searched for my guide but caught no sight of him. That puzzled me. It took less than two minutes for me to empty my shoe.

104

I swore under my breath. Who was he to drag me all over this jerkwater town then abandon me? It wasn't like I asked for all this. I gazed back up the path and considered returning the way I came. That'd show him. He'd come back looking for me and I'd be gone. It would serve him right. Let him worry about me. I dismissed the idea. I doubted that Yoshua worried about much of anything.

On the dirt path I could see the footsteps Yoshua had left behind. I decided to follow. I had a few things to say and I wanted to get in his face when I said them.

Eyes glued to the ground, I started forward. His tracks were evenly spaced, about what I'd expect for a man his size. They were full prints, no signs of running or sprinting, which would leave a different impression.

Ten minutes of careful hiking later, I found my man. He stood with his back to me, his hands clasped behind him. A lifeless tree stood nearby.

"So you felt you had to rush to this, eh?" I snapped. "Couldn't wait a couple of minutes for me? You think you're that important?"

He stood unmoving and silent.

It's difficult to have an argument when the other party won't play along. I set the kits down and moved toward him. That's when I realized that Yoshua stood near a cliff. The ground dropped off just three feet in front of him. I moved closer and gazed over the edge. It was not a huge drop, maybe twenty-five or thirty feet, but certainly enough to injure if not kill a man.

"What are we doing here?"

"Our work." His words were soft and left his mouth as if laden with more weight than they could hold.

The sound of his words was sad enough to take the fight from me.

"Something happened here?"

He nodded.

Unlike the garden I had visited the day before, this place was rough, harsh, uninviting. The ground was hard but covered in an inch or so of loose dirt and decomposed granite. In some ways it reminded me of the terrain in San Diego. That should be no surprise. San Diego and Jerusalem are close to the same latitude.

Why here? What was it Yoshua wanted me to see?

I gazed over the cliff edge again. The ground was the same uniform brown as the rest of the geology in the area. Several piles of stones lay at the base of the cliff, rock outcroppings dotted the ground. A dark, irregular stain marred one batch of boulders.

"What is this place?"

"The people call in Akeldama."

I gave an approving nod. "Seems a nice enough name."

"It's Aramaic," Yoshua said. "It means 'Field of Blood.'"

"That's going to be hard to market."

Yoshua just looked at me. I could tell I was wearing thin on him. Turning from him, I took a quick look around. There was little to see. The slope was sporting new grass and weeds. My guess was the weeds would soon cover the slope.

It was the tree that most caught my attention. In some ways it looked familiar, but it had seen better days. Its bark was dark, its branches naked against azure sky, its limbs gnarled with arthritic twists and bends. At one time it might have been a statuesque tree, its branches full of green leaves to capture the sun and dance on the wind. Now only one branch showed any life. The branch was thin and sported purple-pink flowers—the tree's last grasp at life.

"This is a redbud tree," I said. "We have them in the states. There's one on the street were I live. Not nearly this big, mind you. This tree must be pretty old."

Yoshua kept his opinion to himself, but I could see his eyes fixed on the tree. I tried to follow his gaze.

I saw it. The tree was close to the cliff's edge, and a few of its branches cantilevered over the precipice. One such branch sprouted low on the tree. The branch was different from the others. This one was thick and short. It took a second, but then I realized that it was short for a reason—its distal end had broken off.

I approached, careful of my footing. The end of the damaged limb hung exposed like a gaping wound. Expecting to see the white interior of the branch, I saw dark dry wood. The branch had been dead for some time. Perhaps it gave way under its own weight. That would explain the missing limb but not Yoshua's obvious emotional tie to it.

I looked closer.

The trunk of the tree still held most of its bark, but small sections had been recently marred. I opened one of my kits and removed a hand light. The marks were the result of force applied at an angle to the bark. I knew this—I should say I assumed this—by the odd shape of exposed wood. Retrieving a lighted magnifying glass, I studied the spots where bark had been chipped off. The glass helped, but I would need something more powerful to prove my suspicion.

At the upper end of the reveal, where bark had parted from bark, I could see small fractures and the edge of the remaining bark was consistent with a tearing motion. The freshly exposed sapwood bore several scratches.

Further up the tree I found several fibers that looked to my naked eye like those I had found on the stone wall around the garden. I also found flakes of skin, a bit of blood, and a hair. I verified the blood with phenolphthalein. Although I knew it was a useless task since no crime lab was available, I collected and bagged the fibers and scrapped the thin bits of flesh into a plastic tube. I marked everything. It gave me something to do.

107

Something ate at me. "I have a question, Yoshua. If you wanted to climb this tree, what would be the first thing you would do? I mean, considering that long garment you're wearing."

"Gird myself."

"Gird yourself. What's that mean?"

He removed his cloak, pulled up his long tunic, and tucked it into the cloth belt around his waist. His legs remained exposed. "It is what a man does before he works or if he must run."

"That'd explain how a man in a long tunic could climb a tree."

"Not all tunics are long. You've seen some of the men wear shorter garments."

I nodded. I had seen that. I looked over the edge and saw what I had failed to notice before. The stained piles of rocks below lined up with the rosebud tree. I could also see the limb resting on the ground nearby.

"Is there a way down there?" I asked.

"There is."

Yoshua started walking. I gathered my kits and followed.

The escarpment looked less imposing from its base, but I knew it was high enough to cause serious damage to anyone attempting to fly from its edge. Decomposed granite covered the earth, and rocks that had formerly made the face of the cliff now littered the ground. Years had weathered away much of the material. Rain, wind, seismic activity could loosen anything, and then gravity took over.

At the discolored pile of debris, I found the broken limb from the redbud tree. It had fractured on impact, splitting down the long axis. A handwoven rope held the pieces together. Yoshua stood back several paces. I had asked him to do so.

I tried to focus on the details as I found them, but that is always hard to do. I once worked a case in which an elderly man had been killed and dismembered. Parts of his body were left in different areas of the city—the killer's way of making things difficult for us. It didn't work. Arriving at the scene, my team knew what waited for us: two arms and a leg. No matter how well trained the mind, how instilled the techniques, it is impossible to focus on bits of trace evidence when you know body parts are just a few feet away.

Here, I tried to take note of footprints (there were several sets); other tracks (thin lines from what I assumed was a small cart); disruption of terrain (not much); and signs that the site had been altered. I managed for a while, but soon I had to address the stained pile of rocks. I could see it. Worse, I could smell it. The odor wasn't overbearing, but my nose knew what it was.

"Something puzzles me," I admitted.

"What puzzles you, Max?"

"I have a good idea what happened here, but something doesn't add up. There are several sets of sandal footprints around, all different sizes or sole patterns. There was a group here not many days ago. But up by the tree I could only make out one set."

"What do you think happened?"

"Something out of the wild west, pal: a hanging, and an amateurish one at that."

"Are there professional hangers?" Yoshua asked.

"I don't know. Do people hang other people around here?"

"Not like you're thinking. Jews execute by stoning, but the Romans no longer allow that. Romans kill in many ways, but criminals usually die on crosses."

"Well, this is the site of a hanging. Someone swung by the neck from that tree above, except the tree is old and mostly dead. The branch broke; the victim fell and landed on these rocks. From the mess on the stones, he was busted up pretty good."

"You don't sound puzzled."

"I am. Why so few footprints by the tree? Then there's the matter of bark chipped off the trunk. When I first saw it, I thought it was evidence of a man climbing the tree. That still makes sense. Someone would have to tie the rope on the branch."

I looked at the branch again. The rope had been tied securely around the limb. The other end, the noose end, was missing. I bent and examined the loose end of the rope. I didn't need my magnifier to know that it had been cut.

A picture formed in my mind. "Ah." I stood.

"Ah, what?"

"As if you didn't know."

Yoshua shrugged.

"Okay," I said. "I think I've got this. The reason there are so few foot impressions in the soft grass above is that only one person was there. Judging by the size of the imprint and his willingness to scale the tree, it was a man. He took the rope, shinnied up the tree and onto the limb, tied off one end of the rope and placed the other around his neck. All he had to do then was lean to one side. He'd fall off, the rope would snap his neck, and he'd be dead. It was suicide."

"But the branch is down here."

"A couple of possibilities. The branch looked sturdy enough, but the sudden weight of the man falling snaps the dead limb off the tree and our unhappy victim falls flat on his face on the rocks, which open him up." I paused. "There is no way to tell if he was dead before he hit the ground or not. It's funny in a morbid way. The guy tries to kill himself by hanging but kills himself by falling. He could have spared himself the trouble of climbing the tree."

"Why didn't he just jump?"

My turn to shrug. "We'll never know. Best guess is that he was afraid. The escarpment is fairly high, but our man might have feared falling and being injured but not killed. I wouldn't want to be lying on these rocks, a broken mass, waiting for whatever vultures or critters you have around here to come and pick off hunks of flesh.

"You know," I continued, "if I knew the moment arm, the weight of the victim, the length of rope, I might be able to calculate the force exerted on the tree limb."

"Moment arm. What's that?"

"The perpendicular distance from axis to point of force along the axis ... I guess they don't teach basic physics here. It doesn't matter. The end result is the same."

"What about the tracks down here?"

"Some people took it upon themselves to remove the body. They cut the rope leaving the noose around his neck. I assume that because I can see the cut end of the rope but can't find the noose."

"You truly see what others can't."

"You going to tell me what's going on? You know what happened, don't you?"

"I do, Max. And so do you."

"I told you everything I know. A man successfully killed himself even if his death didn't go as planned."

"Why would he do that? Why here? Why hanging?"

"Last question first: Hanging can be done alone. In the twenty-first-century people kill themselves with drugs or gas ovens or sometimes by slitting their wrists. The last technique is a lousy approach. It usually doesn't work. I don't think this era has the kind of drugs for a decent suicide. Hanging is pretty easy to do. If done right, then the neck breaks and death is close to instantaneous; if done badly, then the person chokes to death. A rotten way to go, but the end result is the same.

"As to why here? It's lonely. No one to talk him out of it. That tells me he was serious about ending his life. I can't answer your first question. Why does anyone kill himself?"

"You should know."

"What's that supposed to mean?"

"Just a comment. Do you know who the man is?"

"No. Not without a witness or a body." Sometimes I think my brain is occupied by elves who work without me knowing it. They're my subconscious. And the elves were making a ruckus. "It's related to Jesus, isn't it? I mean this whole thing is."

"Of course."

"So we're looking at Judas here."

Yoshua folded his hands in front of him. "This is where Judas died." He looked up at the redbud tree. "And after hurling the pieces of silver into the inner sanctuary, he withdrew and he hanged himself."[1]

"More Bible, I see. At least it got part of the story right."

"There's more. In the book of Acts it says, 'Now, this man purchased a piece of ground, the price having its source in wages for wrongdoing, and falling flat on his face, he split open at the waist with noise and his inner organs poured out. The place became known to all the residents of Jerusalem, so that piece of ground is called in their own language, Akeldama, that is, a bloody ground.'"[2]

"So this is the spot of the world's greatest traitor's demise." The thought sat heavy with me.

"He is buried not far from here; in what used to be a potter's field; a place where potters dug their clay. He's the first buried there. Soon it will be a place for indigent burial. It was bought with the money he received for betraying Jesus."

I shook my head. "From betraying Jesus in the garden to

killing himself in the wilderness. Something was terribly wrong with that man. How did he become a disciple anyway?"

"He was called," Yoshua answered and strode away. "There is someone I want you to meet."

"Who?"

He walked on and I, again, trailed after.

✝✝✝

We reentered the city through the Fountain Gate and were soon in the crowded streets of the lower city. The houses were small and the avenues filled with people dressed in clothing that had seen better days. I got the impression that this was the wrong side of the tracks. The poverty didn't seem to bother Yoshua. A child, maybe seven or eight, with a dirty face and bare feet ran through the street weaving between pedestrians. She was chased by another child, a boy, slightly younger. She was laughing and screaming in mock fear as she dodged those in her way. Glancing over her shoulder, she realized that her pursuer had closed the distance. She poured on more speed, but not before checking her direction.

She plowed into a man, bouncing off his right leg and tumbling to the dirty street. He stared at her, then at the boy who had come to an abrupt stop. His eyes were wide and he inserted the ends of two fingers in his mouth. The little girl sat petrified in place. Tears formed in her eyes.

The man, who looked to be sixty but I guessed was much younger, bent over the girl. "You should watch where you're going. You're a menace. What kind of parents allow such disrespect?" He pushed the sleeve of his garment up his right arm. "If your parents won't teach you manners, then I will."

113

He reached for the child who pulled back in fear. A hand—Yoshua's hand—seized the old guy's elbow. "No harm has been done."

"They are undisciplined children—"

"No harm has been done," Yoshua repeated. "Go your way." The last part carried the weight of an order.

The disgruntled man huffed, spun, and marched off. Yoshua squatted and placed a hand on her head. "Does your brother ever catch you?"

"No." She wiped a tear away. "I'm too fast."

Yoshua smiled. "Good." He stood and held out his hand. The young girl took it and he helped her to her feet.

"I'm sorry," she said.

"I know. Eyes forward when you run, little one. People get in trouble because they worry about what is behind instead of what is ahead. Do you understand?"

"Yes. I think so."

"Okay, off you go and don't run into anyone else."

She was gone the next second, the boy close on her heels.

"That was very civil of you, Yoshua," I said.

He looked at me with sad eyes. "These people have enough bad memories. She doesn't need another."

Some of the houses began to look familiar and I realized that we had come to the same part of town we visited yesterday. I was right. Yoshua led me to the same roadside café.

A man was waiting. He sat on the ground atop a thick blanket or rug. In the center was a large platter of food, a pitcher, and some cups. He wasn't eating. I wondered why he didn't choose one of the available tables. To each his own.

When he spied Yoshua and me, he rose, approached, and greeted us, kissing Yoshua on the cheek. "Peace to you," he said in a smooth voice. Yoshua returned the kiss. To me, the man offered a short bow. I returned the gesture.

"Sit. You must be tired." He waved toward the blanket. "Eat."

Last time I was here, I turned down the offer of food, but traipsing around the Hinnom Valley and walking the uphill path back to the city had kick-started my appetite.

Before I could grab so much as a fig, Yoshua offered the same prayer I'd heard at Mark's house the night before. "Blessed art thou, Jehovah our God, King of the world, who causes to come forth bread from the earth."

"Who is your friend, Brother Yoshua?" the man asked after seating himself cross-legged on the rug.

Yoshua looked at me and smiled. "His name is Max ben Odom. He comes from ... far away. HaShem has blessed him with special knowledge and insight into matters of the world."

"I have not seen clothes like his."

And you won't for twenty centuries.

"Brother Max, this is Levi ben Alpheus. He can be of help to you."

The name Levi rang a bell. He hovered a few inches shorter than me, sported a thick black beard, had clear eyes, a trim body, and looked to be in his late twenties.

"Please, Brother Yoshua, I still prefer Matthew. The old name bears too many memories."

"Matthew?" I said. "As in one of the disciples?"

His smile disappeared and suspicion filled his eyes. "I am one of the Twelve."

"We were just at the place of remorse," Yoshua said. "I wanted Brother Max to see it."

115

"I went once," Matthew said. "I do not wish to go again." He poured wine into the cups. I set mine on the lid of one of my kits. "It would have been better had he never been born."

"You knew Judas well?" I took a sip of the wine and reached for a piece of flat bread.

"Judah ben Simon," Matthew corrected me. "Judas is Greek for Judah. Although many called him by that name. Judas Ish Karioth. It means 'Judah, man of Karioth.' Of course I knew him; he walked with the Master for three years as I did."

"What's a Karioth?"

Matthew cut his eyes to Yoshua, but Yoshua said nothing.

"It's a town near Hebron. You know where Hebron is?"

I nodded although I had no idea. "He traveled with you those three years, yet he turned his teacher over to his enemies. At least according to Mark and Malchus, he did."

"I know you have spoken to Mark. Hosah told me. Yes, Brother Max, it is as you say."

Ah, that was how this meeting was set. When Yoshua told me he had to speak to Hosah, he must have asked him to deliver a message and set up this meeting. I had to hand it to him; Yoshua knew how to think ahead.

"What can you tell me about Judas ... Judah?"

"Call him what you will. Son of Perdition fits him." His words were hot but I sensed a deep hurt.

"Were you close to him?" He cocked his head. "I mean, were you friends at one time?"

"Friends? I suppose. In a way. Some men are open to others. Some keep to themselves. The traitor allowed no one close to him. He was different from the rest of us."

"Different? How?" I tried to keep my tone congenial although the urge to interrogate the man grew.

He pulled a piece of dried fish from the platter and tasted it. I recognized a stall when I saw it. "There were ... are many disciples. Hundreds, but the Master selected twelve men to accompany him everywhere. Some, like Peter and Andrew, were related; others were connected in other ways. Some of us were ... outcasts."

"Us?"

He fiddled with the fish. "There is Simon called the Zealot." He laughed.

"What's so funny?"

Yoshua explained. "The Zealots are a party opposed to Rome. They advocate resistance ... and the refusal to pay taxes."

"I don't get it."

"I was a tax collector," Matthew said flatly. "Until the Master came along and called me out of the collection booth."

"What's wrong with being a tax collector? Every nation has taxes of some sort and someone has to collect them."

Matthew looked down at the fish he held in his hand like a man who's appetite has just vanished.

"Does not Rome rule your land? Do they not take taxes from you as they do from us?"

"It's a little different where I live."

"Let me tell you how it is here, Brother Max." Matthew leaned forward. "Here, tax collectors are not paid by Rome. We made our money by taking as much as we can. I paid to Rome what they wanted and kept the rest for myself. Besides ..."

"Besides what?"

"I was a Jew collecting money from my fellow Jews and giving it to a Gentile government that occupies our land, threatens our people, and insults our religion. Add to that my inflating of the taxes due, and you can understand why I am without many friends—except other tax collectors."

117

"Let me get this right: There was one disciple who opposed paying taxes to Rome and one who actually collected them. Man, that must have made for some interesting dinner conversation."

"I don't know how interesting it was, but at first we seldom ate from the same side of the table." He laughed again. "The Master changed all that."

"What does this have to do with Judas?"

Matthew pursed his lips. "Different as we were, eleven of us had one thing in common: We were all Galileans."

"You mean Judas wasn't?"

"Of course not. I've already told you his family hails from Karioth."

"Right. Silly me. So Judas was from …"

"Idumea," Matthew said.

"Galilee is in the north, Idumea is in the south, as we are now." Yoshua sipped the wine.

Matthew stopped playing with his fish and took a bite.

"So he didn't fit in. Always the outsider. Is that it?"

"It was more than his place of birth that put him out. I was an outsider but well received by the others."

"Why is that?"

"Because I was willing to change, to let the Master teach me. Judas never saw Jesus the way we did."

"How do you mean?"

"We traveled with the Master for three years. At first we thought he was a good man, a prophet sent from God, or at least an important rabbi. But we saw the miracles. We heard the teaching. The more we were with him, the more we came to understand—some more than others." He lowered his head; his eyes seemed to be looking through the mist of history. "Lepers were cleansed, their skin made as new as that of a newborn. The lame were made to walk. They leaped—not just walked, but leaped for joy. The blind were given their sight. No prophet has ever restored sight to the blind. I saw Lazarus raised from the dead. I

118

saw vicious storms stopped at his word. We came to understand who the Master was."

"And just who was that?"

He returned his gaze to me. "Peter was the first to say it. It was at Caesarea Philippi. The Master asked who others thought he might be. We told him that some people thought he was Elijah come again, or John the Baptizer come back to life. Then he asked who *we* thought he was. We fell silent. No one wanted to be wrong. But Peter said, 'You are the Messiah, the son of God who lives.'"[3]

"Martha," Yoshua said. He reached for the goat cheese.

Matthew took it as a prompt and nodded. "Yes. It is true that Martha of Bethany said something similar before the Lord raised Brother Lazarus. I was speaking of the Twelve."[4]

"So Peter makes this grand statement and the Master does what?"

"He praised Simon Peter, explaining that HaShem revealed the truth to Peter. He blessed Peter."

"Did you agree?" I pressed him.

"Yes, of course. Very much then ... even now."

"Now that the Master is dead?"

For years I've heard the expression "his countenance fell" but never understood it. Now I did. Matthew looked like a man who had just had his soul stripped from his body.

"There is talk.... Some say he has risen from the dead."

I wanted to avoid that line of thought. I could do nothing but offend Yoshua and Matthew if I voiced my opinion about dead people coming back to life. I tried to right the mental train on the tracks.

119

"Are you saying that Judas did not agree with the rest of you about the Master being the Messiah?"

Matthew shook his head and his eyes darkened. "The highest title I ever heard him use to refer to the Master was rabbi. He never called him Lord.[5] Not once. He never acknowledged the Master as Messiah."

"If his views were so different, then why did he stay around? Better yet, why did you let him stay?"

"It was clear to us that he was different. Not just the place of his birth, but the way he looked at others, the things he valued."

"Like what?"

"Money. He was the treasurer and kept the money box. Once he criticized a woman in Bethany at the house of Simon the Leper. She anointed the head of the Master with expensive perfume. He spoke to her harshly. He thought the money should go to the poor. The Master quieted him.[6] It was not the first time he had done so. At the house of Lazarus in Bethany, the Master reclined at table, and Mary anointed his head with expensive nard and then anointed his feet and wiped it with her hair. Never have I seen such humility. But Judas chastised her in her own home."[7]

"What kind of money are we talking about here?"

"Three hundred denarii—maybe more, maybe less."

That meant nothing to me. Yoshua picked up on my confusion. "Most workers make one denarius a day."

"The perfume cost a year's salary?" That floored me. "So Judas was concerned for the welfare of the poor? Sounds noble enough."

"He never gave anything to the poor," Matthew spat. "He only wanted more money in the box. John told me that the traitor pilfered from the funds."

Yoshua cleared his throat. "Matthew, at Simon the Leper's house, did Judas alone complain about the perfume?"

Matthew looked away. I could see his jaw tighten, and I waited for the sound of cracking teeth.

His head moved back and forth like a slow metronome. "No. Some of us agreed. *I* agreed."

Ah, the money men, tax collector and group treasurer, were more alike than Matthew wanted to let on.

"If Judas was such a pain ..." I rethought my phrasing. "What I mean is, if Judas was a thief, then why did he remain treasurer? For that matter, why did you allow him to stay with the group?"

"Who received an invitation to join and those allowed to stay did not rest with us. It rested with the Master. Besides ..." He trailed off.

"Besides what?"

Matthew frowned. "I do not know if you can understand this."

"Try me."

"When a man walks with the Master, he is more aware of his own sins than the sins of another. We assumed—I assumed that Judas would see as we saw; believe as we believed."

"But he didn't."

"No. After the incident in Simon the Leper's house, Judas left to meet with the chief priests."[8]

"He went alone?"

"Of course."

"Then how do you know where he went?"

"Do you not believe me, Brother Max?"

Time to ease up. "I'm just trying to learn as much as I can."

"The Master had many followers. Some are servants in service to the chief priests. Word has come to us."

"So what pushed Judas over the edge?" I thought of the red-bud tree, the escarpment, and the ugly events that happened there and cringed at my unintentional pun. "Why did he betray Jesus?"

121

"Only HaShem can know the heart of a man," Matthew said.

"You must have a guess."

"Look around you, Brother Max. What do you see?" Before I could answer, Matthew chose to speak for me. "You see an oppressed people. You see men who must step aside for the Roman soldiers; men who are afraid to let eye meet eye. You also see a people whose patience has been worn thin. Too many decades have passed."

"Judas was unhappy with the situation?"

"Everyone is unhappy with the situation. Do you know why many did not follow the Master as Messiah?"

"No."

"It is because they want a Messiah who can destroy Rome and free the people. They want a Messiah with a sword in his hand. The Master spoke of turning the other cheek[9] and to go the extra mile when our oppressors pressed us into unjust service.[10] Such teaching is not what the people want to hear."

"And Judas wanted the Master to do more?" I could see where this was going.

"Yes, Brother Max. The Master taught that he would be mistreated and killed by our religious leaders. Judas preferred it otherwise."

"But how does betraying Jesus accomplish that?"

"Judas saw—we all saw—that the Master possessed the greatest of powers. If he could still a storm with a word or command death to give up those it held, what could he do to the dogs that oppress us?"

"Are those the same dogs you worked for collecting taxes?"

"Yes, but no one would be happier to see our country free. Is your country free of Rome? Of course not. They rule the world."

I didn't bother to correct him. "Are you saying that Judas

betrayed Jesus to put him in a position where he would have to defend himself? He was trying to force his hand?"

"Yes. He always did what was best for him. Judas loved control, but he could not control the Master."

I turned to Yoshua. "Does this seem right to you?"

"It does."

Thoughts danced around in my head and I tried to force them into an order. A picture was forming.

And it was an ugly one.

chapter 8

"I haven't figured you out yet," I said as we worked our way through the streets. As usual, Yoshua walked a pace or two ahead of me.

"What's to figure out?" He kept his stride.

"You ever play poker?" The question seemed stupid the moment it left my lips.

"No. I never felt drawn to the game."

"It's experiencing a resurgence in my country. Even cable sport channels televise high-stake poker games."

"And this is leading where?"

Yoshua moved like a man with boulders in his pockets. He had been in a solemn mood since he woke me this morning. "Poker players have a phrase: 'He keeps his cards close to his vest.'"

"I believe I've heard it." He cast a glance over his shoulder at me. "I'm not wearing a vest."

"I'm aware of that. It's not your attire I'm interested in. It's your cards. You are a man with many secrets."

"Are you speaking professionally?"

"I don't need decades of police experience to know when a man is keeping things to himself."

"And what do you suppose I'm keeping to myself?"

"You knew Judas, didn't you?"

He nodded. "I did."

"How well did you know him?"

"Have I become ... what is it called? An interesting person?"

"You're playing with me, Yoshua. I have a feeling you know the phrase is 'person of interest,' not 'interesting person.' A person of interest is someone who may or may not be involved in a crime but certainly has some knowledge or information. Although I might have to give you that point about being interesting. You're certainly that."

"So am I a person of interest?"

"How well did you know Judas?" I repeated.

"As well as one person could. He was complex—a muddle of a man."

"What does that mean? Muddle of a man?"

He slowed and put his hands behind his back, but he continued forward. We were approaching the shadow of the aqueduct that split the city. "Have you ever known someone with many interests; someone who might love science, but loves art just as much?"

"Yeah. We call someone like that a Renaissance man. Many

125

interests and skills. You're saying Judas was some kind of first-century Renaissance man?"

"Not at all, but he was a man of many thoughts—too many thoughts. Unlike your Renaissance man who finds some way to keep conflicting ideas compartmentalized in his brain and is able to bridge them when necessary, there are people whose thoughts and desires run together like mudslides from opposite slopes of a valley."

"You think Judas was that type of man?"

"He had unquenchable desires. He longed to be part of something special, something grand, something bigger than himself; but he also had views on how that should happen."

"I don't follow."

"Every Jew chafes under the yoke of Rome, but those who live closest to Jerusalem feel it even more. Judas had expectations and realized he wasn't going to receive them."

"So he took matters into his own hands. I got that much from Matthew. What I can't wrap my brain around is why you're so depressed about the man's death. Two thousand years from now, people will still be talking about how traitorous Judas was."

"Who said I felt depressed?"

"No one has to say it. It's obvious: shoulders slightly drooped, head down, empty eyes. Some people would have spit on the site where Judas died. You looked positively mournful."

"I wasn't depressed."

"You could have fooled me," I said. "What would you call it?"

He thought for a moment. "My heart was heavy."

126

"Over Judas? You've got to be kidding. You heard what Malchus said in the garden. Judas led the mob to Jesus and identified him with a kiss. Why would you grieve over a man like that?"

"Because he had been close to the Truth and failed to see it, no matter how clearly it was pointed out to him. He thought he knew better; that he had all the answers. The Master was on the wrong track as far as Judas was concerned, so Judas decided to force the issue—push Jesus into the conquering role."

"So it didn't work and Judas killed himself. Sounds just to me."

Yoshua stopped midstride. "There are many people who can't see the truth when it's right in front of them, Max. Many men who think they have all the answers or that the world has wronged them so they deserve better."

He started walking again. "Judas deserves no adulation, no honor, and no one to make excuses for him. He is as you have described him, and he is responsible for his actions."

"Finally, we agree on something."

"Just like you are responsible for your decisions."

"What's that supposed to mean?"

"Max Odom, it is clear to me that you, too, are holding your cards close to your vest."

Yoshua stopped abruptly and I almost ran into him. My attention had been fixed on the changes around me. The small ghetto housing of the poorer district had given way to a wider stone path and houses made with cut stone. The craftsmanship indicated high-end labor. Mark's house stood large compared to most of the hovels I had seen, but these homes were nothing short of mansions.

"My mother would have called this 'high cotton,'" I said then explained, "It's a southern phrase meaning top notch, good times, expensive."

127

"From there to here." Yoshua was being cryptic.

"From where to where?"

"From the garden to here."

"This is where they brought Jesus?" I looked at the large structure. The same white-gray stone that made up the walls of the city had been used here. Much smaller, of course, but larger than typical brick. I didn't venture a guess as to the square footage, but knew it could hold a large family with ease, not to mention a couple dozen servants.

The walls were straight and plumb, broken only by a few windows, each with wood lattice work. Stepped buttress walls were spaced every twenty-feet to support the tall structure. The building stood three stories in the back and two stories in the front. Like most houses, it had a courtyard, but this one was large enough to park several buses in.

"Who owns this? I'm betting he's got more than a few bucks to be able to afford this place."

Yoshua looked grim. "It belongs to Annas ben Seth, high priest. Here lives Joseph Caiaphas, high priest."

"There are two of them?" That struck me as odd.

"Yes and no. The high priest serves for life, but the Roman occupiers do not like power to reside with one Jew for very long. Annas served in the role for ten years but was deposed by Valerius Gratus."

"So he lost his job."

"In a way." Yoshua turned his attention to me. "Under the Law of Moses, a high priest serves for life. Rome took his title but the people still consider him their high priest. His influence is undeniable. Joseph Caiaphas is Annas's son-in-law. Five of his children have served or will serve as high priest."

"If Rome decides who gets to be high priest, then this Annas guy must have a lot of pull with them."

"He does. He has wealth. He has power."

"It sounds like he has everything."

Yoshua shook his head. "He doesn't have a conscience."

He stepped forward and peered over a shoulder-high wall that marked off a courtyard. A thick wood gate stood locked in place. I joined him and looked in. The courtyard was wide and deep, the ground covered in stone pavers. In a few strategic places that any landscaper would admire, the ground had been left open for plants. Around two sides, where courtyard met home, was a covered walkway. Several chairs and a table rested in the shade. I hadn't seen a chair since arriving. The closest things to it were the benches in Mark's upper room. I imagined chairs were an expensive item in this place.

The center of the open space was dominated by a fire pit. I could see the blackened remains of wood and the soft gray of ashes. Around the pit ran a circular stone bench.

"They brought Jesus here? To Annas or Caiaphas?"

"To Annas first—"

"What do you want?" The words snapped loudly in my ear. I jerked around to face the speaker, but before I could reset my feet, a hand caught me by the shirt, pulled me forward, then slammed me back. My back hit the stone wall and my head snapped back then forward in whiplash fashion. Pain ran both directions in my spine. I dropped my kits and fought for a decent breath.

In front of me stood a tall, thick man, with a black beard, thick lips, and a grimace that could peel paint.

"Easy, friend," Yoshua said.

I'm not good with pain. It makes me angry. Being two thousand years in the past hadn't changed that. The cop in me kicked in. I knocked his arm away but it felt like I had hit a tree limb. Before he could react, I stepped into him, placing a hand to his chest and one foot behind his heel. I pushed for all I was worth, and the big man went to the ground, landing flat on his back.

129

Policemen are taught to avoid fistfights. A uniformed officer carries mace, a baton, and a gun for a reason. When making an arrest of an uncooperative suspect, he is taught to take the perp to the ground and subdue him there—preferably with the help of one or two more other officers. I didn't have other officers, but I wasn't about to let this guy up until I had some answers.

I started my move, but before I could take another step, something drew me back on my heels and spun me around. Before I could regain my balance, I was shoved to the side.

Spinning, I prepared myself to take on what I was certain was a second attacker. I saw only Yoshua between me and the gorilla that knocked me into the wall. The attacker had made it to his feet and took a plodding two steps my way. He started around Yoshua who shifted his position to interpose himself between me and the bruiser.

There was no way I was going to let Yoshua take my fight. I didn't know him well, but I had serious doubts about his fighting skill. He didn't seem the type to throw a punch let alone take one on the chin.

"Out of my way," the big man barked. "I will teach the dog a lesson."

"Bring it, pal. I got your lesson right here." I clenched my hands. If he wanted a fistfight, then I'd oblige. He might give me a beating, but I would make certain he'd remember me for years to come.

I took a step.

"Stay where you are, Max." Yoshua gave the command without changing position, his back still turned my way, his eyes fixed on the problem. Again, Yoshua positioned himself between us. Still, he didn't raise a hand.

"I said, out of my way." Spit sprayed from the angry man.

"No," Yoshua said. "He doesn't understand."

"Then I'll teach him. Now move or I'll move you."

"No."

The man's anger shifted from me to Yoshua. I had to act quickly.

Something grabbed me from behind. I felt a hand on my collar. Again I was turned about. Something moved past my peripheral vision. I didn't wait for an introduction. I threw a right cross that landed hard on the chin of the man who held me. Saliva and blood squirted from his mouth. I allowed only half a moment of satisfaction for landing such a fine knockout blow. Except it didn't have the effect I had hoped for. In front of me stood a man of my height and build but with a very deep anger. Blood trickled from the corner of his mouth.

The next second is still blurry. I felt him grab my shirt and pull. His forehead smashed into my nose and fireworks exploded in my brain. I felt a knee in the groin and the air left my lungs. A hand grabbed my hair and jerked my head up. My brain ordered my right arm to try another right hook, but something was lost in the transmission. My arm didn't move.

A strong hand seized my throat and squeezed. I stumbled backward, pushed by the new attacker. A moment later I felt the block wall that surrounded the courtyard dig into the flesh of my back. What little air was left in my lungs left.

My vision cleared, and I saw the face of the man who seemed to be enjoying the moment. I struck at the hand that pinched my throat closed.

Someone else hit the wall. A glance told me it was Yoshua. Blood trickled from his nose. We were both penned, but I wasn't through. I had to act before I lost consciousness. I reached over my attacker's hand, seized his little finger, and pulled back—hard. I had to dig into my own flesh to get a good hold, but I managed it. I pulled, then yanked.

The knuckle snapped.

The man screamed and loosened his grip.

This time it was me delivering a knee to the groin and I did it with all the strength I could muster, which wasn't nearly as much as I would like. The man folded like a lounge chair. I brought the same knee up catching him in the face.

He went down.

Something hit me on the right side of the head. I felt no pain, just the sensation of falling. The ground rose to meet me.

My head bounced.

Dirt filled my mouth and nose.

Things went gray, then black.

The dream was the same. It always was. Sometimes the setting was different, or the time of day, or the clothes I wore, but the rest of it, the part that really mattered, never altered.

He walked toward me, his green garb a near perfect match to the green walls of the corridor. In the hyper-reality of the nightmare, he approaches, head down as if examining his reflection in the highly polished floors.

His footfalls echo in the hallway.

Everyone is gone.

It is just us. No nurses. No other doctors. No janitors with mop and pail. No elderly volunteers in cheerful pink smocks.

Just him.

Just me.

Why won't he make eye contact? Why won't he look at me?

Maybe he's looking for someone else. Maybe the grim mask he wears is meant for another man, not me.

He stops a pace away from me and raises his head, then shakes it.

"I'm sorry. We did all we could. We used the best equipment and people we had, but it was hopeless from the beginning. There was just too much damage. Much too much damage."

It was my turn to shake my head. "No. You're wrong. You can do more. Please, do more."

He says he's sorry but his eyes are dry. He says he understands but I know he doesn't.

"I wish we could have done more."

Turning, he leaves me standing alone in the wide corridor. A moment later he is out of sight.

Someone begins to turn off the lights in the hospital. First in the waiting room to my right, then above the nurse's station, then those in front of the elevator.

The last lights to go out are those that illuminated the glossy corridor.

With no light to reflect, the hall goes abysmally dark.

I am standing alone. The only sound I hear …

… are my sobs.

Someone was using a jackhammer in my brain. Maybe it was someone beating an anvil. I couldn't tell. I hurt. The side of my head felt caved in, my back ached, my throat bruised. I tasted dirt mixed with the copper tang of blood.

133

I groaned and rolled on to my back. The motion brought new aches. After a couple of deep breaths, despite the siren call of sleep, I opened my eyes and forced the rest of my senses awake.

Something had changed. I was no longer on the street. Instead, I lay on the stone pavers of the courtyard. The cold seeping into my bones told me I had been there for a while.

I pulled myself into a sitting position. Things seemed to spin; my head felt like it was doing cartwheels. I raised a hand and touched the side of my head. It ached and throbbed.

"How do you feel?"

I recognized the voice. "I think I was hit by a speeding bus—twice."

"It wasn't a bus."

I turned my head on an uncooperative and complaining neck. Yoshua sat on the circular stone bench that circumscribed the fire pit. He had bruises on his throat, and his lower lip was swollen. He had taken a couple of shots himself.

I rolled over on to my hands and knees and waited for the courtyard to stop spinning. When I tried to get up, I staggered. Yoshua grabbed me by the arm and led me to the bench. The strength of his grip surprised me.

"You better sit for a while," he said. "I don't think you're ready to be walking around."

"I'll be fine. I just need a couple of … of … Where are my kits?"

He motioned toward the wood gate that led to the street. The kits were there. So were the two men we met on the street. Both eyed me like an exterminator eyes a cockroach. Their mood had not improved during my nap.

"How long have I been out?"

"A long time. The sun is going down."

"I was out the whole time?"

"Off and on. You'd wake, groan, and then lose consciousness again."

I didn't remember any of that. "I shouldn't have been out that long."

"You were."

As casually as I could, I looked around. We were in the same courtyard we had been looking at when Godzilla showed. "We're still at the high priest's house?"

"Yes."

"Are those our only two guards?"

"Forget it, Max. You want to escape, and they want you to try. Same desire, different goals."

"He caught me with a lucky punch."

"Lucky or not, it put you to sleep for a while, and those two men would like to make it permanent. You insulted them."

"I did what?" I bent over trying to relieve the pain that ran from knees to head.

"No one fights with the high priest's men. You started a fight on a public street."

"I didn't start the fight. Big Ben over there did. I just defended myself—and you for that matter."

Yoshua sighed. "You're lucky to be alive."

"It looks like you got roughed up a little."

"Violence breeds violence. I wanted to talk our way out of the problem."

"Talking doesn't always work."

"How would you know, Max? You didn't give it a chance."

Yoshua was getting under my skin. "I didn't ask for this—any of this."

"Still, you have it, don't you?"

"Just whose side are you on, pal?" I stood. A mistake.

135

Nausea roiled in my belly. I lowered myself back to the stone bench.

"Believe it or not, I'm on yours. Whose side are you on?"

"Mine, buddy. Just mine."

"And therein is the problem."

I didn't know what he meant by that, and I felt too sick to pursue it. I changed the subject. "Did you see the back of the big guy's hand?"

"What about it?"

"The back of his hand had a scab on it. His right hand. I saw it when he first attacked me."

"And?"

"It's not just a cut. I've seen similar injuries many times. I didn't have time to examine it, but I'd bet you my last dollar—or whatever you spend here—that he earned the wound by backhanding someone. The shape makes me think that his hand impacted someone's teeth."

"He backhanded someone."

I couldn't decide if it was a question or a statement. I took it as the former. "Yes, and pretty hard, too. Of course, I can't prove it without a proper examination, but I'm pretty confident about what I saw." The pounding in my head began to ease and the nausea went from boiling to a mere simmer.

A young girl approached with a cup of water in each hand. She looked to be about twelve years old. Her face was clean and her eyes a dark brown. She didn't smile. She said nothing as she held out the cups. She never made eye contact. A moment later, she scurried away. Before she did, I caught her stealing a glance at the men by the gate. She frowned. All kinds of thoughts filled my mind, and I felt like renewing the fight.

An urge to pour the water on the ground ran through my

mind, but then I noticed Yoshua suck his down. I took a sip. It had the same wine flavor as what I had at Mark's house this morning. Despite my best efforts to reject the gift, I took a deep swallow. The water was gone in two gulps, and I set the cup down.

"I suppose I should be thankful for that."

Yoshua looked at me. "It is always good to be thankful."

"I can think of a few cases when it's not."

A movement by the gate told me something was up. Our two guards stiffened and their eyes shifted to a spot over my left shoulder. I turned. A man approached.

His shoulders were slightly stooped, his beard gray from root to tip. He wore a blue garment. He also wore phylacteries on his left hand and forehead. He moved with an awkward gait, and one foot turned out farther than the other. He also moved like a man with lower back pain—stiff and with little side-to-side movement.

Yoshua stood and faced the man. I followed suit. Before I knew it, the two men were behind us. I could feel one of them breathing down my neck.

The old man hobbled around the fire pit and faced us. He stopped inches from my face, clearly no respecter of personal space. He looked me in the eyes and tilted his head to the side, like a man trying to understand a piece of abstract art. After looking me up and down a couple of times, his lips parted in an insincere smile.

"You are not from around here." His teeth were brown, crooked, and worn enough that I could see the pulp of his molars. There were gaps where the left incisor had been—and the right bicuspid. His breath smelled of cheese long past its expiration date.

"No, I'm not." I tried to strip away the bitterness from my voice. I had a feeling this guy held my life in his hands.

"He is a traveler," Yoshua inserted, "from a distant part of the kingdom."

The old man nodded. "The Empire is wide." He stepped to Yoshua. "And who are you, my son?"

Yoshua bowed his head an inch. "My name is Yoshua, this is my friend Max ben Odom. I am his guide."

"Well, guide, why were you lurking around my house?"

My house? The pieces of the puzzle self-assembled. Yoshua had said that there were two high priests who lived here. One bore the name Caiaphas and the other, the older one, Annas.

"I was showing him the important parts of our city."

Annas nodded. "Is he of the *goyim?*"

Yoshua nodded. "He is Gentile."

Annas took a step back as if he could see cooties breeding on me. "I suspected that truth. It is why you have not been invited into my house."

Yoshua said nothing, and in a moment of brilliance on my part, I kept my mouth shut.

"We meant no harm," Yoshua said. "My client is unfamiliar with some of our ways. For that, I take full responsibility."

"My men tell me you put up a fight, young man." He directed the statement to me. It was time to think on my feet.

"Your guards mistakenly assumed we meant to harm or rob you. I mistakenly took their aggression for something criminal. I fought back before I realized they were in service to you." I paused. Everyone looked at me. Bile tried to crawl up my throat, but I spoke the words anyway. "I am deeply sorry for the misunderstanding."

He smiled again, and the sight of his decayed mouth made me wish he wouldn't. "Not many men are foolish enough to fight with guards of the high priest. These men are the best of the best. You

CRIME SCENE
JERUSALEM

should praise HaShem that they didn't break your neck." He laughed. "Where would we bury you?" He laughed again.

"Did you know a man named Jesus?" I blurted the words out. The laughing stopped.

"Why do you ask? Are you a follower of the blasphemer?"

I hadn't expected that. "No. I'm not. I heard about him and wondered about his case."

"Case?"

"The things that happened to him and why they happened."

The eyes of the old man scrutinized me. I felt as if he read the thoughts right off my brain. After a moment he nodded. "I met him. He was here not many days ago. He stood in my house."

"I understand he was brought here by force."

"And how would a stranger know that?"

Yoshua fielded the question. "We met Malchus. In the garden where the arrest took place. Malchus found the sword that injured him."

"I gave the sword to your servant."

Annas waved a dismissive hand. "He is Caiaphas's slave, not mine."

"But you did bring Jesus here by force?"

Annas tugged at his long beard. "I encouraged my son-in-law Caiaphas to do so. The blasphemer misled the people and threatened our peace with Rome. As high priest, Caiaphas is duty bound to protect the faithful."

This guy had been practicing his story.

"May I ask what happened when he was brought to your home?" I tried a more civil tone, mindful that there were two men within arm's reach who would like to work me over again.

Annas gave me the eye again, as if determining whether I was worth his time. He didn't answer at first and with every second that passed, the air seemed to drop a degree. I half expected him to look to his bodyguards for opinions, but Annas didn't seem the kind of man who needed suggestions—or tolerated them.

"I wanted to question him. He was to be tried by the court but it takes time to gather the members. We kept him here until the council was ready."

"And you questioned him? About what?"

"About his crimes, of course—his crimes against the Law and against the temple." He paced. "You'd understand if you had seen it. Riding into the city on a donkey, people—hundreds of people—waving palm branches and stripping off their cloaks and throwing them on the ground before him as he rode. On the ground!"

He paused and his face reddened. I would not have been surprised if he popped a vein right there. His mouth grew tight, his fist clenched. "Do you know what the people shouted as he rode along? Do you?"

"No, I wasn't there. Maybe you could tell me—"

"Hosanna. Of all things, hosanna! Oh, not one; not just his close disciples. All of them. Pilgrims from all over the land come to Jerusalem for Passover, and they lined the road and shouted, 'Hosanna, to the Son of David. Blessed is he who comes in the name of the Lord. Hosanna in the highest!'"[1]

He spat on the ground, the spittle landing inches from Yoshua's feet. Yoshua didn't move.

"I don't understand," I said. "What's wrong with saying Hosanna?"

For a moment I thought he would spit again, this time in my face. "Are you so ignorant? Do they not have schools where you come from?"

Yoshua explained. "Hosanna means 'Oh save,' or just 'Save us.'"

"At least one of you knows something," Annas said. "The crowd, mostly Galileans I am told, were singing the Hallel to that commoner, that carpenter from Nazareth. 'Save us, Son of David.' They called him King. A know-nothing carpenter, they call a king. It's blasphemy to HaShem and traitorous to Rome. We have a king, and it isn't the one called Jesus."

"So the crowd got a little excited."

"You idiot! He allowed them to dishonor HaShem and could have brought down the wrath of Rome on our heads. The Pharisees tried to warn him. They pleaded with him to quiet his disciples, but he told them that if the people were quiet, then the stones would sing his praises." He clamped his jaw shut and through clenched teeth added, "He thought he was the Messiah. Now he knows the truth of the matter."

The fury boiling in Annas was clear. If Jesus had been standing with us, I'm certain Annas would have tried to kill him again.

"Let me get this right. Because people sang a song—"

"Not just any song, fool. You understand nothing."

"But that was why you questioned him?"

"Not just that," Annas shot back. "He deserved death many times over. I regret we could only kill him once."

"What other crimes?"

"After he arrived in Jerusalem, he ran off the legitimate business in the courts of the temple. He upturned their tables claiming purification of the temple.[2] Then he worked his magic tricks."

Magic tricks? "What do you mean by magic tricks?"

"So-called healings of the blind and the lame."[3] Annas shook his head. "The children began to sing the Hosanna to him. Children!"

"So you don't think Jesus worked miracles?"

"I had him in my house and he showed me no powers, no

might. He did not look like the Messiah. He looked like a common carpenter with dreams of being something his kind can never be. Trickery. It was all trickery. They said he raised Lazarus from the dead. I doubt Lazarus was ever dead. Yet, the people believed him, and it was my job to put an end to it before he could do any more damage."

"Is it a crime to work miracles, real or otherwise?"

"It is if you, a man, make yourself out to be God."

"So you questioned Jesus?"

"I did. Of course I did. The judgment rested with Caiaphas, but I had questions."

"What kind of questions?"

"Pertinent ones. It's beyond your understanding."

"Try me," I pressed him.

He sighed. I figured he chose to answer because of the culture of hospitality that Yoshua had described. Still, I knew that he had limits.

"I asked questions about his teaching and about his disciples. I wanted to know everyone close to him."

"Did he give you names?"

"No. His arrogance prohibited him. Instead, he suggested that I ask the hundreds who had heard him teach. He said he spoke openly, and that he taught in synagogues and in the temple."[4]

"So he suggested that you interview those who heard him teach. Sounds reasonable."

"It is not reasonable to evade a question—especially *my* question." He looked at the big man I had tussled with earlier, then back at me. "That's when I had him struck."[5]

That explained the cut on the bruiser's hand. It appeared that Annas shared the same bad temper.

"How many times did you allow him to be hit?"

142

Annas shrugged. "A few. I did not count."

"Did you torture him?" I expected Annas to blow up over that question, but he took it easily.

"Of course not. We let the Romans take care of such things."

Sweet guy. "Then what happened?"

"I grew weary of him. In my presence he did not seem so mighty. He was just a man in dirty clothes, weary from his many lies."

I thought back to the garden and the suffering that Jesus must have endured to experience hematidrosis and sweat blood. Having agonized in prayer, been betrayed, bound, and led here, must have crushed the man, yet I knew enough to know that it hadn't.

"Maybe you can tell me—"

"No. I've wasted enough time with you. Do not come to my gate again."

Before I could speak, the old man shuffled off, looking more worn and tired than when he arrived. The memories of that night must be heavy.

"It's time to go, Max," Yoshua said.

The two men in front of us refused to move, but they made no effort to stop us as we walked around them and I retrieved my kits.

Once we were well beyond the gate, I said, "Not a very pleasant man."

"No, there is nothing pleasant about him."

chapter
9

We walked in silence, the sun inching toward the horizon, the azure sky slowly darkening toward cobalt and the inevitable blackness of night. The wind had picked up and carried with it a chill that made my already-sore body ache. The problem with injuries is that the pain grows for the first day. Shock and adrenaline dulls the sharp edge but that soon wears off, leaving ribs to complain with every breath, bruises to grow more sensitive, and muscle aches to ratchet up their complaint.

It had been a long day, and I yearned for a bed—even the itchy wool blankets of the pallet where I slept last night. My legs were weary of walking, my shoulders and hands made known their impatience with the weight of my field kits.

Yoshua had been roughed up, but he made no complaints. He moved slowly through the streets with his head down. The broader avenues and larger homes were left behind us.

"I don't know this city very well, Yoshua, but shouldn't we be headed the other way to reach Mark's house?"

"Yes."

"Then why aren't we?"

"Because we're not going to Mark's house. We have another stop to make."

"Where?"

"Near the temple."

The temple complex was not far ahead. I could see the large structure glinting in the fading sunlight. Its white stone and gold trimming made it stand out. That and its size. Tall walls of massive stone formed a plaza. A tall building dominated the middle of it.

"So that's the temple that got Jesus in so much trouble," I said. "Look at the size of it. How big is it?"

"The complex is about forty acres. The temple itself is much smaller."

"And they built all of this by hand?"

"Yes. Herod rebuilt the temple and its structures. It has stood like this for nearly thirty years."

"You said it would be all torn down."

"In a few decades from now. All of it gone, except that retaining wall." He pointed in the direction of the west side of the complex.

145

The amount of people going and coming from the area amazed me. Yoshua had told me that pilgrims had filled the city, but the numbers I saw startled me.

"Annas mentioned Jesus committed crimes against the temple. What did he mean by that?"

"To the Jew, the temple is the center of the universe. It is God's house. Any crime against the temple is a crime against him."

"The center of the universe." I mulled over the comment. It seemed absurd to me. How could a building contain God? "I still don't understand what Jesus did that could be construed as a threat against this place. It would take a lot of men to do any real damage."

Yoshua kept us moving. "It isn't what he said; it's what others *thought* he said."

"And what was that?"

"There is someone I want you to meet. We must hurry."

Fifteen minutes later we stood in front of a small bazaar. Outdoor shops sold everything from fruit and bread—what I assumed to be the first century's idea of fast food—to sparrows, which Yoshua told me the poor used for sacrifices. I had to admit that it was a good location. People going from the residential part of the city to the temple passed this way. Even in the first century, retail success was spelled location, location, location.

A middle-aged man and a boy, who I took to be his son, manned an open-air storefront filled with sandals. He called out to those who passed by. Most ignored him, but some came to look at his wares. Yoshua nodded at the man and patted the boy on the head as he moved from the street into the "sales area" and through a tentlike flap at the back of the store. As always, I followed.

Once through the flap I was surprised to see three other tent walls. We were in the storage area. A blanket on the ground marked off the "lunch room." A woman inside set a plate of flat bread and cheese in the middle of the blanket. A ceramic pitcher sat nearby. The moment we entered, she rose and left.

146

"I take it you know the cobbler." I set my kits down, glad to be free of the weight. I sat on one. Yoshua sat cross-legged on the floor.

"I know him. He was expecting us."

"He's the guy you want me to meet?"

Yoshua shook his head. "He'll be here soon." Yoshua poured water into a cup and passed it to me. I took it. He offered the platter of bread and cheese and I didn't hesitate to take some. The walking and fighting had left me starved. Besides, I hoped eating would ease the throbbing pain in my head from the blows I took. At the moment, I would have traded everything in my field kits for a handful of ibuprofen.

I had finished off my second piece of bread and third cup of wine-laced water when the flap opened and a man entered.

"I'm sorry I am late."

Yoshua stood and put his hands on the man's shoulders and they exchanged kisses on the cheek. The man stood four inches shorter than Yoshua and looked ten years younger. His hair was dark, his beard black and untouched by gray. His skin bore the dark, leathery features of an outdoorsman.

"You have been hurt, brother," the man said. His voice was clear and youthful.

"Nothing to worry about," Yoshua said. "We spent some time at the house of Annas."

The concerned look on the visitor's face switched to one of anger. I could see he was working hard not to say what was on his mind.

147

"His men attacked you?"

"Yes, and my friend here put one of them on his back."

He raised an eyebrow. "Is this true? You fought back?"

"Not for long, I'm afraid."

For some reason, that fact tickled the man and he let slip a loud laugh. He then regained control of himself. "I am sorry. I shouldn't have laughed at the violence." Apparently the image played in his mind again because another guffaw erupted. "I wish I had been there to see that. Bless HaShem that you are safe." He chuckled again. I doubted he would be laughing if he saw the rest of the fight. I know I had no desire to laugh.

"Sit," Yoshua said and offered the food and water to the man. "I want you to meet my friend," he continued. "This is Max ben Odom. He is here from a land far away." He turned to me. "Max, this is John ben Zebedee. He is one of the disciples of the Master."

"Shalom," John said.

"Um, shalom. I guess."

"John," Yoshua said. "How is Mary?"

He shook his head. "She grieves terribly. I do what I can. The Master entrusted me with so much. I wish I knew better what to do."

"Mary?" I asked.

"The mother of the Master," John said. "From the cross he said … he asked …" His eyes filled with tears.[1]

Yoshua explained. "When the Master hung on the cross, he gave responsibility for his mother to John. She has been staying with him. He has rented a home in the city."

"That's very noble." I didn't know what else to say.

John gave me a thank-you nod but turned his attention back to Yoshua. "There is much talk about the tomb. Mary of Magdala went to—"

Yoshua's raised hand cut John off. "I know. We can talk of that later. It is important for Max that things be done in order."

"What things?" John asked.

"Max has special gifts and training. He is following the Master's last hours. He has questions for you."

"What kind of questions?" Both men looked at me.

It was showtime and I didn't know enough to ask pointed questions. I began with something general. "When you heard that we had been to the house of Annas, you looked angry. Do you know Annas?"

"Oh, I know him, and Caiaphas, too. Better than most."

I studied him closely. He wore clean clothing but not the fine weave I had seen on the wealthier citizens. His face and hands were sun darkened. He struck me as a man familiar with hard work.

"May I ask what you do for a living?" I asked.

"For the last few years I have traveled with the Master. Before that I fished with my brother and our father."

"How does a fisherman come to know someone like Annas? Isn't there some kind of class distinction?"

I caught Yoshua smiling. John just tilted his head. "Fishing is an honorable and lucrative business, Brother Max. My father owns several boats. He has done well for himself and our family. He has made many contributions to the synagogue in our town and to the temple treasuries in Jerusalem."

"What are you smiling at, Yoshua?" His grin irritated me.

"You've made the same assumption that many twenty-first-century people do. Not everyone in this century is poor, uneducated, and without influence. Many people make a good living by the sweat of their efforts."

"Had I known I was going to land in this time, I might have prepared a little better, but as you know I wasn't advised of the travel plans."

John looked confused and I knew why. He could not conceive

149

of the twenty-first century or someone like me. I didn't feel like explaining it.

"So, you know the high priests because of your father?"

John nodded. "We have been to his home before. Annas and Caiaphas sometimes invite large contributors to share a meal." He paused. "There was a time when that mattered to me."

"But not now?"

He lowered his eyes. "Not since that night. Not since ..." He choked back a sob then buried his face in his hands. I had seen the toll trauma takes on survivors of a crime. Too many times I had walked through the rooms and halls of someone's house that had been blackened by a violent murder: painted walls splattered with blood; pools of blood absorbed by carpet; flesh blown away from the body by a bullet or jerked free by some kind of object like a tire iron. Sometimes those who remain behind suffer more than the victim. John, although he looked strong and vibrant, was a man of tissue paper; a flimsy shell, gutted of confidence and life.

I waited a moment before asking my next question. "You were at the house when they brought Jesus in?"

It took two full minutes before the man could respond. He seemed unembarrassed by the breakdown. He inhaled loudly and let the air out in a long, slow exhalation, then pushed the last of the tears from his eyes.

"I was with the Master in the garden. We had gone there to pray. The hour had grown late and we were all weary from the day's travels, the excitement of Passover.... When we reached the garden, the Master chose three of us to join him inside while he prayed."

"Who were the other two?"

"Peter and James. The Master often pulled us aside for special things, so it didn't surprise us. He went off a ways to pray. We sat down on the ground to wait ... we fell asleep. I have never been so tired." Tears began to flood his eyes. "He needed us to pray for him, but we ... we could not. We slept. Had we known ..."

I didn't want him to lose control again. "I know this is difficult but try to focus. You're at the garden, Jesus is praying, then what?"

"He woke us and told us that the hour had come for the Son of Man to be betrayed into the hands of sinners."[2]

Having been to the site and examined what remained of the evidence, I could see the events unfolding. "You went with him? Toward those who had come to arrest him?"

"Yes." John said it without pride.

"Why not go the other way? Why not flee?"

"He had been talking about betrayal and about dying. I thought he meant it figuratively. He often taught in stories and examples."

"But you changed your mind when you saw the crowd?"

"There were so many of them. At first I didn't give it much thought. Crowds often followed the Master. At times there were so many people we could hardly breathe. When I first saw the torches, I thought some of the pilgrims from Jerusalem had come to see the Master or perhaps seek healing for themselves or their family. But then ... then I saw the Roman guards and the temple police, and the scribes and priests ..." He trailed off.

"Go on."

"Then Judas came out of the crowd and approached the Master. It made no sense. Judas had left the table earlier. For a moment I thought he had been taken captive, but he approached the Master and kissed him on each cheek then on the mouth."

"Then?"

"Then someone in the crowd stepped forward and took the

151

Master by the arms. Peter lost his senses and drew his short sword. He charged and struck a slave."

This was material I already knew but it was good to have support for Malchus's testimony. "What did you do?"

John was slow to answer. He looked down at the blanket as if the answer had been woven into the fabric.

"We ran. All of us. We abandoned the Master to the hands of the mob." His lip shook and he seemed to shrink before my eyes.

Yoshua leaned forward and said softly, "But you found your courage, didn't you?"

"I cannot call it courage. Peter and I did not run far. We saw that they had no interest in us, just the Master. We turned back and began to follow, staying some distance away."

"No one saw you?"

"No. We stayed well back and moved quietly. They were easy to follow. The moon was still up, and they carried torches. Also there were many of them, and many people make much noise. Some were laughing. Some mocked him as they walked. I could not hear most of what was said."

"How far did you follow them?"

"To the house of the high priest; the house of Annas."

That confused me. "You mean the whole mob went to the house?"

"No. Once we passed through the gates, most went their own way. The Romans were the first to leave. They were unneeded and would not be welcome at the high priest's home."

152

"So the temple police kept custody of Jesus ... the Master."

"Yes, Brother Max. When the crowd was small, we approached more closely. They led the Master into the courtyard. Since I am known to the high priest and his staff, I could pass beyond the gate. Peter was afraid to try. I spoke to the maid who kept the gate and she let Peter in."

"The maid?" The image of the young girl who brought us water came to mind. "I think we met her."

"Her job is to open and close the gate for guests and to see to their comfort."

"Okay, so now you're in the courtyard. What did you do next?"

"You saw the courtyard. You know the space then. It has a fire pit in the middle. The night was cold, like tonight is going to be. The maid had a fire in the pit and was keeping it lit. We were not allowed in the house. We had to wait outside."

"So you have no idea what went on."

"I know some things. I could see the Master through the lattice of the window and hear the questions being asked. I also saw ..."

"You saw what?"

"I saw a big guard strike the Master across the mouth." He pursed his lips. He was living a painful recollection.

"What did you do?"

"Nothing. I did nothing but watch and listen. Annas asked question after question but the Master refused to answer. He told Annas to ask those who had heard him speak. Annas refused and with good reason."

"Good reason? What good reason?"

John's face hardened. "Annas and the others wanted the Master dead, but they no longer have the power of execution over men except in rare circumstances such as blasphemy or when a Gentile crosses the barrier in the temple going where Gentiles are forbidden."

153

"So Annas was trying to get the Master to blaspheme in public."

"Yes," John answered. "He knew that he could not find witnesses who could agree that the Master had offended HaShem."

"What would be considered blasphemy?" I wondered. He looked at me like I was an idiot. I was getting used to the expression.

"If a man speaks evil of HaShem, it is blasphemy; if a man pretends to be HaShem, it is blasphemy; if a man worships a false god, it is blasphemy."

Yoshua spoke up. "Today it can mean to speak evil of Moshe—Moses and the Law."

"And Annas believed Jesus was a blasphemer."

"But he could not prove it," John said.

The information puzzled me. "Didn't Jesus claim to be the Son of God? Isn't that blasphemy or at least a form of it?"

"Not if it's true," John said.

"And you think it's true?"

John glared at me. "I do. Do you not?"

"This isn't about me," I countered. "I'm just trying to figure out what has happened."

John's face turned to stone. "It is about you, Brother Max. It is about everyone."

Time to sidestep the issue. "Can you tell me what happened next?"

"They took him, bound like a criminal, to the Hall of Hewn Stones."

"Did you and Peter follow?"

"I did."

"But not Peter?"

John shook his head. "He left."

154

"Why?"

"It is best that you hear from him. I will not talk of it."

"But—"

"No. Do not ask. I am not his judge."

"I don't understand," I admitted. "You were there. Did Peter do something I should know about?"

"I don't know what you should know."

He was getting defensive. I needed to back off and give him room to open up. I took a different approach. "Okay, forget Peter. What about you? You said you followed them to this hewed stone place."

"*Lishkat ha-gazit* in Hebrew," John said. "The Chamber of Hewn Stone. It is on the north wall of the Temple Mount. It is the place of the Sanhedrin: the council chamber."

"And what happened there?"

John's shoulders dipped.

"Evil overcame good."

chapter
10

T ell me about this Sanhedrin, Yoshua." We were back at the home of Mark and his family. Again we were in the wide upper room where we had eaten and slept the night before. I could see my pallet in the corner. Someone had spread the blankets smooth.

Around the table reclined Yoshua, Hosah, and Mark. Hosah's wife was not present. The meal turned into a gathering of men. I had seen enough women walking several paces behind men and seen the discomfort of the woman at the sandal shop to know that women had a very well-defined place.

"They are the ruling council of the land," he replied as he

sipped wine. "Much like your Supreme Court with its nine judges. The council in Jerusalem numbers seventy, plus the high priest."

"Seventy-one judges. That sounds like a recipe for confusion."

"There are other councils throughout the land that rule in local matters. The council in Jerusalem is supreme over them. They are the highest tribunal.[1] They debate matters of religious law and interpretation, and sometimes civil matters."

"And Annas leads this group?"

"No, not Annas," Yoshua corrected. "Remember, he remains high priest for life, but Rome has replaced him in the daily functions. That now falls to Caiaphas."

"So that is why John said they took Jesus to the Chamber of Hewn Stone. Annas has no official power to try Jesus."

"You are correct," Yoshua said.

"Yet he had enough power to demand that Jesus appear before him."

"Annas is still a man of great influence," Hosah interjected. "Rome cannot keep the old man from exerting his influence."

"He is as evil as the Romans," Mark offered.

"Mark! Watch your tongue, Son. He is still a high priest."

Mark opened his mouth to reply but stopped. Some silent communication was exchanged between him and his father. No words came out.

Yoshua continued. "*Sanhedrin* is a Greek word meaning 'to sit together.' When they meet, they sit on stone benches and in a semicircle."

"Have they been around long?"

Hosah chuckled. "They date back to the time when HaShem commanded Moshe to select seventy elders to help him govern."[2]

"Rome doesn't interfere with them?" I wondered. "I would think that a conquering nation would want to control the legal system."

157

"No, Brother Max," Mark said. "Rome is happy as long as there is peace and the tax money flows beyond our borders."

There was bitterness there, not that I could blame the young man. No country likes to be invaded and domineered for decades on end.

"Still, they have limits," Yoshua said. "While they are the highest court, they can exert little pressure outside of Jerusalem. Local councils are responsible for those areas. When the Master taught in Galilee in the north, the council could do nothing—"

"But he came to Jerusalem," I interjected.

"For Passover," Hosah said. "Like the thousands of other pilgrims."

"More than that, Father," Mark said. "He spoke of his death in this very room, of a traitor and of betrayal. He knew."

Hosah nodded. "True, Son."

"Okay, I apologize if this offends you, but why would a man go to a town where he knew that one of his own would betray him and where he would die? Why not stay in Galilee where it was safe?"

"'Greater love no one has than this, that a man lay down his life on behalf of his friends,'[3] Mark recited.

"That sounds familiar." Mark gave me a puzzled look. I gave a moment's thought to telling him I was from a time just a couple thousand years in the future, but I imagined insane asylums in this era might not be pretty. I let the comment stand without explanation. He was too polite to ask what I meant.

"I heard him utter those words right in this room," Mark said. "I helped serve the table. His heart was heavy when he said it. I could see it on his face."

"So how does one get a position on this council?"

Yoshua answered. "The high priest and any who had been

high priests sit on the council; the others are drawn from the influential families, scribes, elders, and other leaders."

"So Jesus wasn't tried by a jury of his peers? He was tried by aristocrats."

"He was condemned by his enemies," Hosah spat. "It was a sham. It was nothing more than pretense."

"A kangaroo court," I said.

The room fell silent. Finally, Mark asked, "Brother Max, what is a kangaroo?"

Yoshua looked at me then raised an eyebrow. He offered no help. A thin smile worked the corners of his mouth.

"It's an old expression from the land where I live. It means a court that has no interest in justice, just condemnation."

††††

We were on the move again. The moon, a sliver less than what it had been the night before, hovered in the coal black night. Thin clouds had drifted in covering stars and moon like a gossamer garment. My feet ached from the day's hiking, and the thought of one more trip out had no appeal. Unfortunately, Yoshua didn't ask my opinion.

"You know what's popular in my time, Yoshua? Conspiracy theories. Kennedy, Roswell, Area 51, secret wars, forbidden genetic testing, government programs to alter the weather. That's the thing about humans; we love a good conspiracy."

We plodded toward the high walls of the temple complex, moving to its southern wall.[4]

159

"Why tell me this?" Yoshua asked.

"Because you're trying to get me to believe in a conspiracy. Truth is, most evil in the world is done by individuals. Granted there are exceptions. Hitler had to have help; Stalin needed his minions; but most of the time conspiracies are the work of fiction-rich minds."

"You don't believe a group of men can conspire to end the life of another man?"

"In some cases yes, but such things are usually done by gangs. What I'm hearing is the religious leaders hated one man so much as to formulate an elaborate effort to entrap him and then ramrod a case against him."

"And that's not possible?"

"Well, of course it is possible, but it seems unlikely. Why get in a huff over an itinerant preacher? It seems to me this Sanhedrin you mention would have bigger fish to fry than a former fisherman turned preacher."

"Carpenter. The Master was a carpenter. Four of the disciples were fishermen."

"Yeah, that's what I meant." I knew Jesus had been a carpenter but I wanted to get a rise out of my guide. He was too passive for my tastes ... no, not passive ... too *steady*. That was it. I had seen some range of emotion from him, but he was always so controlled. That bothered me. What bothered me more was the way he controlled me. Here I was, pounding down another street, fighting off a chilling breeze, carting my kits in sore fingers, all because Yoshua had "something to show" me.

"Do you know what your problem is, Max?"

That was direct. "Since you say problem in the singular, I'll take the question as a compliment."

"Let me rephrase. Do you know what your *chief* problem is, Max? You're a chronic doubter. You doubt the intention of those around you; you doubt the reality of this wonderful event."

"I've seen too much deception to believe everything I hear.

Evidence is my standard. Evidence has no prejudices, no agenda. A fact is a fact; nothing more and nothing less."

"You speak the truth about facts. Evidence is powerful."

"That surprises me," I said. "You strike me as a man of faith. It's as clear as the sandals on your feet."

"You think faith is the opposite of evidence?"

"Faith is a belief that demands no evidence, no facts. That's why they call it blind faith."

"Who calls it blind faith?"

He got me. "Everyone. You know, believers like you."

Yoshua shook his head. "Now faith is the title-deed of things hoped for, the conviction of things which are not seen."[5]

"I think you just lost me."

"It's from the Bible. The verse means faith is based on facts in evidence, not on assumption. Some translations use the word 'assurance' instead of 'title-deed,' but the word came to have a business meaning. You know what a title-deed is?"

"Of course. It's a document that shows ownership of property."

"If someone came to you and said you didn't own your home ..."

"I'd produce the title-deed and point at my name."

Yoshua nodded. "Faith is the result of a conviction that something is true. Conviction is from evidence. The disciples believed the Master was the Messiah, why? Because he told them he was the Messiah."

"Maybe. People will believe almost anything. In 1997 in San Diego, twenty-one women and eighteen men consumed a snack of apple sauce and phenobarbital, then washed down the sedative with vodka, lay down on beds, and put plastic bags over their heads. Thirty-nine young people committed suicide. Why? Because they had been taught that through death they would be transported to a spaceship hiding behind the Hale-Bopp comet."

"And you think they acted on faith?"

"Yup. What would you call it?"

"Self-deception. It has nothing to do with faith. What evidence did they have that a spaceship followed the comet?"

"None."

"Then they did not have faith, they had blind obedience to a lie."

"Exactly! That's my point."

"And your point is wrong. The followers of Jesus in this era followed because of what they saw, learned, and knew to be true. Followers through the centuries have come to believe based on the evidence given in the Bible coupled with personal experience."

"Personal experience is subjective ..."

"Facts are objective. A belief without objectivity lacks a brain; a belief without subjectivity lacks a heart. Together, they give birth to faith."

"It's too much for me to believe."

"Which is why I say you're a chronic doubter. You find comfort in doubt; you find security in avoiding the dangerous work of belief."

"Don't hold back. Tell me how you really feel."

The comment must have irritated him. He punished me by walking faster.

The temple complex towered before us. The masses of people who clogged the arteries of the city had thinned. What few still navigated the streets did so with oil lamps in hand. The smell from cooking fires filled the air, moved by the cold breeze. Smoke, once cooled by the night air, settled on the city like a thin, velvet fog.

Without comment he marched on, as if the dark streets were

bright with sunlight. Men dressed in ankle-length white robes with white turbans perched on their heads milled around the massive stone stairway that led to the dark stone walls surrounding the complex. Lighter, nearly white stone capped the wall. A thinning crowd moved away from the complex, the day's business done.

Yoshua plowed forward, never looking to the right or left. He walked like a man with a clear destination and limited time to get there. I couldn't tell if his quick steps were meant to get us somewhere by a certain time or if he just didn't want me by his side. Maybe I had shot my mouth off a little too much. It wouldn't be the first time.

At first I thought he would lead me up the worn stone stairs. Instead, he veered to the right and led me to a nearby building. Like the perimeter wall of the temple complex, this building was made of tooled stone. The craftsmanship impressed me.

From the open door and glassless window poured a warm yellow light. Several men stood near the opening, chatting in low tones. Their clothing was distinct from what I had seen so far. The material looked expensive compared to the barely-above-burlap I had seen the poorer folk wearing. These men wore mostly white outergarments lined with blue trim. Tassels hung from the tunics.

Yoshua stopped ten yards away from the structure. My eyes were fixed on the men and I almost ran into him.

"You asked about the Sanhedrin," Yoshua said. "The Chamber of Hewn Stone."

"It's beautiful."

"On the outside, yes. It's what goes on inside that is ugly."

He motioned to the men by the door. "Sadducees. The others are Pharisees and rabbis."

163

"Are they getting ready to meet?" I asked.

He shook his head. "The Sanhedrin does not meet after dark.

It looks like most have gone home." He started forward, moving at a much slower pace.

We passed a group of three men, dressed in nearly identical garb. I caught a snippet of conversation as we passed.

"The story spreads."

"It will die like all rumors. If such were true, certainly, we would know it."

"But what if it is true—"

"It is not. Not even the goyim would believe such nonsense. It is only a lie by his disciples."

"Some of the people believe it."

"Do they? Will they believe it tomorrow or next week? No, they will not. Things will be normal soon...."

The man caught sight of me and bit off the end of his sentence. If looks could kill, then I'd be in ICU. Yoshua paid them no mind.

I had felt out of place since I arrived here. What man two thousand years out of time wouldn't? But for the first time I felt the electricity of nerves, maybe fear. The others in his circle turned to stare at me. I knew I stood out. My clothing was wrong, the kits I carried were unlike anything they had seen, I wore shoes that looked nothing like sandals, and my face sported only a day's growth of beard. I was a giraffe in a herd of horses—and I had a sense that these horses didn't like giraffes.

A man, four inches shorter than Yoshua and twenty pounds heavier, approached. His shoulders curved forward, his posture had a slight but noticeable forward lean, and his face—what I could see in the moonlight—gave testimony to a life of at least fifty years. He kissed Yoshua on the cheeks, and his eyes danced under bushy gray eyebrows.

"It is good to see you, my friend," the man said. "I do not see enough friends these days."

"Has it been hard on you?"

He looked at the few remaining men of the Sanhedrin and nodded. "I have spoken too often of the wrong things."

"But truthful things," Yoshua said.

"Yes, of truthful things, but too many prefer their own truth."

I cleared my throat. Yoshua looked my way then said, "Brother, this is Max ben Odom. He has traveled from afar. HaShem has given him special skills." He turned back to me. "Brother Max, this is Naqdimon ben Gorion,[6] also called Nicodemus."

The name tickled a brain cell. I knew the name appeared in the Bible somewhere but couldn't pin it down. Naqdimon gave a gracious nod and a wide smile.

"A new friend is a blessing," he said.

I said I was glad to meet him and tried to size him up. He stood like a man comfortable with himself and others. When he spoke, he made eye contact, and he listened like a man getting directions to a difficult-to-find location. His speech came across smooth and easy. Still, he looked tired, worn by some yet undisclosed event or trial. Age had certainly taken its toll, but something more bowed his shoulders.

A movement to the side kidnapped my attention. The small group I had overheard talking moved off into the dark streets, their backs turned to us. Another motion brought my eyes back to the open door of the chamber. A small mob of five men exited the building and started down the road. I recognized three of them. One was an old man who walked with an awkward gait. Two of the other four were familiar. I had left some of my DNA on their fists and had taken a forced nap on the old man's stone courtyard.

"Rumor has it that you have met Annas and his bodyguards,"

165

Naqdimon said. "Even without the light of the sun, I can see that is true."

I touched the side of my head and looked at Yoshua's busted lip.

"Yeah, we met," I said.

"They misunderstood our intent," Yoshua said.

"I'd like to try and explain it again," I said.

Yoshua caught my meaning. "No you wouldn't. They'd have no hesitancy in killing you."

"Your friend is feisty," Naqdimon said, "but not all that wise. Come, the night is cold and is going to get colder. Let's move out of the wind."

Naqdimon led us to the chamber but didn't enter. I looked through the open doorway and saw a wide room with a stone bench laid out in a gentle curve. Opposite it rested another bench. This one lacked the curve. A man in a blue robe stood surrounded by the same kind of men that traveled with Annas. Another man dressed like Naqdimon was talking to him.

I faced Naqdimon again. "This is where the Sanhedrin meets?"

"Yes," he answered. "Have you heard of the Court in your land?"

"Yoshua explained it to me. You just finished a meeting?"

"At sunset. Some of its members remain to discuss matters informally."

"This is where they brought Jesus after Annas was finished with him?"

Naqdimon raised a hand to silence me. "We should not speak of that yet."

"And why is that?" a voice said over my shoulder. The words had the same effect on me as the cold wind. They were delivered with a bite. I snapped around. Standing a foot away was the man in the blue robe. He wore a turban. His eyes were dark and fore-boding. A thick gray-streaked beard hung from his face. I backpedaled a few steps.

"Why should we not speak of the rebel, Brother Naqdimon?"

Naqdimon did not answer the question. Instead he said, "We have guests. Max ben Odom is from a land far from here, and this is Yoshua ben Yoseph. Brothers, I introduce you to Yosef bar Qayafa, high priest of God to Yisrael."

High priest? Qayafa? Caiaphas. Joseph Caiaphas. Yoshua had told me a little about him. I wasn't sure how to address a high priest, and my last encounter with one didn't work out very well.

"I know who they are," Caiaphas said. His mouth remained tight as he spoke. I half expected a forked tongue to snap out now and then. "Annas told me about your ... visit. He assumed you might come by. You have an interest in the heretic?"

I had regained my composure after being startled and set my kits down. The man's attitude was getting on my nerves. As I straightened, I noticed two of his bulldog guards were two steps closer to me. Perhaps they assumed I was setting my kits down to better pop the high priest on the nose. I had no such intention. I left my fighting form on the ground at Annas's. Maybe one-on-one, I'd go toe-to-toe, but my mama raised me better than to take on a handful of bone-breakers at the same time.

"Yes, sir, I do." My response surprised me. Truth was, the only thing I was interested in was returning home. I followed Yoshua up and down the streets of Jerusalem and trekked the valleys beyond the walls because I hoped it would put an end to the nightmare.

"You are a follower of his? You number yourselves among the rebel's disciples?"

I answered for myself. "No." Yoshua would have answered yes, and I gathered that Naqdimon would have been obliged to do

167

the same. "In my land, I study criminals and the people who punish them. I investigate crimes."

"And just where is your land?" the high priest wondered.

Go straight through two thousand years of history and make a right at the Pacific Ocean. "San Diego, California." What did I have to lose?

"I have never heard of it."

"It is beyond the borders of Rome," Yoshua explained without really saying anything.

"That far?" Caiaphas raised an eyebrow. For a moment I thought he'd press for more details, but that would indicate that there were things he didn't know.

"We committed no crimes, Max ben Odom. We dispensed justice as is our right and our responsibility."

"You oversaw the trial?"

"Of course I did. It is part of my duty." He looked at me like a man looks at an annoying fly that has just landed within swatting distance.

"I wish to tell the tale correctly when I return to my land." Best to couch this in positive terms even though my police instincts told me I was staring at a man guilty as they come. "They brought Jesus from the house of Annas to this place." I motioned toward the stone building.

"My father-in-law had every right to interview the prisoner while I called to session the council."

"So Jesus was taken into that room and stood before all seventy-one of you?"

He didn't answer right away. I caught him glancing at Naqdimon. "Not all attended."

I nodded. Something wasn't being said. "But you did invite all the members to attend. I mean, that's the way to do it, right?"

His eyes narrowed and the temperature plummeted. "How would a goy like you know how we conduct our business?"

"I don't. That's why I'm asking."

"The only answer you need is that we saved the nation from a false teacher."

"You saved the whole nation?"

"You know nothing. It is expedient that one man die for the nation so that the nation may not perish."[7]

"So you made him your sacrificial lamb."

I don't know what I said, but before I could react, the high priest snarled, screamed something I didn't understand, and back-handed me hard enough to stagger me. The pain of it exploded through my head. Flickers of light that had nothing to do with stars flashed in my eyes like tiny strobes. Growing up with old-fashioned ideas of manhood, I refused to touch my jaw; but it took several seconds of solid concentration not to do so.

My teeth clenched, and I took a step forward. Before I could take a second step, I was moving backward. A pair of strong hands seized my shirt, spun me, grabbed me by the back of my collar, and trotted me away from Caiaphas and his barracudas. The hands belonged to Yoshua. At first I thought he was just putting distance between us and them, but then I realized that he didn't intend to stop.

"What are you doing?"

"Saving your life. Shut up."

"But—"

"No talking." His strength surprised me. I wiggled to get out of his grasp, but his hands were unyielding vises.

As we moved away from the Chamber of Hewn Stone, things grew darker. Moments later, we were in an alley between two rows of large structures. Houses maybe. Only then did Yoshua release me.

The alley was a good deal darker than the street. The buildings around us were two stories tall and blocked much of the moonlight we depended on for sight.

"What is the matter with you?" I snapped.

"That's a question you should ask of yourself." He rubbed his face in frustration. "Do you remember the beating you took earlier?"

"Of course. Your high priest landed a blow on a very sore spot."

"You should bless HaShem that that was all that happened. The beating you took earlier was nothing compared to what just about happened. You approach the high priest with violence in your eyes and his guards will gut you like a fish."

"So you were saving my life. Thanks." I'm sure he picked up on the sarcasm.

"Why are you so self-destructive, Max?"

"Who says I am?"

"You do. Your actions do."

"Well, that's too bad. In case you've forgotten, I didn't ask to be here. If I'm doing it wrong, then send me home or let me die or whatever is happening. Just make this nonsense end."

He started to speak but then swallowed his words.

"What did I say that was so wrong anyway? I was just asking questions. That's what I'm here for, right? To find out things? To investigate? I thought I was being pretty civil." I gave in and rubbed my jaw. It hurt. I felt a new bruise being born.

Yoshua stepped away from me. He didn't look afraid. Anger wasn't the right word. Maybe perturbed. Watching him watch me then directing his attention to the place we had stood a few minutes before made me feel adrift. This wasn't my time, this wasn't my doing, and this wasn't my choice. I was a twenty-first-century man not only twenty centuries misplaced but in a land and a culture I didn't understand. Clearly, I had tipped over the apple cart, but I wasn't sure why.

"What did I say anyway? It wasn't like I was grilling him."

Yoshua looked at me like a father looks at a slow child. "You said Caiaphas made Jesus a sacrificial lamb."

"Yeah, it's an expression of speech."

"An unfortunate one, albeit accurate." Once again the way Yoshua spoke to me when we were alone surprised me. When others like Mark, Hosah, or anyone else from this time were present, he adopted their speech pattern. With me his comments were straight, fast, and low.

"I don't follow."

"Jesus died during *Pesach* … Passover. On Passover, a lamb is slain for the sins of the people. You equated Jesus with that lamb."

"And made Caiaphas liable."

"Right. It so happens you're right, but Caiaphas … took exception."

I touched my jaw again. Exception was one way of phrasing it.

The sound of slow-moving footfalls approaching made me tense. Out of the lighter street and into the dark alley a man appeared. At least it was just one man. By his size and posture, I realized it was Naqdimon.

"They're gone," he said. As he neared, I could see him better. His face bore the strain, shock, and shame of what had just happened.

"Did they trouble you, Brother?" Yoshua asked.

"No. I am a man of great wealth and much influence. They keep their distance, but I am not likely to be invited to dinner anytime soon." For some reason that made him laugh.

He stepped closer to me. "Are you injured, Brother Max?"

"I've been hit harder. And not many hours ago."

171

Both men chuckled. It was forced; not the kind of laughter that comes from good humor but from unsettled nerves.

"Yeah, laugh it up, guys. At least your jaw is still hinged."

Naqdimon stifled the laugh and looked guilty—but only a little. It is what men did after a stressful situation. I had seen cops do it many times. After a shooting or a difficult arrest in which one or more officers were in danger, laughter was the first recourse after the situation had been contained. Some things never change.

"Come, Brother Max, I will show you the Chamber of Hewn Stone."

"Are you sure that's wise?"

"We are the only ones left. All others have gone to their homes."

"Let's get this over with," I said, and marched out of the alley.

†††

We stood in the council chamber. I wondered what Caiaphas would think if he knew that I stood where he had been standing not long before. Darkness pressed at the window and door, kept at bay by a series of large oil lamps.

"Nic— Brother Naqdimon," I began, "I take it you weren't here when Jesus was brought in."

He shook his head. "I was not informed until too late. Not that I could have stopped the evil."

"Any ideas why they excluded you?"

"I know very well why they left me out. I defended the Master in their midst many months ago."

"Really?" I walked around the room, my eyes fixed to the surfaces of floor and furniture. I had no hopes of finding anything of use in this room. Men had been in and out of the building. Even if only a portion of them came through at any time, then fifty to seventy pairs of feet had walked on this floor.

"I spoke with the Master once. I went to him at night."

"Why at night?"

He hesitated at first. "I could tell you that I am a rabbi, a Pharisee, and by custom we study at night as well as by day. I wished to learn from the Rabbi. If I said such a thing it would be true, but not complete."

"You were afraid of what others would think?"

"It shames me, but yes."

"Tell me about it."

He took a deep breath. "Night had fallen, and I approached.[8] I said, 'Rabbi, we have known that from God you have come—a teacher, for no one can do these signs that you do if God is not with him.'"[9]

"Nice beginning. Butter him up. How did he respond?"

"I had no butter with me, Brother Max, just a heart filled with questions. The Master looked at me, and I felt that he was gazing through me, into that heart of questions. Before I could speak, he said, 'In truth I say to you: If anyone is not born from above, he will not see the reign of God.'"

"What? What does that mean?"

"He was saying that I needed to be born from above, to be born again. It made no sense to me and I said so. I asked how a grown man could be born again. It is impossible to climb back in the womb."

"I don't imagine Mom would appreciate that."

He ignored the comment. "You are not from here, Brother Max. Perhaps you do not know that we Pharisees are taught to learn through debate and argument. I was not being rude. I was being inquisitive. I expected the Master to enter my debate. He didn't. Instead, he said, 'Truthfully I say to you: If one is not born of water and the Spirit, he is not able to enter into the kingdom of God; that which has been born of the flesh is flesh, and that which has been born of the Spirit is spirit.'"[10]

"He wasn't talking about a new physical birth but a spiritual one."

"Yes, Max ben Odom. You are wiser than I. I didn't understand that at first."

"Then what did Jesus say?" I noticed some spots on the stone floor. Some were dark, others were barely visible.

"He called me a bad teacher."

I looked up. "Really? Straight to the point, eh? I can admire that."

"He said that if I could not understand earthly things, how could I understand heavenly ones. I had no answer. Then he surprised me. He said that as Moshe held up the brass serpent in the wilderness, so the Son of Man must be lifted up so that those who believe will not perish but have life unending."[11] He paused and looked down at his hands as if something stained them. He began to quote from memory:

"'For God did so love the world, that his Son, his only begotten, he gave so that everyone who believes in him may not perish, but may have life everlasting. For God did not send his Son into the world to judge the world, but that the world may be rescued through him; he who believes in him is not judged, but he who does not believe has been judged already, because he has not believed in the name of the only Son of God.'"[12]

I had to ask. "Do you believe him?"

I expected him to look around to see if unwanted ears were listening. He didn't. "Yes, I believe. He knew me although we had never met. Saw inside me where even I am afraid to look."

He stepped my way. I wanted to warn him off, telling him not to contaminate the scene, but he couldn't do worse than what had already been done.

"I have a question for you, Brother Max. The Master said to me that evil hates the light but those who practice the truth come to the Light. Why do you suppose he said that to me?"

"Well, since you made a point to mention that you went at night, I would say that he had a double meaning in mind. First, he thought you needed to leave the darkness behind and come to him as the Light. How'd I do, Yoshua?"

"Very well."

"Something of Sunday school stuck."

"You speak strangely, Brother Max," Naqdimon said.

"There are many things strange about Brother Max," Yoshua said with a thin grin.

"I see. So now you're going to gang up on me." I opened my second case and removed a boxy black plastic light, four filters, and a pair of orange-tinted wraparound goggles. My kit contained three other pairs of goggles: yellow, red, and UV clear. The filters were red and orange.

I donned the eyewear and turned on the high-intensity light. A fan in the case came on with a soft purr. I shone the light on the stone floor and faint spots became bold and clear.

"Brother Max, what is that ... thing you hold?"

"It's a high-intensity alternate light source ..." I looked up and saw Naqdimon several paces back from where he had stood a moment before. It was my turn to chuckle. "It won't hurt you, Naqdimon."

175

"What kind of witchcraft is this?" he muttered.

I turned the light off. "It's not witchcraft, it's science." That carried no currency with him. I looked to Yoshua for help. He offered none, but he did seem amused by my predicament. Naqdimon looked ready to bolt. How could I explain this? I decided to try again.

"You have built fires haven't you?"

"Of course."

"Have you ever studied the flames of the fire? Are they one color or many?"

"Many. The flame changes sometimes depending on what is burning. Damp wood burns differently than very dry wood, and cloth brings a different color."

"Now look at the oil lamps. Is the flame one color or many?"

"One."

In point of fact, the flame was a mixture of colors not distinguishable to the human eye, but I saw no sense in bringing that up now. I could bend the truth a little to make a point.

"The lamp flame is one color because it burns one material: oil. Wood burns with several colors because wood has different parts, bark, heartwood, and so on." *Keep it simple.* "The light I hold is like the oil lamp. It shines one type of light. But with these," I held up a filter, "I can change the color of the light, and the lamp inside allows me to change colors in a different way. Where I come from, it's called a poly-light."

"Poly-light?"

"It means 'many lights.'"

"I speak Greek, Brother Max. I know what poly-light means."

Yeah, but you don't understand what it is. "Let me show you something. Come here."

He hesitated and looked at Yoshua who gave an encouraging nod. Naqdimon approached.

"These are called goggles." I removed the eyewear and slipped them on Naqdimon's head. His eyes widened. "What do you see?"

"Everything is different. One color."

"The goggles filter out certain wavelengths—stop certain colors from reaching your eyes—and allow you to see other colors." I shone the poly-light on the area I had been studying. "Now what do you see?"

"Spots. Spots on the floor."

"Let me see if I can explain this. Every biological can be made to fluoresce ..." Another bad start. "Everything associated with our bodies can be made to shine under certain lights. With the right light and goggles you can see things that you can't under normal circumstances. I use this special, um, torch to see what has happened at crime scenes. Those spots you see are blood and saliva. The light allows me to see blood, saliva, inks, certain drugs, fingerprints, and semen."

The last word brought Naqdimon's head up with a snap. "Brother Max, it is not appropriate to speak of such things." The shocked expression on his goggled face was comical, but I managed not to laugh.

"The spots on the ground tell me that someone was mistreated here. Very mistreated." I removed the goggles from his face and placed them on mine. "Someone stood here and took a beating. The saliva tells me that they spat on him. Judging by the amounts, the beating was fairly light, but there's a lot of spittle." I thought about taking samples. Back home I would. Much could be learned from DNA, but I had nothing with which to process the samples.

"They beat him," Naqdimon said. He seemed to have hunched over another few degrees.

"I thought you said you weren't here." I removed the goggles.

"Several of the elders told me what happened. Some were very proud of it. They spit upon him and some struck him.[13] Then it got worse."

"Worse?"

177

Naqdimon took a seat on the curved stone bench. "The Master stood where you stand now. They brought witnesses to speak against him. They testified that they heard him say that he would destroy the temple and build another without hands.[14] But the witnesses could not agree on details. Agreement is required. When asked to defend himself against the accusations, the Master said nothing. He stood silent."

"That probably went over well."

"No, Brother Max, it didn't."

So much for sarcasm.

Naqdimon continued. "Caiaphas demanded that the Teacher tell him if he was the Messiah, the Son of the Blessed.[15] The Master said, 'You will not believe even if I tell you.'" He paused. "Then he said something that put ember to kindling. He told them that from now on the Son of Man would be seated at the right hand of the Power and coming with the clouds of heaven."

"I don't understand why such a comment would be so inflammatory."

"To sit at the right hand of God is to claim a position only Messiah can claim. When he mentioned coming with the clouds, the council knew he was saying that he was the one mentioned by the prophet Daniel." He closed his eyes then began to rock as he quoted, "I saw in the visions of the night, and lo, in the clouds of the heavens one as a son of man coming, and to the Ancient of Days he has come, and before him they have brought him near. And to him is given dominion, and glory, and a kingdom, and all peoples, all nations, and all languages serve him, his dominion is everlasting, and does not pass away, and his is a kingdom that is not destroyed."[16]

178

"And David the psalmist also," Yoshua added. Now he recited some Bible verse. "The affirmation of Jehovah to my Lord: 'Sit at my right hand, until I make your enemies your footstool.'"[17]

"So they understood that Jesus claimed to be the Messiah?"

"Caiaphas flew into a rage, tore his cloak, and declared the Master a blasphemer. The elders present rushed him and began to treat him with contempt, spitting upon him and slapping him. Someone tied a blindfold around his head. They slapped and punched him, telling him to prophesy who it was that hit him. Then the guards ..."

Naqdimon lowered his head. For a moment I thought he was going to vomit. Yoshua put a hand on the man's shoulder but said nothing.

"Guards?" I prompted.

"Temple guards assigned to the high priests. Caiaphas let them—" He took a deep breath. "Does your special torch work outside, Brother Max?"

"Yes." Odd question.

Naqdimon rose and walked to the door. I grabbed my kits and followed. A few strides later and around the corner of the building he stopped and pointed. In the dim moonlight I could see only the stone pavement and wall. I slipped on my goggles and flipped the switch on the poly-light. I anticipated what I would see and set the filter and light to fluoresce blood.

I saw plenty of it.

There was blood evidence on the ground: Gravity splatter and force splatter indicated that Jesus received a measured but thorough beating. The gravity splatter was consistent with blood dropped from about six feet, the height of a man. The spray was similar to other scenes where a beating had taken place. I once investigated the murder of a man pummeled to death by a gang. There were similarities. Blood spatter on the wall indicated that Jesus stood near it while the guards beat him.

"What time did this happen?"

179

"Some of the trial took place before sunrise. That's when the beating happened. After the sun rose, the Sanhedrin met officially.[18] The council can only meet officially during the day."

The scene began to form in my mind. "So Jesus was first taken to Annas's house where the former high priest grilled him. He was beaten there, then brought here at night where he was tried and beaten again—more than once."

"I should have been here," Naqdimon said. "I should have been here."

"What could you have done?" I asked.

"I do not know. Reasoned with them. Reminded them that they were acting against the Law and the traditions. Just like the first time I met the Teacher, I remained in the darkness."

"That's very noble, Naqdimon," I said, "but my experience says that once a gang is intent on doing harm, reason no longer matters." I packed up the kit. No reason existed to look for more evidence.

Yoshua spoke. "You were there for him when he needed you, Brother Naqdimon. You stepped into the light when the time came."

What was this all about? "I don't follow," I admitted.

Naqdimon let out a sigh so long that I felt sure he had just expelled his very soul. "I saw the Master one more time. I buried him."

chapter
11

The walls were different this time. And the odor. The halls smelled unlike the last time I stood in the hospital corridor. Everything—the lighting, the doors, the sounds—was wrong. Only the deep hollow in my gut was familiar. That's when I realized my error.

I wasn't in the nightmarish, soul-sucking hospital.

I stood in a place far worse.

The corridor was empty. No men and women in white; no surgeons in green scrubs; no visitors coming and going from the rooms, just the long hall with its shiny linoleum floor, pale white walls, and seemingly endless string of florescent lights overhead. One light buzzed and flickered, hurting my eyes.

Something gnawed at my stomach, chewed my innards as if they were a Thanksgiving meal. My mouth was dry as a bag of cement, and my knees begged to buckle.

I knew this place. I had been here many times, but the recollection fluttered out of reach.

I turned around. The corridor stretched endlessly back as far as it did forward.

"Hello?" The word came out like a croak. I cleared my throat. "Hello?" The lone word rolled down the hall and echoed back, a muted version of itself. "Is anyone here?"

No answer. I started forward, my dress shoes squeaking on the polished floor. Step followed step, the only sound being my footfalls and the noisy florescent light that struggled to live just a few moments longer.

A pair of double doors at the end of the hall beckoned me. I moved toward them as if drawn by an invisible rope.

Where was I? Why couldn't I recall this place? Why was it familiar?

Ice water circulated up and down my spine. My hands felt as if uncountable ants crawled on the flesh. My stomach ached with acid. My throat burned, raw from something I couldn't recall. Bile tried to climb up my throat. I swallowed hard.

Five steps became ten, and the end of the hall neared.

Music, some form of hideous Muzak with every third note flatted, every tune in a minor key.

The air turned cold as if a freezer door had been opened.

My steps devolved to the shuffling of a drunken man too inebriated to lift sole from ground. Despite the cold, my face burned with a fire kindled internally by the oxidation of some unknown fuel.

I pulled my fingers into a fist and was surprised to discover soaked palms.

I wanted to close my eyes but couldn't.

I wanted to turn and flee in the other direction, but the doors held me in their trance, inanimate sirens calling me closer and closer to certain destruction.

A soft voice percolated through the doors, too soft to be understood, too loud to ignore.

My hand shook as I raised it to press back the door. What lay beyond was as evil and hurtful as hell itself. I don't know how I knew that, but I did, and I knew it more in gut than in brain.

Mucus filled my nose, tears inundated my eyes. I didn't want to go in. Better to die right here; better that my heart should decide to stop beating or an aneurysm on my aorta give way than I should cross this threshold.

This place was familiar.

This place knew me.

This place was branded on every brain cell.

The voice on the other side continued.

I didn't push the door. I had no strength to do so. Still it opened at the touch of my fingers. First one door opened then another.

They made no sound as they swung on their hinges. As they completed the arc of their opening, cold white light washed over me, as did the pungent, stomach-turning smell of disinfectant. I wretched but the contents of my stomach stayed in place.

My pupils constricted in the strong light, but soon my eyes adjusted. I was looking at a wide room filled with metal tables. I stepped in and the doors closed in silence behind me.

Then the voice. The awful words.

"Female, twenty-two years of age, five foot six inches, one

183

hundred twenty-five pounds ... no discernable birthmarks ... no tattoos ... a single gunshot wound from a large-caliber weapon as indicated by point of entrance one-point-five inches from the median of the sternum ... exit wound is large and ragged as would be expected by a hollow-point bullet...."

"No," I whimpered. She lay naked on the metal table; naked for the world to see, unable to cover herself, to protect herself.

"A sexual trauma kit has been taken and pending results. Gross examination indicates ..."

"No, no." I tried to shut my eyes but they were glued open. I moved forward. I tried to dig my heels into the linoleum but step still followed step.

"I'm beginning with a Y incision...." I could hear the scalpel cut the flesh.

"Please, please, no ... no more."

The medical examiner peeled the flesh back then reached for a pair of long-handled garden sheers. He placed the parrot-beaked cutting blades into the woman's chest and forced the handles together with a loud crack.

I whimpered and tried to force my eyes away. I couldn't.

There was another snap as the garden implement, designed to separate branch from trunk, made quick work of delicate rib bones.

As the medical examiner removed the front of the rib cage and set it aside, the blonde head of my daughter turned to face me.

"It's okay, Daddy," she said.

I screamed.

184   ✝✝✝

I was on my feet, the coarse wool blankets of my pallet puddled on the ground. My heart pounded so hard I expected ribs to crack and breastbone to explode from my chest. Air came in gulps, sweat dripped from my face.

An earthquake of shivers ran through me time and time again. I couldn't stop shaking. I fought back tears. I fought down the gorge in my stomach. I fought back the images my subconscious had painted. I fought ... and fought.

Seconds ticked by like months as I tried to acclimate myself again to my surroundings. Where was I? Not the autopsy room. That had been a dream, although I had been there many times. Not my home. Not the hotel in Jerusalem. Then where? The other nightmare came back—the one where I was stuck in first-century Jerusalem. It took a few seconds, but I began to recognize the pallet that served as my bed, the table, and the walls.

Slowly, I looked to the corner where Yoshua had slept the night before and where I had seen him settle after we returned from the Sanhedrin building. His bed was empty.

I rubbed my eyes and let my heart settle to a more leisurely pace. Then I turned toward the window. Yoshua stood in the near darkness. The ivory light of the setting moon painted his face. Smoke came from his mouth. For a moment I thought he was smoking then realized how stupid an idea that was. I was seeing the condensation of his breath. The sight of it reminded me how cold the night had become. I picked up one of the blankets and wrapped it around me. It felt damp with perspiration.

My muscles ached from yesterday's activities; my jaw complained the most. The high priest had a pretty good backhand. Too tired to stand and too frightened to attempt sleep again, I moved to one of the benches by the table and sat down.

185

"I'm sorry if I woke you," I said, shivering beneath the blanket.

"You didn't. I was already up."

"Couldn't sleep?"

"No better than you," Yoshua said.

"I know why I'm up, but why are you up and staring out the window?" Unlike me, Yoshua had not donned a blanket to fend off the cold predawn temperatures.

"I've been thinking about Naqdimon ... Nicodemus."

"What about him? He seems like a resourceful man."

"He is, but he carries too much guilt. He thinks he could have made a difference in the outcome of the Sanhedrin's decision, but he's wrong. What was to be would be. Naqdimon could do nothing."

"I hadn't taken you for a fatalist."

"It has nothing to do with fatalism." Yoshua never turned. "Guilt is a weight that gets heavier with time. Too much for too long can crush a man."

"I suppose, but he has nothing to feel guilty about. Like you said, he was powerless to change anything. The best he could do was endanger his own life. He's smart. He'll figure it out."

"Maybe."

"You can't do anything about it. A man must face his own guilt."

"Like you are?"

That froze me. "What do you mean?"

"Why are you here?"

"Where? Here in the first century? Beats me. You'd know better than me. I can't see any reason for me being here. It doesn't matter what I find, nothing will change. It's not like I can influence the trial of a man and save his life. Your teacher is dead already."

"Why are you in Jerusalem?"

"Because you brought me here. What kind of question is that?"

He sighed like a schoolteacher with a disobedient child. "Why were you in Jerusalem in the first place?"

"I was sent to teach new field forensics techniques to the local police."

"Why you?"

"Because I'm one of the best and I've done these seminars before."

"But someone else was scheduled to come. Why did you come in his place?"

I wondered how he knew that, but I had learned that wondering seldom brought answers in this place. "My superior felt it was better that I come."

"Because—"

"Because I was messing up a case. Is that what you want to hear? I was in the way and they wanted to put some distance between me and the case before I could ruin it for the investigators."

"You're a professional, but they don't want your input. Why?"

"There are reasons."

"There always are. Do you agree with their reasons?"

"I don't know." I stood. Sitting close to the window made me all the colder. Cold air and perspiration don't mix.

"Guilt is heavy—"

"This ends now," I snapped. "I'm here against my will. I'm under no obligation to answer your questions, so stay out of my business."

I kept my back to him. I didn't want to see his face. He had a way of looking at me. I crawled back onto my bed pallet, rearranged the blankets, and pretended not to notice the uncomfortable wetness left by my perspiring body. Rolling over, I faced the wall and pretended to seek sleep. The truth was, I feared sleep.

It came anyway.

I could still smell the autopsy room.

†T†

It was the largest home I had seen. Mark's house was a good size, the high priest's house twice as large, but this stretched my imagination. Before me towered a series of structures on a platform that I guessed was a thousand feet north to south and almost two hundred feet east to west. Red tile covered the various roofs and stood in remarkable contrast to the wall of Jerusalem behind it. People bustled about the street in front, but none approached the large, open colonnade. Clearly the average joe didn't walk these grounds.

"Who owns this place?" I asked Yoshua.

"Herod Antipas, tetrarch of Galilee and Peraea."

I had no idea where Peraea was, but I had heard of Galilee and had the impression that it was some distance from Jerusalem. While interviewing Matthew, I learned that Galilee was someplace well north of here and that all the disciples except Judas were Galilean.

Yoshua must have detected my confusion. "Peraea is south of Galilee and on the other side of the Jordan."

That didn't help much. "So this is King Herod's place."

"Sort of."

"What's that supposed to mean? Is it or isn't it?"

"Herod Antipas isn't king, not in the usual sense. His father was a king, but when he died, Rome divided the kingdom. Antipas is a tetrarch, although some call him king because of his father."

"So he got just a piece of the inheritance pie."

"That's one way of putting it. The palace belongs to the family. He stays here whenever he's in Jerusalem."

"Like during the holy days," I guessed.

"Exactly."

A man came from the compound to the street. He looked to be in his midthirties. Unlike most of the Jews I saw here, his beard was trimmed. He and Yoshua exchanged greetings and then I was introduced. Yoshua gave the man's name as Chuza. He greeted me like I was his long-lost cousin.

"Shalom," he said and kissed me on both cheeks. "Please come, I will show you the house of the great Herod."

"So Herod Antipas built this place," I said as I fell in behind Chuza.

"Oh, no, Brother Max, this and many other buildings, including all the improvements to the temple, were built by his father. He built aqueducts, fortresses, sanitation systems, pools, palaces, and the Antonia Fortress. The list is very long."

Chuza talked nonstop, acting every bit the docent at a historical landmark, but I got the impression he was putting on a show. He pointed out pools, bronze fountains, and a lush garden in a wide court that separated the two wings of the complex.

It took no effort to act impressed. I had never seen anything like this. People whom I took to be servants worked at various tasks. A gardener tended the plants, a young woman swept dirt from the tile-decorated stone floor.

I saw banquet halls, sleeping quarters enough to house hundreds of guests, baths, and more. The interior walls were covered in white plaster in which small, colored tiles had been pressed to form decorative shapes and patterns. I knew very little about first-century life, but I knew opulence when I saw it.

"Is the …" I dredged up the word Yoshua had used, "… tetrarch here?"

"No," Chuza answered. "He had pressing matters in Galilee and has returned to his palace there."

For some reason I felt relieved. I'd met two high priests and took a beating each time. I had no idea what an angry man of Herod's wealth and power might do.

"I will show you something else," Chuza said with enthusiasm.

189

He led us into one of the banquet halls. A workman was patching a crack in the plaster. "Finish that later," Chuza ordered. "And close the door after you."

The man didn't question his dismissal. He gathered his tools and shuffled from the room. Once the worker was gone, Chuza relaxed. His manic behavior rushed from him like air from a balloon.

"We can talk here," he said. "Out there are too many ears and too many mouths to whom HaShem gave no sense, may his name be praised."

He looked at me and waited. Yoshua took up the conversational slack. "Chuza is a respected steward of Herod Antipas. His wife is a follower of the Master."[1]

Odd phraseology. Start simple, I thought. "Exactly what is a steward?"

"Stewards are managers of another man's property. Herod has many stewards. I am responsible for the preparation of his households. It is my job to travel before him to be certain that his palaces are ready for him and his guests. I oversee repairs and use. Do you understand?"

I said I did. "So you're still here because ..."

"Several repairs needed to be made. I will travel back to Galilee when the work is done."

"Excuse me for asking, but Yoshua said your wife is a follower of Jesus."

"Of Jesus the Nazarene, yes. My woman contributed to his teaching and needs."

190

"Needs?"

"Financial support," Chuza said, almost embarrassed. "She is among the women who supported the Rabbi."[2]

"The way you say that makes me think that you disapprove."

He shrugged. "My woman believes the Rabbi to be the Messiah. I have no opinion."

"You have no opinion because it is better for you not to have one considering who pays your salary?"

He smiled. "You are wise, Brother Max."

So he was supporting Jesus through his wife. "Still, if your wife is a known supporter ..."

"It matters not. She is a woman. No one pays attention to her."

Harsh. "Do you mean that because she is a woman, she can do what she wants?"

"I mean that because she is a woman, no man cares what she does, as long as she is faithful to me and to the Law."

Yoshua explained. "You have already noticed that women here act differently than women in your land."

I thought of the veiled young women, the wives walking several steps behind their husbands, and the cobbler's wife who scampered away when we met with Matthew behind the shop. I also thought of Mark's mother, whom I had only seen at the first meal, and the way she avoided eye contact.

"I have noticed that."

"Here, women have very few rights or privileges. Strict social custom governs what can and cannot be done. A woman seldom speaks to a man who is not her husband, and most men won't address a woman directly. Instead, they communicate through the husband or some other male."

"So this ... woman ... does she have a name?"

"She is called Joanna," Chuza said.

"So Joanna can support Jesus and no man gives it much thought?"

"Yes," Yoshua said. "It is different with the Greeks and Romans."

191

"I guess that's why they're considered enlightened."

Yoshua replied, "Here, the Roman women are considered … loose."

"Do the women act differently in your land, Brother Max?" Chuza asked.

"You have no idea, pal." I considered telling him that the United States has had two female secretaries of state, but thought better of it. He wouldn't know what the United States or a secretary of state was.

"I am sorry for you," Chuza said.

I wasn't going to go down that path. "Was Jesus brought here?"

Chuza's imperial attitude softened and his gaze shifted to something only he could see. "The chief priests, the scribes, and the elders brought him to Herod."

"How did he look?" I already knew the answer. I had seen his blood in two spots of the council building.

Chuza bit his lower lip. "He had been … mistreated."

"In what way."

"I don't like to think about it."

I said nothing, giving the steward an opportunity to twist up a little courage.

"His face was swollen and bloodied. I could see that someone—many people—had been spitting on him. It is a great insult to spit on another man. Is that true in your land?"

I had seen this trick before. Chuza didn't like the questions so he made an effort to change the subject.

192

"Yes, it is. Could Jesus still stand?"

"Yes, although two men—guards from the high priest, I think—held him by the arms."

"Did they bring him to this room?"

"No. The courtyard. The night was cold. The Rabbi shivered."

That might be a result of shock as much as cold. Still I thought about how chilled I had been last night. "Herod came out to meet him?"

"Herod was very glad to meet Jesus. He had wanted to meet him before but the Teacher had left Galilee. John the Baptizer had died at Herod's hand. I and others assumed Jesus was afraid."

"Herod killed John the Baptist?"

"It was Herodias's idea," Chuza explained.

"Herodias?"

Yoshua filled in the gaps. "Herod-Philip, Antipas's half-brother, married Herodias. He divorced his wife, the daughter of Areatas IV, king of Nabataea."

It took me a moment to fit the pieces together. "Wait a minute. Herod threw off one wife so he could marry his sister-in-law?"

"Yes," Yoshua said. "Correct."

"He's a real peach."

Chuza tipped his head to the side and gave a puzzled look.

"Never mind. Can you tell me what happened next?"

The house-steward looked embarrassed. "The court was filled with the leaders of Yisrael. They told Herod that Pilate the governor had sent the Rabbi to him for judgment." He took a breath. "Herod asked questions, but the Rabbi gave no response. None whatsoever. Herod has never been treated so rudely. No matter how many questions Herod asked, no answer was given. He demanded the Rabbi perform a sign."

"A sign?"

"A miracle," Yoshua said.

"So Herod wanted a performance and Jesus wouldn't dance to his tune."

"No, Brother Max. There was no music that night."

"I meant ... what happened next?"

"The elders shouted out accusations against Jesus. Most often they said, 'He claims to be the King of the Jews.'"

"They said that because it would irritate Herod?"

"My master was appointed to rule over two regions. If anyone has a right to be called king, it is he."

"You think he should be king?" I pressed.

He cut his eyes away. No, he didn't think so, but he could never admit it. It occurred to me that almost everyone in this time lived in fear of someone else.

"Because of the accusations, my master put one of his best cloaks on the Rabbi and mocked him. 'Now you look like a king instead of a beggar,' but still the Rabbi said nothing." He studied the ground. "After they mocked him more, Herod sent the Rabbi back to Pilate dressed in the royal garments. Pilate killed him."

"Pilate? So far it sounds like more than Pilate was involved."

It was clear that there was no new evidence to gather here beyond the testimony of Chuza. The treatment of Jesus was beginning to make me feel ill. A part of me understood his tormentors. I had seen enough crime and violence that I had sometimes been tempted to let my service revolver save the taxpayers the cost of a trial and sustaining a killer for the rest of his life. Despite the temptation, I knew how wrong even the thought was.

For some reason Chuza irritated me. I couldn't put my finger on it but the man set me on edge. "I bet it was difficult to tell your wife what you saw."

He looked away.

"You did tell her, didn't you?"

"She knows the Rabbi was executed. One of the women told her."

"Is she home in Galilee or does she travel with you?"

"It is Passover season. She came to Jerusalem with me."

"Does she know you watched him being mocked?"

"I could do nothing." He became defensive.

"You could have an opinion."

He gave that puzzled look again. "I don't understand."

Maybe it was my interrupted night's sleep or the still-burning brand of the dream, but I felt my temper slipping. "Your wife ... your woman may not have many rights in this time but she has one thing you lack. She knows what it means to hold a conviction."

I walked from the room.

"I don't want to do this anymore," I told Yoshua as we left the wide expanse of the palace and exchanged it for ever-narrowing streets.

"Don't want to do what? Walk?"

"I don't want to play this game. I don't want to go from place to place to look at evidence that makes no difference to anyone. I don't want to talk to people who I barely understand and who think I'm from some other planet. And I really, really don't want to put up with your nonsense."

"What nonsense?"

"That. What you're doing right now. Pretending not to know what I mean. Speaking cryptically. Standing by while I pretend to be a homicide investigator in another millennium."

"You don't look like you're pretending. You come across very professional."

"So what? What am I going to do with what I find? Test blood for DNA? With what? DNA won't be discovered for centuries and the process for examining it even longer. I can't carry a mass spectrometer with me, I can't do electrophoresis, I can't do any chromatography work or anything else. If I find fingerprints, it makes no difference. There's no fingerprint database to search. I'd have to line up every suspect, print 'em, and then do a by-eye comparison. Imagine how that'd go over."

"It's hard having limitations."

"You don't understand. All I have is a pair of customized field kits to use in a presentation. Besides, none of it matters."

"It matters," Yoshua said.

"How? Tell me that, pal. How does anything I learn or find change the events? It's clear that Jesus was killed by conspiracy. So if I prove that, what changes? Does he not die? I know very little Bible and even less theology, but I'm pretty sure that Jesus dying was part of the cosmic plan."

Yoshua continued on without comment.

That did it. I shouted, "I WANT TO GO HOME!" I threw my cases down and they skidded along the stone-paved road. One tipped to its side. I no longer cared. I stopped in the middle of the street and rubbed my temples. Passersby stared. I overheard someone say, "He has a demon."

Yoshua stopped, turned, then surprised me. He picked up the cases and walked to me.

"Max, it's time you learned to trust."

He pivoted and resumed his journey. I watched him for a few moments then followed.

As I walked, I waited for the nervous breakdown to begin.

It arrived.

I quickened my step, which turned into a jog. I reached Yoshua, grabbed his shoulder, and spun him hard. "Don't walk away from me, pal. I'm losing my patience."

"So I see."

I pushed him, and he took an unwilling step back. "No more

cryptic wordplay. No more smug answers. I've reached my limit."

He said nothing, but a flood of sadness filled his eyes.

I shoved him again. With each outburst my anger grew. For a moment, for the briefest fragment of a second, I fought to control myself. But I didn't want to be controlled. This place with its backward people, crowded streets, its smells, its impossible to understand cultural dictates … Here, in a place not of my choosing—worse, in this time not of my choosing—my mind was eroding, eaten by an illusion that struck me as too real.

I said, "I want to quit. Do you understand that? I'm done. Finished." I seized the front of his cloak and pulled him close, nose to nose. "I don't understand. I don't pretend to understand, but I do know that I have been kidnapped—snatched against my will—and forced to be your flunky."

"Max, you need to stop—"

Something snapped. I shoved with anger-fueled strength. My kits fell from his hands and Yoshua stumbled a step, then two, and then landed hard on the ground.

"You. Stop!" The voice came from my right but I didn't turn, didn't look, didn't invest a second of caring.

I took a menacing step toward the fallen Yoshua. If I couldn't talk him into returning me to my time and place, then I'd force him to do so—even if I had to beat him to within an inch of his life.

"Stay put," the new voice commanded.

I didn't.

Yoshua looked up. "Max, stop. Please stop. Before—"

"Before what? I've already taken a beating and a backhand to the face for you. You gonna get up and give me a little too? Well, come on, mystery man. On your feet. Let's see what you've got."

To my surprise, Yoshua was on his feet in a second and I

197

braced myself. A perverse pleasure ran through me. Whatever broke in my mind had snapped clean in half.

"Max, don't move."

A powerful hand grabbed my right arm and squeezed my bicep. The pain of it ran to my shoulder and down my back. I gave no thought to my next action. I leaned toward the hand then pulled away, swinging my arm in a tight circle. I now had the new attacker's arm pinned between my arm and body. The next motion came on the heels of the first. With my right leg I kicked the attacker's foot from beneath him, pulling back on his arm. I let go so I wouldn't fall with him.

He hit the ground hard and his metal helmet clanged against the stone street, his javelin rolled a foot or two away from him. The Roman soldier looked stunned, but no more than me. In the second of inactivity that followed, I knew I had made a colossal mistake.

The few times I had seen the leather armor-clad soldiers patrolling the streets, they had done so in pairs. There wasn't time enough for the thought to fully form, but I intuited the next event.

Something hard hit me just above the kidney. My knees went weak and I stretched for the injured area, but before my hand could reach my back, another pain erupted just right of my left shoulder blade. The pain was electric, a million volts of lightning along every nerve. My stomach convulsed into a knot of burning as if I had swallowed a hot coal.

"STOP." It was Yoshua.

My knees gave way, and I dropped to the unyielding stone. I made an attempt to get up but the soldier I had flattened had a different idea. On his feet, he had reclaimed his javelin and brought the butt end of it around in a sweeping arch to the side of my head.

Lights flashed.

Glitter filled my eyes.

Things faded. Except the pain. The pain.

My head bounced when it hit the ground. A sandaled foot caught me in the ribs, another found my groin, and another my belly.

Then I felt something touch me, cover me like a warm blanket. I thought it was death. I hoped it was death. But it wasn't. The body of a man sheltered me. On hands and knees, Yoshua interposed his own body between me and the bludgeoning.

It didn't stop the beating; the only thing that changed was the target. I could hear the air forced from his lungs; I knew when one of his ribs broke.

Between blows, Yoshua muttered, "I'm ... sorry, Max."

The sun and blue sky fled, leaving the black of unconsciousness.

For the first time in my adult life, I prayed. "Dear God, let me die. Let me die."

chapter
12

I shivered.

Cold.

The room spun, revolving on some unseen axis. The rough floor drank the heat from my body. I was still alive, and I regretted it. Every breath came with sharp pain, as if I were wearing a shirt of razor blades.

Why hadn't God let me die? I had no reason to live. Not here in the first century and certainly not in the twenty-first.

I rolled on to my back. No relief. My breath came in short gasps. A deep inhalation made my ribs crackle. Something stiff pulled at the stubble on my chin. Gingerly, I raised a hand and touched my face. I felt a crust of dried blood. I could also tell my face was swollen.

I started to sit up.

"Easy, friend." Yoshua? No. The voice belonged to a younger man. "Do not rise too fast. It makes things worse."

Not being in the mood to take advice, I pressed myself up to a sitting position. The man had been right. It did make things worse. I was able to shift positions and lean back against a stone wall. I felt sick to my stomach. My kidney and back throbbed like a bass drum in a rock band.

I willed my eyes open. One complied. The other was suffocated by a mountain of swollen tissue. Four stone walls surrounded me. An iron gate sealed off the only narrow door. A shaft of light pierced the dusty gloom. I coughed and a new tsunami of pain rolled from head to foot.

I blinked my one good eye, trying to force a sharper focus. It took several moments, but I began to see clearly. A man stood, leaning against the opposite wall. He was dressed in the plain clothing I had seen the poorer citizens of Jerusalem wear. He was maybe five foot eight or nine, thin and young. I guessed that he was in his very early twenties.

As I studied him, I realized we had more in common than a jail cell. The right side of his face was bruised and swollen. His lower lip puffed out like he was a five-year-old with a good pout going on. It also had a nasty-looking red tear in it.

"Do I look as bad as you?" I asked.

"Worse. Much worse. Dead men look better than you."

"Thanks, pal. That was just the kind of encouragement I was looking for."

He gave a crooked smile that looked like it pained him. "My name is Yohanan."

"What? No Yohanan ben Something-or-another?"

"My family is unimportant."

"I'm Max Odom, human punching bag."

"I'm not certain what that means, but I am very sure you crossed the path of the wrong people. You must have made someone very angry."

"I knocked a Roman guard on his back."

That made him laugh, which he cut short and touched his tender mouth. "That would explain it. These Roman dogs have no sense of humor. What made you so foolish to fight with a trained killer?"

"I didn't know who it was. He grabbed me. The rest was instinct."

"And you really knocked him to the ground? Without a weapon?"

I nodded. "His partner took exception to it."

"You are a lucky man, Max Odom. There are some of the invaders who would have killed you where you stood."

"That's me. Mr. Lucky." I rested my head against the wall. My neck grew weary of doing its job. "I take it you got on their bad side too. Why are you here?"

"More important, what is a Roman like you doing here, sharing a cell with a Jew?"

"I'm not Roman."

He gave me a critical look. "Greek?"

"No."

He looked doubtful. "Not many Jews shave their faces, Max Odom."

So that was it. I ran a hand over my stubbled chin. "I'm not from around here."

"That much is obvious." He moved toward me then slid down the wall and sat three or four feet away.

"Exactly where am I?"

"You really are not from around here." He motioned around the room. "This, my friend, is one of the finer cells in the Antonia Fortress."

"Antonia Fortress?"

"Yes. It is the barracks of the dogs from Rome and where the governor rests his feet when he is in Jerusalem."

"Governor?"

"Are you testing me, Max Odom?"

"Listen, pal, I'm working on staying conscious. Testing you is not on my 'to do list.'"

He frowned. "His *Excellency* Pontius Pilate. You have not heard of him?"

"I've heard of him, but not the way you're thinking."

"It matters not. You'll meet him soon enough."

"I take it that you've already had your time before the governor?"

"I did. Yesterday." His gaze shifted to the iron gate that kept us prisoner.

"Since you're still here, I assume you've got more time to spend in lockup." The spinning in my head slowed and my stomach settled.

"I will not be here long."

"Planning to break out?"

His confident demeanor evaporated like water in a frying pan. "I am to be crucified today."

"Crucified?" I started to say they wouldn't really do that, but what did I know? Pilate's men had come near to kicking me to death on the stones of the street.

"No need to worry, Max Odom. They won't crucify you. You look too Roman. Romans do not crucify their own."

"I suppose I should be relieved."

"They behead them."

"Oh, that's better." I shifted my weight and wished I hadn't.

"In many ways it is. I will die slowly. Even stoning is better than the cross. This is especially true for some of us."

"I don't understand."

As if he flipped a switch that detached him from his own reality, he explained. "A few days ago, on the eve of the Sabbath, three men died upon the crosses. Mercifully, the Sabbath was so close."

"What difference does that make?"

"It is an affront to our laws to have men hanging from crosses on the holy days. At the instigation of our religious leaders, the guards broke the legs of the crucified so they would die at a more expedient rate."[1]

The longer I spent in this time, the more convinced I became that it was impossible to distinguish between the criminals and those who dispensed justice.

"The Sabbath is several days off. I will not receive the benefit of broken legs."

How does a man respond to that? What could I say? "I'm sure you'll die quickly. Try not to worry." No, that wouldn't do at all. So I just admitted, "I don't know what to say."

"What is there to say, Max Odom? Today they will take me and tie me—or maybe nail me—to a cross. I will die when I die." He paused. "Some have taken days to breathe their last."

The image made me sick again. Despite Yohanan's assurances that I would not be crucified, I wondered if I was doomed to the same fate. My temper got the best of me; my fear overcame me; now I might pay for it with my life.

"May I ask what you did to deserve the death penalty?"

"I killed a man. A Roman man."

I had no words.

"A centurion mocked my father. My father delivers food to the barracks. He's a baker and brings bread. Two days ago he was here making his usual delivery when his cart overturned. The bread fell to the ground and was soiled. One of the centurions became furious with him. I was there. He slapped my father, then told his men to shave the beard from Father's face."

"His beard?"

"An unbearable insult. I watched as they raised a knife to his face. I had a knife too. The foolish centurion turned his back to me. I cut his throat and ran. They chased me, but my father was free. Bread is a small thing in the sight of murder."

"You killed a man because he ordered his men to shave your father."

"They are dogs, not men, not worthy to breathe the air of Yisreal. HaShem gave us this land. He did not give it to them."

"Yohanan, a beard will grow back, but once a child is gone, he is ... gone." Flimsy images of my dreams flickered in my brain.

"If I did not act, I would never be able to face my father again."

"Your father would have understood."

He shook his head and I made no attempt to convince him. Maybe his courage in the face of death was the belief that he had done the right thing no matter how wrong it had been.

Like the light through the window, silence streamed into our small cell.

I felt very cold, very small, and very alone.

†Ť†

"On your feet." The voice echoed around the cell, jarring me from the thin sleep that had overcome me. I blinked awake. The sunlight had dimmed but still filled the cell. "I said, on your feet."

Two soldiers stood at the iron gate. I recognized my friends from the street. It took me a second to realize that they were talking to me.

I folded over to my knees and tried to struggle to my feet. I faltered. A second later Yohanan's hands were on my shoulders, helping me rise.

"May HaShem be merciful to you, friend."

I raised a hand to the side of his face and gave it a gentle tap. "And to you, Yohanan ben ..."

"Yohanan ben Yakov."

"See. Family does matter."

He helped me walk to the gate, which the soldiers unlocked and opened. Once free of the room, I was led down a narrow corridor and up a short flight of steps, one guard before me and one after.

Every step I took came with effort and the endurance of pain. Earlier, before dozing off in pain-laced sleep, I tried to estimate my injuries. My ribs were bruised and the intercostal tissue was sensitive to movement, but the best I could tell no ribs were broken. My lungs were clear and I hadn't coughed up any blood. A good sign. There was a knot over my right kidney where the guard had brought home the butt end of the javelin. I told myself I should be thankful he hadn't used the business end, but a very large part of me wished he had just gone ahead and run me through. My head throbbed and I could feel the place where the first guard wound up and took his aim-for-the-fences swing. I wondered if he cracked my skull. It didn't matter. What was, was. Still, I'd trade my field kits for a bottle of Vicodin.

My thoughts ran to Yoshua. Last I saw him, he had tented himself over me to protect me from the pummeling the guards were giving me.

That was a picture that played across my mind in a constant loop. I had just pushed him to the ground and was ready to go the next step, yet when I was in trouble, he sacrificed himself for me.

I didn't think it possible, but I could swear my soul was hurting.

"Stand there," the lead guard said pointing to the middle of the room. Unlike the cell I had spent the last few hours in, this room was wide and deep. As I entered, I saw open doors hinged to an arched passage leading to a long set of stairs leading to the street. To the side was another pair of doors opened to a plaza. On the court, soldiers milled around; some had gathered into small groups.

Directly before me rested a raised platform with a single thronelike chair. Logic dictated that the chair wasn't for the likes of me. The guards stood to each side, hands resting on one of the two swords they carried. They must have been standing at the first-century version of attention, because a blind man could see that I couldn't fight a toddler let alone these two knuckle draggers.

I swayed and my head went light. I took a few deep breaths and waited for my mind to clear. It did, but not quickly. Seconds oozed into minutes, taking their own sweet time. The thought occurred to me that I might not be able to stand as long as my hosts would like. What was the punishment for passing out in front of the judge?

From a door in the distant wall a man entered, accompanied by a woman of dark hair, deep eyes, and smooth olive skin. No veil covered her face, and her hair was visible for all to see. She was breathtaking. He, on the other hand, was two inches shorter than she, his hair cut so close to the scalp I couldn't be certain of the color. Like the soldiers, he was clean shaven. He wore a white robe decorated by a red-purple sash. His face bore the evidence of a man grown weary with the years. Then again, I had grown weary of life, so who was I to judge?

When he entered, the guards on either side came to attention, moved their hands from their swords, struck their chest with a closed fist, then extended an arm in a salute.

"Hail, Caesar," they said in unison.

The man didn't respond to the guards. He took a seat on the throne, wiggled until he was comfortable, then stared at me. The woman stood to his side.

"You're not Jewish," he said flatly as if commenting on the weather.

I swayed in silence. The guard to my right shot a sharp elbow into my arm.

"What?"

"His Excellency has spoken to you."

"Perhaps," the man in the chair said, "you do not know who I am. Forgive me for not introducing myself. I am the man who holds your life in his hand. Pontius Pilate, procurator of this desolate, useless land. Do you understand me?"

"I do."

"Good. That will make things simpler. You are not Jewish, are you?"

"No, sir. I am not Jewish."

"Well, that's one thing I can thank the gods for. I am beginning to lose my appetite for killing Jews. What is your name?"

"Odom. Max Odom."

"From where do you hail?" Pilate asked.

"California," I answered before thinking.

"I do not know of California."

"It is in the far west."

"Gaul?"

Sure. Why not? "Near Gaul."

He nodded as if he had just figured out that California was somewhere in Europe.

"Max? Is that short for Maximus?"

"Would it help?"

He frowned.

"Maxwell," I said before another elbow could be delivered.

"Maxwell Odom, you have delayed my departure to Caesarea Maritima. I should be on my way to the coast, yet here I sit in this pigsty city."

I considered being insulting or even attacking the man in the chair in hopes that someone would have the common decency to kill me, but I remembered Yohanan's description of crucifixion. He said they would never crucify me, but with my luck they'd make an exception.

When I said nothing, he continued. "I am told that you fought with two of my men. Do you like fighting with my men?"

"No, sir. It was unintentional."

"But you confess to knocking one of my men to the ground?"

"Yes, sir. Before I knew who he was."

"You are not one of the daggermen?"

"No. I've never heard of daggermen." My lips hurt with every word.

"Zealots. Fools who think they can intimidate Rome into leaving this place. Daggermen sneak through the streets and stab Romans in the backs. Cowards, every one."

"I am not a daggerman. I am a traveler."

"A traveler? What brings you to Jerusalem, traveler?" He leaned back, looking bored. I was not a man to him, I was an inconvenience.

209

"I've been ... retained to investigate something that happened a few days ago. That's what I do where I live. I'm a detective. I detect things."

"What kind of things?"

"Crimes. My job is to put criminals in jail based on the evidence they leave behind."

"It is your job to jail criminals, yet here you become a criminal yourself. Ironic isn't it?"

"I had no intention of attacking your men. I apologize if I hurt him." The guard to my left cut a hard look my way but said nothing. Clearly, this was Pilate's time and not his.

"Are you injured?" Pilate asked the guard.

"No, your Excellency. I am more than able to serve. It would take more than the likes of this dog to injure me."

Pilate smiled, apparently hearing what he wanted. "Max Odom, what do you investigate here in Jerusalem?"

This was dangerously ironic. I had hoped I wouldn't have to answer this. I had a patchy understanding of the Bible, but I knew that Jesus stood before this man and ultimately received a sentence of crucifixion.

He saw my hesitancy. "You do not wish to answer?"

One of the guards slapped me hard on the back of the head. "Answer!" The additional pain fired the nausea in my stomach.

"I've been looking into the death of Jesus who died on a cross a few days ago." There, I said it. Now the ball was in the court.

"Jesus? The Hebrew?" He laughed and the sound of it rebounded off the hard surfaces of the room. "The King of the Jews. Of course. I remember him." He looked at the woman standing next to him. The color had gone from her face. Unlike the other women I had met in this time, she looked me straight in the eyes. I saw fear.

"He was an odd one, that Jew. He never quite understood the

trouble he was in. I asked questions and got almost no answers. There I was holding his life in my hand and he looked at me like I was a child.[2] The world is better off without him. Still ..." He trailed off.

I risked a question. "Still, what?"

"I found no guilt in him. It was *his* people that brought him to ruin. They were intent on seeing him die—not just die, mind you, but crucified. That has puzzled me."

"Why?" Then I quickly added, "Your Excellency."

"Every time I crucify a Jew, the people complain." He shook his head. "I bring justice and peace to this land. That means the guilty must die, but the people complain when it's one of their own who hangs in the hot sun. These Jews have caused me trouble in Rome. They won't be happy until I'm exiled to some hole never to be seen again. Yet, their religious leaders come to me asking for a favor."

He stood and paced in front of the judgment seat. "Do you know they wouldn't even step inside this fortress to bring their charges?[3] To step foot in this place would defile them. Defile them!" His face reddened. "I asked them what the charges were and all they could say was that he was guilty or they wouldn't have brought him to me."[4]

"But you tried him anyway?"

He snapped his head around to face me. "Careful with your tone. I am a fair man but not a patient one."

"I meant no dishonor." Easy does it, I reminded myself.

He looked hard into my eyes, then continued. "Yes, I judged him, but I did so against my will. I told them to take care of the matter themselves, but they said they were not allowed to crucify. That's true, of course, but I would have tolerated a quick stoning."

Nice guy.

211

ALTON
GANSKY

"They were persistent. And they say we Romans are cruel. I would not like to be alone and in the hands of Annas and Caiaphas."

"I've met them," I said. "It wasn't pleasant."

"You are on the bad side of those two pigs?"

I nodded. "We didn't hit it off well." Maybe I shouldn't have used the word *hit*.

A smile pushed the edges of his mouth back. "In that case, I'm starting to like you."

I couldn't say the same so I muttered a quick, "Thank you."

He rubbed his hands together as if he had just discovered something sticky and unpleasant on them. "They would not yield. I learned that this Jesus was from Galilee. Herod the Tetrarch was in Jerusalem for Passover. It made sense to send the accused to him. Let the tetrarch of Galilee deal with a Galilean."

"But he sent him back to you," I said.

"You have been investigating, Max Odom. Yes, Herod sent him back." He smiled. "He sent him back dressed in a king's robe."

"They must have made quite a game of it."

"It was humorous, I must admit," Pilate said returning to his seat and adopting his imperial air. "I've always disliked Herod, but seeing how he handled one of his own with such, such … aplomb—well, I have a new respect for him."[5]

This guy's elevator didn't go all the way to the top. Knowing that made me all the more uncomfortable. I had fleeting wishes for death, but I had no hunger for torture, and he seemed the kind of man who would consider such an act entertainment.

"Excellency, may I ask what happened after Jesus was returned to you?"

"He had been roughed up some. They had beaten him before

they brought him to me the first time. Herod let his men have some sport at Jesus' expense, but that is his privilege. Still it gave me an idea. Maybe all his accusers wanted was a little blood."

And you thought you'd provide it, you animal.

He leaned forward and began to rub his hands. The silent woman looked thinner, as if she were evaporating before my eyes. "I turned him over to my men. They delivered some punishment. They even wove a crown out of a thornbush and thrust it on his head."

I pictured that. I had seen enough scalp wounds to know that they bleed in profusion.

"They dressed him in purple, called him King of the Jews, and spat on him. All of it, of course, an effort to save the man's life. Maybe a thorough beating might satisfy the bloodlust of the leaders. My men are quite good at inflicting pain and punishment."

"Yes, your Excellency. I've noticed."

That made him laugh again. "Yes, it seems you have. I'm afraid it did no good. I gave it one more attempt to free the poor Rabbi. I release one condemned man each Passover. It makes the people happy for a short time. I had Jesus and three others. I chose a man named Barabbas. He was a thief, a scoundrel of the worse kind." He looked at the woman. "What does his name mean, Claudia?"[6]

"It is from *bar abba*," she said. Her voice was sweet, but I could hear the strain. "It means 'son of the father.'"

My spine seemed to melt. If Pilate was willing to allow a man to be tortured and beaten to save his life, what would he do to the likes of me?

213

"I allowed the beating to go on for a while. They used rods to pound the accused around the face and head and to hammer down the crown of thorns. No matter how pitiful I made him, no one rose to his defense. Nothing to do but hand him over to exe-cution. I finally had to wash my hands of the whole situation."[7]

This was one of those situations where wisdom demands silence, or a simple nod of the head implying agreement even if no agreement is felt. Instead ... "You knew the man was innocent, yet sent him to the cross anyway?"

His face frosted over. "Innocent is a subjective idea, Max Odom. Just like truth. What is truth? Do the Jews have truth? If so, which Jews? The Sadducees, who make up the chief priests, or the strict Pharisees? What of the Essenes in their monastic complex? Did that poor rabbi have truth? What of the Greeks?" He leaned forward. "Max Odom from Cally-Forna, do you have truth?"

There was a time when I thought I knew what was true and just. Things had changed. I knew nothing and the more I learned, the less I seemed to know. "No."

"Then don't judge me. It is impolite and ..." His face softened with a smile that was just a step away from a sneer. "Besides, judg-ing is my work, not yours. What am I to do with you, Max Odom?"

He stepped down from the platform again and came close. He smelled of flowers, and his skin was a moonscape of pores. This close to him I could see the ridge of his nose was crooked, the result of some break, I supposed. I fought the urge to break it again.

All my adult life I have waded through the world of criminals, both as a cop and a forensics investigator. Here was a man who was a law unto himself. Guilt and innocence for him were mere judgment calls, directed and redirected by whim or convenience.

He studied me like a man deciding if the week-old meat in the refrigerator had turned.

"My men hurt you?"

That should be obvious. "I took a bit of a beating." I hadn't seen a mirror but my fingers told me that blood caked my face, my lip was swollen, and the tissue beneath my face felt as if it were orchestrating an escape.

"A bit? I can arrange more."

"Your Excellency." The voice was familiar. I looked over my shoulder and saw Yoshua standing beneath the arch of the doorway. He leaned forward a few degrees and slightly to the right. He held his right arm across his chest, a clear sign of fractured ribs. Blue and red splotches marred his face. The guards hadn't gone any easier on him. "I have come to speak on behalf of the accused."

Pilate looked annoyed. "Enter." He returned to his chair, plopped down, and rested his head in one hand, advertising the boredom he felt.

"Your Excellency, I am Yoshua ben Yoseph, guide to Max Odom."

"I take it you were the one he was fighting with."

"He became frustrated with my manner of work. He meant no harm to me or to any of your Excellency's men."

"My men did that to you?" He pointed at Yoshua's face.

"Yes."

Pilate turned to the guard on my right. "Why did you beat the Jew?"

"He was interfering with us as we carried out our duty."

"He was trying to save my life," I said. Yoshua gave me a look that suggested I shut up.

My eyes traveled to the beautiful woman at Pilate's side. She looked as pale as a corpse.

"Why should that matter to me? This man attacked a soldier of Rome. At the very least, I should have him beaten."

"As your Excellency can see, he has already been beaten," Yoshua countered. "As have I."

Claudia's gaze was frozen on Yoshua. Pilate started to speak again, but she put a hand on his shoulder. She leaned close to his ear and whispered something. He straightened, turned, and stared into her face. He frowned.

"Please," she said.

Pilate turned our way again. "My wife is given to dreams. The night before your Jesus was brought before me, she had been troubled in her sleep.[8] It seems it has happened again."

I allowed myself a moment of hope.

Pilate fell silent and I watched as a war of desire raged within him. Finally, he sighed. "I have a long journey to begin and would like my wife to be comfortable. Only then will I be comfortable." He stood. "I suppose we will have to be satisfied with the beating you've already received. You are free to go."

"But your Excellency—" the guard to my right began.

"You have my praise," Pilate interjected. "I will see that your centurion is made aware of my pleasure. You will also receive extra rations and pay." That seemed to quiet him.

Pilate wasn't done. "A word of wisdom, Max Odom. Stay out of trouble. My wife will not be here to turn the ear of your next judge. Leave."

We did.

chapter
13

"What happened to you?" I asked. "After they took me away, I mean."

We had been escorted from the hall where I stood before Pilate, bracketed by a pair of guards who had been hoping for a different decision than I received. I sensed their disappointment as they crushed my arms in their meaty hands and led me from the building. The shove at the end was unnecessary, but they added it nonetheless.

"I lost consciousness." He led me down the long flight of stairs that led from the entry doors and stopped next to a short stone wall that formed the perimeter of a courtyard for a small building.

The stone had been cut with great skill, as had the pavers beneath our feet and in the courtyard itself. Had I been a tourist, I would have been more impressed. At the moment I felt a brief giddiness at being released, which a flood of depression soon extinguished.

Yoshua leaned against the stone and lowered his head. It was the body language of a man in pain. He took a few shallow breaths and continued.

"When I regained consciousness, I was in a small room of an inn. A man, a Samaritan, had found me. He and his family carried me back to their rented quarters. I slipped in and out of consciousness for hours. When I could stay awake, I went looking for you."

His words were red-hot swords to my heart. I caused the problem. I lost my temper and tried to force my will upon him with violence, and when my life was being pounded and kicked out of me, he laid himself between me and the blows. Now, like me, his body bore the wounds, bruises, and breaks of the beating. I wanted to take him to a hospital. He needed X-rays, painkillers, maybe more, but nothing resembling a hospital existed in this time. He needed more than herbs and leeches or whatever they passed off as emergency medicine here.

I tried to speak, but my throat closed up. My eyes burned, and my heart seemed to transform into putty, flopping more than beating. In the bright light of a spring sun, darkness surrounded me like a mist, seeping into my pores, flooding the orifices of my head.

The world receded from me. I could no longer think. Linking progressive thoughts one after another became impossible. *Think of something else. Anything else!* Useless. I no longer controlled my mind. Emotion bubbled, roiled, frothed inside me. The genie was out of the bottle, and I couldn't find the cork.

I lowered my head. I didn't want to make eye contact with Yoshua. Maybe it was the dreams; maybe being so far from home

CRIME SCENE
JERUSALEM

in time and in space; maybe it was the physical beating I had taken, or the sights I had seen, or the hatred I had heard, but my control, my iron-willed control, rusted into powder.

My shoulders shook.

My stomach blazed.

My sinuses flooded with mucus.

I wanted to run, to escape, to flee to a place of solitude, empty of humans, void of emotion, silent as the inside of a tomb. But I couldn't move. Emotion welded me to the wall.

I heard a sniff. It came from Yoshua. Out of the corner of my eye, I watched him wipe away a tear, then drag the same hand beneath his nose.

Yoshua wept.

No words were spoken. No verbal apologies given. Yet, something bridged the distance between us. He stood no more than eighteen inches from me, but light years separated us—a chasm so wide that I could not see the distant edge where he stood. But in that moment, when soft tears burned our faces, when a force like deep ocean pressure threatened to squash me like a soda can under the tire of a truck, the distance closed.

I stood not by a guide, not by a time-traveling abductor, but by a friend. It made no sense. I wanted to hate him, wanted to cry out how unfair all this was considering what I had just been through, and it was his fault. His, not mine.

But I couldn't. No matter how vigorously I stoked the coals of self-pity, no matter how hard I fanned the flames of resentment, I could no longer hate the man—not the man who covered my body with his to absorb blows meant for me; not the man who left the warm, supportive bed of a stranger who took the time to comfort him to come looking for me; not the man who marched into the judgment hall of the Jew-hating Pontius Pilate.

219

And he did it all for me, a man who had given him nothing but grief.

Finally able to move, I turned toward the courtyard, more to hide my face from onlookers and Yoshua. The court was empty of furniture. No fountain, as I had seen in some, no large jars of water, nothing but an expanse of brown stone and one object: a post. It looked like a telephone pole that had been cut so that it stood no higher than eight feet from its base to its crown.

The pole puzzled me. It supported nothing. It just stood there. I studied it closer. An iron ring, rusted by its exposure to the elements, hung six inches or so from the top. I began to see things I previously missed. Two other iron rings were attached to the base of the wood column by a chain I judged to be twelve to fourteen inches long.

My first thought was that soldiers used the post to tie up an animal, maybe a horse, but the iron ring at the top made no sense. I wasn't a horseman, but I felt pretty sure one didn't tie a horse to a ring a foot above its head.

I started to ask Yoshua about it when other details caught my eye. Dark stains surrounded the pole as well as dotting the length of it. The post was close to a stone wall and I saw stains there—familiar stains.

The mystery was short lived, and the truth that replaced it nauseated me. The stains were familiar because I had seen similar markings hundreds of times before.

Blood splatter. It was all there: gravity drops on the ground, velocity splatter on the walls, and cast-off splatter emanating from the post to a spot four or five feet away. Now the iron rings made sense—ugly sense. My mind conjured up the image of a Roman soldier with whip in hand and an unfortunate man chained to the post.

A sound broke the garish image. To my left a woman was weeping. Next to her stood a man with half a beard and next to him a boy of twelve or thirteen years and a girl a year or two younger than that.

My mind exploded with the realization of what was happening. "No, oh no. Yoshua, we have to—"

A sharp pain silenced me. The hard, cold point of something pressed into the swollen tissue over my kidney. It didn't pierce the skin, but the slightest nudge would remedy that.

"Still here, Maxwell Odom?"

I turned enough to see the soldier who I had dumped on his back, the one who minutes before stood by my side hoping Pilate would order more punishment rather than letting me go. A glance to my right showed the older soldier standing directly behind Yoshua, a sword pressed into his back exactly like the one that dug into my flesh just right of my spine.

"We were just leaving," I said.

"Not now," the soldier said. I had no doubt that he enjoyed the situation.

Over the next few seconds more soldiers gathered around the outer limits of the wall. Some joked. One made a crude joke about Jewish women and the sons they bore.

My heart began to beat again, but with bass drum percussions that I suspected others could hear. A few soldiers stood behind the half-bearded man, and in what had to be one of the coldest acts of cruelty I have ever witnessed, pushed the family close to the wall, sealing them in. There was no escape. Perhaps they had come to plead for the life of their oldest son but instead were condemned to watch everything.

221

Two guards walked Yohanan around the corner of the building into view of the sadistic crowd.

The Romans cheered.

Hatred filled me.

Yohanan didn't struggle. His hands were bound in front of him with rope, and another rope tied around his ankles hobbled him, allowing only small steps. As he walked, he made the short strides as fast as the rope would allow. I had seen prisoners hobbled with leg shackles walk the same way.

They stood him in front of the post and turned him to face his family. I fought the urge, denied its existence—but an invisible hand turned my head to see his mother, father, and siblings in tears. Mother pleaded for his life; Father begged them to take his own life instead. Sister wept uncontrollably; Brother stared dry-eyed at the guards. I knew the look. The Romans had just made a new enemy, maybe a new daggerman.

The pleas went unnoticed, neglected.

New faces appeared in the crowd, perhaps drawn by the commotion. Faces. Jewish faces. Roman faces. Other faces came to the wall to watch.

I looked at Yoshua. Tears ran like rivers. My tears had dried, replaced by a murderous rage, a rage that would never be satisfied. The wrong motion from me and a short sword would be rammed through my back until stopped by its own hilt. I held no doubts that the same would happen to Yoshua. If my anger won, Yoshua and I would be wounded shells on our backs, bleeding our lives out on dry ground, and tomorrow no one would care.

Yohanan looked at his mother and father. "Do not weep, Imma. Do not cry, Abba. My life is in the hands of HaShem. May he avenge my death."

One of the guards spat in his face.

The other pulled a dagger from his belt and placed it near the neck of the young man. For a moment I thought he meant to slit his prisoner's throat. He didn't. Instead, he cut Yohanan's garment from neck to fringe and ripped it away.

Yohanan stood naked before the crowd. Bruises covered his body. The Jewish women turned away. The men averted their eyes in reflex. Seconds later all eyes were back on the nude youth. The humiliation radiated from him. The guards let him stand there for long minutes. Several crude remarks were made. I choose not to repeat any of them.

After a suitable amount of time for ridicule and embarrassment passed, the soldiers inside the courtyard spun Yohanan around and drew him to the post. First they secured his hands above his head, tying the rope to the high iron ring. Next they secured his feet to the iron rings on the ground. It took a moment for me to realize the purpose of the lower rings. Yohanan would not be able to hide behind the post when the whipping began. The chains would keep him in place.

I knew the purpose of the post. The blood splatter told me all I needed to know. The cast-off—blood splatter made by the instrument that caused the injury—lay in such a pattern that only something like a whip could create it. Judging by the amount of splatter visible, this post was used often.

Yohanan's mother wailed. His father started over the wall but a guard pulled him back.

The crowd fell silent for a moment. From overhead an eagle's cry pierced the air.

The lull lasted only a few seconds. A man appeared and the soldiers cheered. The noise of it hurt my ears. The new actor walked onto the stage of his play. He wore the same leather body armor as the other guards, the same greaves, the same bootlike sandals, the same cape, and the same style helmet.

He held a whip in his hand.

223

Now that they had Yohanan strung up, the two courtyard guards approached the new man. They helped him remove his belt and swords, his cape, and his helmet. Then they stepped to the side.

The whip-bearer was bald as a stone and thick around the middle. He had a chest the size of a barrel and arms like a pro athlete with a steroid problem. A dark growth of skin cancer clung to his forehead just above the right eyebrow.

The whip unfurled. I had never seen anything like it. It resembled other such devices except the end of it deviated into multiple strands. I could see bits of glass, metal, and bone woven into the ends.

The man tasked with brutalizing Yohanan swung his right arm around in circles, limbering the shoulder like a major-league pitcher.

He positioned himself in just the right spot, something easy to do. All he had to do was place his feet in the only clean spot of the cast-off blood spray.

The scourging began. The first few blows seemed light, leaving only scratches on Yohanan's back. He tensed with each impact, gritted his teeth, but refused to give the onlookers the satisfaction of seeing him cry in pain.

The man with the whip had not just been going light; he was warming up. After three strokes he put his back into it. Yohanan's flesh shredded. Blood splattered the ground and wall.

Yohanan screamed. The tone was violent, pitiful, originating from a place most men don't know they have. The sound of it ripped a hole in my soul. I wished for deafness.

And I could do nothing but watch. When I looked away, the sword point in my back dug deeper.

Every time the whip landed, Yohanan screamed to God to die.

In a merciful act, Yohanan's mother fainted. A moment later his sister pushed through the crowd and fled, wailing with every step.

I watched as the skin was removed from the young man's back. The muscles were laid bare. The bald man expanded his target, striking not just back but buttocks and the back of the thighs. That tissue gave way like butter before a heated knife.

The soldiers laughed and cheered.

Yohanan's father melted to his knees and pleaded that God would take his son rather than let him feel any more pain. He, of everyone present, felt the blows as much as his son.

Some of Yohanan's blood splattered my face.

I bent forward and vomited.

†✝†

I lost track of time. The world had lost its center and no longer turned on its axis. Instead, it tumbled end over end through space.

Yohanan's screams stopped. I looked up in time to see the whip land two more times. Sweat dotted the bald man's head and his breathing came in ragged gasps. He had worn himself out.

Yohanan had lost consciousness and hung by the ropes around his wrists. His hands were blue, the ropes having cut off his circulation. I didn't want to look at his back but my eyes had ceased obeying my brain. What I saw looked like nothing that belonged to a man. Blood, trashed tissue, sinew. I had no idea how it was that Yohanan still drew breath.

As one guard helped baldy don his helmet, belt, and cape, the other brought a wood pail of water and poured it over Yohanan's head. He came to, and I wished for all I was worth that he wouldn't.

He blinked a few times, groaned, then writhed as the pain

reintroduced itself to his mind. He began to weep, sobbing with a pathos that ripped my heart from its place with icy fingers.

The guard with the pail walked around the young man, examining the damage. He shook his head and looked to the crowd. The man with the sword in my back spoke up.

"I have a volunteer."

The guard nodded and motioned to something around the corner and out of my sight.

"Come with me, Maxwell Odom. Give me a moment's trouble and the blood of your friend will decorate the end of a Roman sword." He jerked his head in Yoshua's direction. I looked at Yoshua and saw the shell of a man, a human cored out by the violence he had seen.

I reached deep into my bag of quips and sarcastic remarks, the tools I had used all my life, and found it empty. There were no words to say. What could be said?

I let him lead me around the stone wall. We passed Yohanan's family. His mother had come to, and his father held her close in a viselike grip that buried her face in his shoulder, preventing her from seeing the torn body of her son, but not even her weeping could drown out the sounds of her boy, the fruit of her flesh.

As we walked by, Yohanan's brother faced the soldier who kept his sword in my back. I saw the kid look at the sword and I saw the pure hatred in his eyes. I don't believe in telepathy, but I knew exactly what he was thinking, and those thoughts could cost him his life. I stared at him, willing him to look at me. He did, and I shook my head. I cut my eyes to his parents, and he followed my motion. He knew what I was saying. His brave, revengeful act might bring a moment's satisfaction if it worked—which it wouldn't—but it would cost him his life and the life of his parents.

Don't do it, son. Don't make your parents lose two boys on the same day.

He stayed in place.

We followed the wall another ten paces around the corner. Where the front portion of the court was free of objects except the whipping post, this area was cluttered with objects including dark beams of wood. I caught a glimpse of the bald man washing the blood from his hands, face, and the front of his leather armor. He looked at us.

"Who is this, Lucius?"

"A volunteer. Once again you have done your job too well. The prisoner will not be able to carry his cross."

"If he had the decency to die, it would save us a trip to the hill."

"That's my favorite part," Lucius said. I believed him.

"You are young. It grows old with time." He wiped his hands and face with a cloth. "Are you sure this one can do the job? He does not look strong."

"With the proper motivation, he'll be strong enough."

The bald man raised an eyebrow, the one with the hovering cancer. "I see. This is the one who upended you in public." He laughed. I don't think Lucius appreciated the humor. He gave me a push. Apparently word had gotten around.

A few steps later we stood by a pile of timber. Each piece looked to be eight feet long and four inches by six inches. It would be a struggle to carry it, even if I hadn't been beaten unconscious a few hours before.

He pointed at the top beam. "Pick it up."

"Tell me you're kidding."

227

He backhanded me. One knee gave away.

"I'd pick it up," the bald man said. "Lucius has no sense of humor. But then, I guess you know that."

I staggered to the beam and gave it a test lift. It was lighter than I expected, and I guessed it to be pine. I felt thankful that it wasn't oak or some other hardwood. In the middle of the beam was a one-inch hole that someone had taken the time to auger. On the end closest to me the wood bore marks of ill treatment, of hammers and nails.

My first plan involved lifting the beam onto my shoulder and balancing it there. A half dozen of my ribs told me that was wrong thinking. There was no way I could lift the beam that high. Maybe a man in good shape could, but I ceased to be such a man hours ago.

"You might as well kill me now, buddy, because there's no way I'm going to get that hunk of wood on my shoulder."

"Drag it."

Again, I lifted one edge and pulled. Despite its weight, it moved fairly easily. I tugged until it came off the pile and began to move forward, one end of the beam in my hands and the other dragging the ground.

Every step hurt. Every muscle screamed in protest, but I managed to pull the beam along with me. By the time I returned to the front of the fortress, the crowd had divided into clumps of similarity: Jews with Jews; soldiers with soldiers; unescorted women with unescorted women. Yohanan's family stood alone. The little girl was still gone. Gone home I hoped.

Yohanan stood swaying in the sun, the running blood on his back, buttocks, and thighs drying to stiff cakes. He was still naked. They didn't have the decency to dress the condemned. How he stood I didn't know, but I suspected that he had gone into shock.

People began moving down the road toward a destination known to them.

I was forced to follow.

chapter
14

My load became lighter. Someone had picked up the other end of the beam. A glance confirmed my suspicions. Yoshua had taken it upon himself to help. I doubt he asked permission. In that quick look I could see the pain on his face. Carrying a load, any load, with busted ribs was agony. I could attest to the fact.

We fell in behind Yohanan, or the shell of what had once been a man. I couldn't see his face but his zombielike steps told me all I needed to know.

· The procession of guards, family, and the curious moved along the stone path that led from the Antonia Fortress through the streets of the city. I think we headed east, but to be honest, I couldn't tell and didn't much care.

As we walked, people stood to the sides. Most watched in silent horror. Children stood near their mothers. The weight of the beam made my injuries burn, but I left little room in my mind for complaint. The sight of Yohanan made every pain, every hurt, every trial seem trivial.

With every step Yohanan took, he left a bloody footprint. He walked barefoot and naked through the public streets. His tormentors would not afford him the decency of tunic or sandals.

The wood rubbed my hand raw as I carried it, but I paid it little mind. My brain occupied itself with the impossible: how to make this end.

A thought oozed to the forefront of my consciousness. More than a thought, an image. Jesus had walked this path a few days before, and if my imperfect understanding of biblical events was correct, he had carried his own cross, at least part of the way. Looking at Yohanan, I couldn't imagine any man taking such a beating then walking through the ever-narrowing streets of Jerusalem toting such a long piece of wood. I had seen paintings of Jesus dragging a full cross behind him. Now I knew that was impossible. I didn't have to be an engineer to know that I held the cross member of a cross to be, and it felt heavy in my hand. The upright had to be at least this large and probably a good bit larger. That would amount to a couple hundred pounds.

The most unsettling sound filled the streets. Yohanan's mother wailed, an ululation that quick-froze my burning bones. Along the way, women joined the procession adding their voices to the siren-loud howl.

Mourners, I thought. *Mourners come to grieve over a dead man walking.*

His father held his mother so tightly her feet barely touched the stones of the street. Grief spread through the procession like fire through dry brush. Even the Romans had ceased their mockery. Perhaps they had mothers as well, or children.

I grew numb. Everything was shutting down. I could no longer look at Yohanan, no longer view the agony of his parents and younger brother. I searched the ground for relief. Every stone, every joint, every crack was a nanosecond of distraction I felt grateful for. I tried to project myself down into the cracks I saw, as if I could shrink out of sight, and if lucky, cease to exist.

Wide streets gave way to narrow paths, and then we passed through one of the gates and out of the city. The road widened again and continued down the slope of the hill Jerusalem called home, but we veered to the left. Near the juncture of two roads was a flat lot. Travelers parted on the road as we worked our way through pedestrians. Some decided to delay their travel to watch the horrid act being staged at the crossroads.

Crossroads. The location told me more of the Roman mind-set. They were going to kill this man on a cross in a place where every traveler could see. It was more than an execution, it was a statement.

Several Roman guards huddled in the center of the lot, tall poles surrounding them like an anemic forest. I counted six uprights, each spaced about ten feet apart. The posts had been roughly hewed to a square cross section and were about half as large as what Yoshua and I carried.

"This way," Lucius snapped.

We followed him to one of the posts.

"Set it down." We did. "Not that way, fools. The center hole faces the ground."

Yoshua and I turned the beam until the side with the augured hole rested on the ground.

"Now step away. Leave if you want."

I wanted but couldn't. My feet wouldn't budge. I studied the posts, the tops of which stood ten feet above the ground. A thick peg protruded from the side facing the street. Now the augured hole made sense.

A pair of soldiers took Yohanan by the arms and forced him to the beam we had set down. One kicked him behind the right knee. Both knees buckled and he dropped like a stone, his legs folding under him. Then in what had to be a practiced motion, they bent him until his head rested on the beam.

Yohanan moaned as his raw back impacted the dirt and his head bounced on the beam. The gorge in my stomach rose. Each soldier pulled a short piece of rope from his belt. As he did, another soldier stepped forward, bent forward, and lifted one end of the beam so his partner could slide the rope beneath it. With hasty motions the guard tied Yohanan's wrist to the beam. A few moments later the guard on the other side had done the same.

Then I saw it.

The nail was square. The nail was rusty iron. The hammer looked like a two-pound blacksmith mallet. One man held Yohanan's hand open. The other placed the nail in the palm....

The sound. Oh, dear God, the sound.

Yohanan screamed from a place no man should know exists. "HaShem! HaShem!"

He began to weep.

His mother wailed; his father howled.

No longer able to watch without action; no longer in his right mind, the father charged, ready to take on the whole Roman army. A young guard flattened him to the ground with the shaft of his javelin. Still in pain the father rose to shaky feet.

The other nail went in. I have seen the worst that life has to offer, but this shook me beyond words.

I could see the father readying himself for another desperate attempt to free his son.

"Yoshua ..." I began.

Yoshua pushed past me and moved toward the father. Before the soldier could land another blow, Yoshua had interposed himself between the father and the young guard. Taking the father in his arms, Yoshua held him in place. I have no idea how he did it, but despite crippling injury, Yoshua held the man still. The father could see over Yoshua's shoulder. Yohanan's mother raced to her husband's side. Losing a son this way was unbearable; to lose a husband would be more than a woman could stand.

I returned my attention to Yohanan. Blood ran from his palms. His skin had paled, his lips parched. The loss of blood had left him dehydrated. His shock was deepening.

Two Jewish women whom I had seen join the procession moved to Yohanan and knelt. One held a pitcher, the other a bowl and sponge. As the first woman poured water into the basin, Lucius raised his javelin.

"Back away."

I grabbed the javelin. "The man's dehydrated. Leave them alone."

"I don't take orders from the likes of you."

My brain ran out of control like a car with a jammed accelerator. I said the dumbest thing in my life. "You want to go again, pal? I'm ready. Bring it."

I wasn't ready. Injured as I was, I couldn't beat a preschooler in an arm-wrestling match.

His eyes flashed.

"Step away, Lucius."

233

He snapped his head around ready to let the imposer know what he thought of the suggestion, then stopped. His expression changed. "Yes, Centurion."

Standing a short distance away stood an older man who wore an outfit similar to the one worn by Lucius and the other soldiers, except this man had circular metal plaques on his chest, something I took to be analogous to war medals, a long red cape, and he held a stick in his hand that looked like a thick branch from a vine. His helmet was different too, sporting a crest. I hadn't seen him before, but he no doubt led the procession through the streets.

Lucius stepped away and so did I.

The women helped Yohanan drink from the sponge, but he choked on some of it. He had little strength to cough. The women moved away, their act of mercy finished for the moment.

"On your feet," one of the soldiers who had driven a nail demanded. It was an impossible request. No man could sit up nailed and tied to that crossbeam. Apparently the executioners knew this. A soldier on each end of the beam lifted the weight of the wood while Yohanan did his best to sit up. "Now stand."

They lifted the wood and Yohanan's screams rolled down the valley. A second later he stood, then vomited on himself. The soldiers paid no attention to it.

They backed him to the post and lifted the crossbeam as high as they could. Two other soldiers, each carrying a long pole with a Y-shaped construct on the end, stepped forward, while a third set a wood ladder on the back of the post and climbed it. He held a rope in his hand.

The pole-men placed their poles beneath the crossbeam. Someone said, "Now," and with loud grunts they lifted.

Yohanan's feet left the ground. He bit through his lip.

The man on the ladder began to give orders. "Up, up … left.

More. Up. There." He pulled the crossbeam toward him and it dropped on the pin in the upright. "Hold it."

With adroit hands he tied the crossbeam so that it couldn't slip from the pin or twist to one side. A second after he had finished, someone handed him a hand-lettered sign on a thin handle. He nailed it to the top of the cross. It was written in Latin, Greek, and Hebrew.

I thought the cruelty must certainly be over but it wasn't.

The guards who had driven the nails in Yohanan's hands each were handed a square iron spike by the centurion. The spike, I guessed it to be six inches long, had been driven through a small, thin square of wood. I didn't know why, but I figured it out soon enough.

They took Yohanan's legs, bent them, and placed them on the sides of the upright. With the help of others, they drove the nails through the young man's ankles. I heard the hammer hit the spikes time and time again; I heard bone crack; I heard again the screams of a tortured man.

Yohanan's head fell forward as the pain drove consciousness from his mind.

And I felt insanity knocking at the door of my brain.

Four guards remained, as did Yohanan's family. The latter huddled at the foot of the cross, weeping and praying. His mother stroked Yohanan's feet and legs, which were just a few feet above the earth. His blood covered her hands. Dad stood next to her, bobbing as he prayed. The younger son sat motionless on the ground, his emotion pressed down in the dark places of his soul.

If my mind had been glass, it would have shattered long ago.

235

Yoshua and I stood a short distance away. I wasn't able to leave, and I didn't know why. It just didn't seem right. I had sat in a cell with the man who hung on that cross. Our time together was measured in minutes, but I connected with him.

"What does the sign say?" I asked.

Yoshua, who looked like a wrung dishrag, glanced at it. "It says 'Murderer.'"

Those entering and leaving the city stopped to watch the heartbreaking scene, but no one stayed for long. Apparently seeing people on crosses wasn't new.

"How long will he live?"

Yoshua shrugged. "Some live for days, but he has been impaled. That makes a difference."

"I don't follow."

"There are many ways of crucifixion. Sometimes a man is just tied to the cross and left to die of exposure or shock. Some are impaled with nails. Those die faster, usually in less than a day or two.

"A day or two?"

"Let's pray that he dies quickly. Do you remember how cold it was last night?"

I did and said so. "I can't imagine hanging naked through the night. Is that why they left him nude?"

He nodded. "It is very insulting to a Jew, especially a religious Jew. It's a way of insulting the condemned and hastening death."

"They did this to Jesus?"

"Yes. Worse."

"Worse? What could they do that was worse?"

"They beat him several times. His scourging was longer, and he bore his own cross much of the way. Simon of Cyrene carried it the rest of the journey."

236

"Like we carried Yohanan's."

"Yes."

I forced myself to look at Yohanan again. He remained unconscious, probably from blood loss. One thing had changed. He leaned farther forward than before. The reason unsettled me. His arms were out of joint.

"The women who gave him water. Who were they? I saw them join us."

"The Daughters of Jerusalem.[1] They minister to the condemned, giving them water and sour wine."

"Sour wine?"

"When mixed with water, it helps cut thirst."

The deathwatch continued. The guards huddled together and told jokes, sharing the light of laughter in the midnight of someone else's sorrow.

As the sun began to set, four men came with a wood pallet with four handles. The stretcher could only have one purpose. They set it down, then—like the soldiers—stood together passing the eternally long minutes with talk.

I had fallen silent. My words had run out. My thinking was muddled. I wanted to do something, but there was nothing to do but wait. A brief madness swirled in my mind, an insanity that made me consider the odds of attacking and overpowering four trained killers, removing Yohanan from the cross, and taking him somewhere safe.

Somewhere safe? And just where was that? Even if the impossible happened, Yohanan would not survive his wounds. He was a dead man whose heart still beat out of habit. He was a corpse yet unburied. His life ended when he came to the aid of his father and his father's pride. Great bravery; admirable strength; foolish act that had cost him his life and driven his family mad.

Yohanan coughed weakly. I stepped closer. He opened his eyes—mere slits.

"Imma ... Abba ..."

I heard an exhalation, long and wet.

A gurgle bubbled from his throat.

His eyes no longer moved.

I steeled myself for the wailing to follow, but his mother fell to her knees; his father rested his head against the post; his stoic brother who had tried so hard to be brave, resolute, and strong for his parents plopped to the ground, rolled to his side, pulled himself into a ball, and began to weep uncontrollably.

I turned away.

†T†

Taking the body from the cross equaled the violence of what put him there. The soldiers motioned the family back. Papa gathered his family and led them a few paces away. How he could see this was beyond my understanding. The weight of what I had seen had dropped my heart in the blender, and I had only known the young man for a few hours.

One ankle spike came out with a sickening sound. The other, however, refused to budge. The soldier hammered the nail up and down several times trying to dislodge it but to no avail. All he managed to do was mangle Yohanan's ankle. Finally, at the instruction of one of his compatriots, he chiseled the wood away from the iron using his short sword. It took fifteen minutes for him to chip away enough wood for the post to give up its grip on the spike. The sword cut the dead Yohanan's flesh time and time again. Thankfully, he could feel nothing.

The third soldier replaced the ladder, climbed to the cross

member, and cut the rope. I assumed he would work the beam lose while the others used the long poles to steady it until they could lower the victim to the earth.

I was wrong.

They used the poles, but instead of lifting the member off the peg, they stepped behind the cross, put the ends of the poles to the horizontal beam, and pushed. Yohanan dropped to the ground still tied and nailed to the wood.

Bones snapped.

In the minutes that followed, they cut the ropes that held him to the crossbeam and pulled the smaller nails from the palm. Two of the men lifted the beam to their shoulders and started toward the city gate. The remaining two spoke to the men with the wood stretcher then walked off holding a hammer, two nails, and one spike. The other spike remained in Yohanan's ankle.

I watched as the four men straightened the lifeless body, lifted him, and set him on the makeshift stretcher. The family fell in behind them, and the men moved quickly away.

"Why are they rushing?" I asked as we worked to close the distance between us.

"Jews bury their dead the same day they die. They have only a few hours of daylight left to prepare the body." He laid a hand on my shoulder, slowing me. "This is their time, not ours," he said.

"But ..." *But what?* I had nothing. Yoshua was right. The family didn't know me and I didn't know them.

I stopped on the road and watched them disappear into the city.

"Come," Yoshua said. "There is more to see."

"I don't want to see any more. I've seen too much."

"We are close. Now is the time. Before the sun sets."

He placed a hand on my arm, turned me, and walked me away from the city wall.

239

chapter
15

We traveled a short distance. I'm not certain how far. My brain had ceased to take into account such things. The sights and sounds of the brutality I had seen replayed themselves in an unending loop. No matter how hard I tried to quiet Yohanan's screams, I could still hear them, and each time the marrow in my bones melted. Death had stilled his voice, but memory kept it alive and just as real as if it were all happening again.

Yoshua led the way, his steps lacking the spring I had come to expect. My preference would be to find a place to hide, a place where I could curl up in a ball and not see, not hear, not smell—not feel. Instead, I forced one foot to lead the other. I no longer had the urge to resist Yoshua's demands. Nothing I did changed the situation. For now, I would do as told.

For now.

The path led to a garden. I stood in a cultivated lot similar to the garden of Gethsemane I had seen my first day here. This place, however, was smaller. It didn't look like the kind of place one held a picnic. Trees stretched out wooden arms to the sky, green grass carpeted the uneven ground. Shrubs and bushes the local gardener might be able to name but that were beyond my knowledge formed a perimeter hedge.

Any other day I might have called it pretty, lovely, pleasant. But the garish images of flayed flesh, pierced hands and ankles had so damaged me that I doubted that I would ever be able to appreciate beauty again.

A steep hill rose to my right, a portion of it excavated to unveil the rock base beneath. Someone had carved a door out of the stone. It stood open before me like the maw of some prehistoric animal. To the side, a massive wheel of stone rested, blocking about a third of the opening.

Near the disk-shaped stone rested my two kits. The Samaritan had delivered. Standing near the cases was a man of deep age. His beard had grown fully gray, his posture had yielded to the weight of years of life, his face bore the plow marks of a life long lived, of an existence full of joy and trouble. His clothing matched what I had seen on the public-praying Pharisee a few days ago. It was the style of clothing Naqdimon wore.

A few days. It seemed a decade ago.

"That's not your Good Samaritan is it?" I asked.

"No. Come, I'll introduce you." Yoshua kissed the Pharisee and gave a warm hug. "You look well, friend."

The man laughed. "I haven't looked well for many years,

Brother Yoshua, but I'll take your exaggeration as a compliment. This is the friend I heard about?" He pointed a painful-looking arthritic finger in my direction.

"Max ben Odom," Yoshua said. He turned to me. "Brother Max, this is Yoseph of Arimathea, a disciple of the Master."[1]

He gave me the traditional slight bow I had come to expect. "Shalom, Brother Max."

"Shalom."

Addressing Yoshua, Yoseph said, "I received your message. I am sorry things have gone badly for you. I can see the work of the oppressors on your face."

"I will heal, Brother. Time is a good physician."

"As is our heavenly Father."

It took longer than it should but I finally put two and two together. "You're the man Naqdimon mentioned. The one who helped bury Jesus."

Yoseph nodded. "Brother Naqdimon told me of your visit and your questions."

I replayed my conversation with Naqdimon. "You're part of the Sanhedrin?"

"I am and of no small standing, if I'm not being immodest."

"So you were in the Chamber of Hewn Stone when they held trial over Jesus?"

"No. I received word far too late. I suspect that was intended."

"I'm sure it was." Standing in front of what I now recognized as a tomb, I made the connection. "You buried Jesus here?"

His head dipped. "With the help of brother Naqdimon, yes. We laid him here." He aimed the same bent finger at the tomb.

242

"This is the tomb of Jesus?"

"Technically," Yoshua said, "the tomb belongs to Brother Yoseph and his family."

"You buried Jesus in your own tomb?"

The old man nodded. "Time was short and the Master had no tomb of his own. If we had not claimed his body, it would have been taken beyond the city walls on the Hinnom and dropped in the dump like that of a criminal."

"But, the tomb is open. You mean ... his body is in there?"

The old Pharisee straightened his spine more than I thought possible and surprise painted his face. "Have you not heard? All Jerusalem is abuzz about it."

"About what?" I asked, then stopped. Of course. This was the story told every Easter, but I had never bought the tale. I had seen too many dead bodies to believe that one could spontaneously come back to life. Such things were for fantasy writers, not forensic specialists. "You mean the resurrection."

"Of course, Brother Max. Why would the tomb be open if the body were inside? Think of the odor and the animals."

"Jews do not embalm," said Yoshua. It painted a clear picture. "May I look around?"

"Yes, Brother Max. Look all you wish." Yoseph smiled, revealing several places teeth used to be.

"I won't be desecrating your family's remains?"

He looked puzzled, then his smile widened. "The ossuary box is empty, Brother Max. The tomb is new."

"Ossuary box?"

Again Yoshua came to my rescue. "A limestone or marble box used to store the bones of family members. After ... a suitable time, the family returns to the tomb and places the bones of the deceased in the box so the rest of the tomb can be used again."

"So no one has been buried here, or should I say entombed here, except Jesus."

243

"You are correct, Brother Max." The Pharisee gave a nod.

"Have many people been here since the alleged ... since the resurrection?"

"Yes. I know of several," Yoseph said. "I am told that Mary of Magdala and the other women of support visited the tomb, and so did Cephas and Yohanan."

The last name seized my attention. "Yohanan."

"The disciple you met at the cobbler's market. John."

I sighed. "I'll never get used to these names. Sometimes it's Yohanan, sometimes John. Sometimes Naqdimon or Nicodemus."

"We are a people of long history and live with many languages."

Glad to have something to do other than revisit the brutal death of young Yohanan, I let my eyes trace the ground. The sun made its way to the horizon. My light would soon be gone. I opened one of my kits and removed a standard flashlight and played its beam along the ground.

Some footprints were visible in the soft dirt but nothing that I would bother taking a cast of even if I had casting material. The ground was too firm and covered with grass to allow much of a print. What I didn't see was any sign of a struggle.

I was eager to enter the tomb, but years of experience reined in my enthusiasm. I heard whispering behind me and turned to see Yoshua and his friend talking. I guessed that Yoshua was trying to explain what a flashlight was. I left that his problem.

The mouth of the tomb was square like any door opening. I could see tool marks where iron chisel ate away the stone one chip at a time. The tool marks didn't look fresh. Some curved scratches at the head and both sides of the opening looked as if they had been made recently.

At the threshold of the opening I saw a channel. It, too, had scratches. The channel had been cut several inches lower than the base of the door. I ran the light along the groove from door to round stone. A slope was clearly visible. The stone stood uphill of the gradient. It would be easy to roll it into place but a ton of work to move it up the grade. I doubted one man could do so.

Following the trench, I saw a smaller stone had been placed beneath the larger to wedge it in place and prevent it from rolling. I saw something else.

A white wad of wax looking like chewed bubblegum had been pressed into the face of the stone near the edge. I found another on the opposite side. As I looked closer, I verified the wad was wax and that some image had been pressed into it. I couldn't make out the details but it looked official. A thin cord dangled from one of the wax pressings.

Returning to the door, I examined the jambs a little closer. Sure enough, another seal had been pressed into the rock face. This one was damaged as if a cord had been pulled through it.

The grave had been sealed, and I bet I knew by whom. "Pilate?" I asked Yoshua.

"Pilate," he replied.

"To break the seal is to risk death," the man from Arimathea added.

"Apparently that didn't matter to someone. The seal is broken."

I surveyed the grounds again, working in a zigzag pattern. Fifteen feet from the opening, I found the remains of a campfire. Who would spend the night in front of a tomb? "Yoshua, is it customary to sit at the tomb after burial?"

"No, Max, it isn't." He joined me.

"Someone did.... Hello, what's this?" Around the cold remains of the campfire were round depressions as if someone had been using a cane. No. Not a cane. It came to me. "Roman soldiers?"

"Yes," Yoseph of Arimathea said.

"Then these indentations are from their javelins. They were guarding a dead man? They thought someone would steal the body?"

"Yes. The Master spoke many times of dying and being raised from the dead."

"So the Romans believed it enough to post guards."

The Pharisee shook his head. "Not the Romans; some members of the chief priests and my Pharisee brothers asked Pilate to post the guards."

"Yet the tomb is open and the seals are broken. They didn't do a very good job keeping people away."

"That's one explanation," Yoshua said.

"That sounds like a loaded statement."

He shrugged.

I faced the tomb. "Let's go in."

"I have a lamp," Yoseph said. "The sun will not provide enough light. It is too late in the day." He shuffled off to a place near the open tomb. We followed.

Moments later I warned them not to touch anything without first talking to me, then entered. Yoseph asked why, but I didn't bother explaining.

The tomb was larger than I expected and composed of two compartments. As we passed through the door, we entered the outer room. The ceiling was a little over six feet from the floor. Just high enough for me to stand without hitting my head. The space was tight, maybe seven feet wide and eight feet deep. An open arch stood before us.

The light from the two oil lamps brought by Yoseph gave the space the unwelcome feeling of a haunted house. No matter how rational a person, no matter how logical a life he leads, walking in a tomb is unsettling. I traced the floor in front of me. Dust had covered the stone and I could make out several footprints.

"Who has been in here?"

Yoseph answered. "I was here, and Naqdimon. I've heard that after the Master was risen and appeared to others, Cephas and Yohanan visited the tomb and came inside to see for themselves."

"Peter and John," I reminded myself. "That would explain the tracks." I stooped for a closer look and saw several prints made by different sandals. I also saw one set of tracks made by bare feet.

"You really believe in this resurrection stuff, Yos ... Brother Yoseph?"

"I do, Brother Max. I'm a Pharisee not a Sadducee."

That made no sense to me. "Meaning?"

Yoshua explained. "Pharisees believe in a bodily resurrection. Sadducees, who make up the chief priests, do not."

So he was defending a theory. To one side sat a white stone box with a Hebrew inscription on the side. The lid to the box rested on its side against the wall. The ossuary I assumed. There was nothing else in the "lobby" (as I thought of it) of the tomb.

Out of instinct conceived in repetition conducted at scores of crime scenes, I moved forward, stepping to the side of the barefoot prints. My shoes left their own unique mark, but by staying to the side I did less damage to the evidence.

A wide opening led to the next chamber. I had to duck to clear the head of the doorway. A sweet yet pungent odor greeted me. I shone my light around. The ceiling here was a foot shorter than the outer chamber and I had to bend at the waist to keep my head from leaving bits of my scalp on the rock above.

The dust here captured the same impressions as I saw in the other room. Jutting out from the opposite wall was a stone bier, a shelf seven or so feet long and four feet deep.

"That's where the body rested?"

247

"It is," Yoseph said. "Naqdimon and I put the Master there ourselves."

Several items rested on the rock ledge. I shed my light on it, moving the beam from left to right. What I saw made no sense.

"A chrysalis." I muttered the word but the hard surfaces echoed the utterance well enough for the others to hear.

"I do not know the word, Brother Max."

I made eye contact with the Pharisee. "A chrysalis. Certain insects make cocoons. A chrysalis is a cocoon."

"Like the butterfly."

"Yes, Brother Yoseph, just like the butterfly, but this is different." My light, aided by Yoseph's lamp, illuminated the object—a hollow object in the shape of the feet, legs, and torso of a man. A close examination revealed the human-shaped cocoon was made with strips of linen held together by some substance. Lying loose on the chrysalis was a band of linen, a loop with its ends tied into a knot. To the right rested a folded linen cloth. I could also see piles of powder covering the bier.

It was confusing.

"You say you prepared the body for burial, Yoseph?"

"Yes, Brother Max. As I said, Naqdimon and I made the preparations."

"Walk me through that, will you?"

"Walk you through it?"

"Tell me what you did starting from the beginning."

"They crucified the Master. Naqdimon and I watched from a distance. We could not stop it. The people were calling out for his crucifixion, but we knew that the chief priest had arranged that. Someone had to deal with the body."

"Doesn't family do that?"

"Yes, normally, but only Mary his mother was in Jerusalem.

The rest of the Master's family was in Galilee. Mary could not handle such a thing. HaShem has blessed Naqdimon and me. We are men of some means and so decided that it was the least we could do. Naqdimon went to gather what we would need. I went to Pilate the moment the Master died and asked for the body."[2]

"You asked Pilate for Jesus' body?"

"I did. Someone had to take responsibility for him. It became my honor to do so. Pilate gave his permission although he was puzzled why I, a Pharisee, would want such a thing since it was my brethren who called for crucifixion. I think it confused him."

"He's not the only one."

"The governor sent word with one of his men to release the Master to me. Pilate released the body to me, which allowed me to take the body down without interference. Friends and servants helped. We brought the body here, to a place just outside the tomb."

"Naqdimon met you here?"

"Yes, he brought some of his servants as well. He had the linen and spices."

"So what happened after you arrived? What steps did you take?"

"We did as is done for the dead."

I tried to be patient. "It's done differently where I come from, Brother Yoseph. I want to know how *you* did the work you did."

"I see. We quickly washed the body. The sun was setting and the Sabbath would soon be upon us." I thought of Yohanan's bloodied, bruised body being dropped to the dirt. "After the body was washed, we anointed it with aloes and myrrh. We then wrapped the body."

249

"With the linen strips I'm seeing?"

"Yes. It is our custom to wrap the body from the feet to under the arms. First we tie the feet together, then wind the linen cloths around the body, rubbing myrrh and aloe in each layer. Does this make sense?"

"It does. So Jesus' feet were bound by a linen tie, then his body was wrapped in these strips, which are glued together with aloe and myrrh."

"It is not glue, Brother Max, but it is sticky."

"Then what?"

"After the body was wrapped, we placed the Master's hands in front of him and tied them with that linen strip you see there. After that we placed coins on his eyes and covered his face with a linen napkin."

"The coins are to keep the eyes closed?"

"Yes, Brother Max."

I stepped closer to the bier and looked. Two coins lay near where Jesus' head must have rested. I hadn't seen them at first because of the powder.

"Tell me about this stuff, the powder."

"Spices, Brother Max. It helps disguise the ... unpleasantness of death. Naqdimon brought about a hundred pounds of spices, aloes, and myrrh.[3] We used it all. The expense did not, does not matter."

"The odor, you mean."

"Said crudely, yes."

"I'm a crude guy, Yoseph. Just ask Yoshua."

"Yes, he is very crude."

I gave my guide a frown.

"I can't make sense of this," I admitted.

"What troubles you?" Yoshua asked.

"This chrysalis. If a man were wrapped in this, then how did he get out without destroying it? Not only that ... wait. Did you say you tied his feet?"

"I did."

"With a linen strip like this one?" I pointed to the binding on the chrysalis.

"Yes."

Carefully, I stepped to a place where I could shine my light into the cavity of the cocoon. There it was; a strip of linen exactly like the one used to tie the deceased's hands.

"Okay, you guys are having fun with ol' Max, aren't you? Tell me the truth, who put the linen tie inside there? It had to be you, Yoseph. Yoshua has been with me ... except when I was in the cell."

"I did no such thing." Yoseph deserved an Academy Award. Great acting. He looked shocked, hurt, and puzzled all at the same time. "Why would you accuse me of such a thing?"

"Because, I'm being asked to believe that a man who had been brutalized and nailed to a cross, was wrapped up like a mummy from foot to armpit with feet and hands bound, somehow worked himself free."

"I cannot tell you what it means," Yoseph said, "but I can tell you that I am not a party to lying and trickery." He started to leave but Yoshua laid a hand on his shoulder then burned a hole in my soul with his eyes.

"What?" I protested. "Am I supposed to believe that a man swooned on the cross, came to all tied up, freed himself from these linen bonds, and wiggled free without disturbing anything?"

"Swooned?" Yoshua said. "You saw Yohanan die on the cross not one hour ago. Did it look like he had swooned?"

"No. I can guarantee you that he was dead, as dead as they come."

Yoseph glared at me. "I helped take the Master's body down. With my own hands I washed the blood and dirt from his body.

251

With my own hands I wrapped him. He was dead, Brother Max. I've seen death many times. There is no doubt that the Master had given up the spirit."

"I don't believe in miracles," I said.

Yoshua shook his head. "Max, you're standing in a first-century tomb."

"A delusion."

"Do you really believe that?"

"I have to."

"No you don't. Use your brain."

"I *have* been using my brain. It's just not working well."

Again I looked at the resting place of Jesus. When I had looked inside the chrysalis, I noticed dark stains on the linen that touched his back, and one where his side would have been. I moved up and down the bier hoping to make sense of it. During my second pass I noticed something I should have seen earlier.

"The spices are disturbed at the head and foot of the ledge. The powder had been flattened and some of it lay on the ground."

"Not that you will believe this, Brother Max, but some of the women say they saw angels sitting there."

"Angels. As in heavenly beings?"

"The Sadducees would welcome you, Brother Max. They don't believe in angels either. No resurrection. No angels. Only the Torah. If you want, I can introduce you to some."

"Don't bother. They wouldn't want me either. May I talk to these women?"

The suggestion stiffened Yoseph. Talking to women made him uneasy.

"I have already arranged for it," Yoshua said. "Do you want to take samples, Max?"

"Why bother?"

I brushed by the two men and stepped from the tomb into a night that darkened as fast as my mood.

It couldn't be true. I knew that. Corpses don't come back to life. Not like this. It couldn't be true.

Something in my mind didn't agree.

chapter
16

I took another look around the grounds outside the tomb. The sun perched on the horizon, ready to take its final bow for the day. The sky above darkened like a bruise, and the breeze began to chill.

We had bid good-bye to Yoseph and watched him leave the garden and plod up the path toward the walls of the city.

"He's a gutsy man," I said. "I'm not sure I'd want to ask Pilate for the time of day, let alone the body of a man he condemned to the cross."

Yoshua agreed. "History does not give him enough credit. Hardship awaits him and Naqdimon. It is hard to be a member of the Way and sit on the Sanhedrin."

"The Way?"

"The name for the early church. Maybe I should say it *will be* the name of the early church."

"How do you do it—keep the time correct in your mind?"

He shrugged. "Practice."

A sound to my right caught my attention. Maybe the beating I had taken made me jumpy but the noise startled me and I spun to face the cause of it. At first I saw nothing.

"I heard something."

"So did I." Yoshua smiled.

"What are you grinning at?"

He pointed to a clump of dense bushes ten yards away. "You are safe here," he said to the plants.

"Who are you talking to?" I scanned the foliage and caught a hint of brown on the other side of the flora. It moved. At first I thought a dog had been crouching, ready to pounce once we turned our backs. Paranoia had become my companion.

Yoshua gave a come-here motion. "We are friends of the Master."

Seconds stumbled by before a figure rose from behind the brush. A woman approached, her head down. She wore the same Jewish clothing I had seen the other women wearing. Her hair was covered, and she walked with her hands folded before her. Stopping a short distance away, she looked up. Her eyes met ours but only for a moment. Her face bore the wear of at least three decades, and her thin-lipped, pale mouth looked more familiar with frowning than laughing.

"I am Yoshua ben Yoseph and my friend is Max ben Odom."

She stole a glance but quickly cut her eyes away.

Yoshua gave a little laugh. "Yes, he does look strange."

"Oh, thanks, pal."

"He is a traveler here to learn about the Master."

"You are a disciple of the Rabbi?" Her voice carried a hint of fear.

"You have nothing to fear from us, Miriam."

Her head shot up. "How do you know my name, sir?"

"I know all the Master's followers." He addressed me. "Brother Max, this is Sister Miriam, of Magdala, also known as Mary Magdalene."

I wasn't certain what to say. Aside from a brief meal with Mark's family, which included his mother, Mary was the first woman of this time that I had spoken with. "Um, hello, Sister Mary."

She bowed but said nothing.

"Why were you hiding in the bushes?" I asked.

"I did not know who you were. I feared you might be one of those who killed ..." She choked up.

I felt pity. "You feel the need to hide? Do you think that the men that killed the Master will come after you?"

"It is not safe. Many of us are hiding. They took the Master. Some think they will come for us next."

"I see," I said. "If you fear for your safety, then why are you here by yourself?"

"I ... I had to see again." A drop of sadness trickled from her cheek.

"See what again?" Was she one of the women who had seen what they thought was a resurrection? The name Mary Magdalene was familiar to me, but I knew nothing about her.

"The Master. I thought maybe he might return and I could see him one more time."

"You saw him after they buried him?"

"Yes. Right here. He stood where you stand now."

For some reason that chilled me.

"Can you tell me what happened?" She looked at Yoshua as if she trusted his guidance but still doubted my sincerity.

"Go ahead, child."

She took a deep breath, raised her head, and looked me square in the eyes. I hoped my face didn't show the shock I felt.

"After ... when they took the Master down from the cross, I followed as Naqdimon and Yoseph took his body. They are Pharisees, the party that troubled the Master so. I feared what they might do."

"But aren't they followers of Jesus?"

"I did not know that at the time. They had been secret disciples."

"Well, it's no secret now," I said.

"They prepared the body for burial but they worked so fast. Sundown was coming and the Sabbath about to begin. I worried that they did not prepare him as he deserved."

"You didn't see all they did?"

"No. I stood too far away."

"But you saw them place the body in the tomb."

Another tear and a nod. "Once they rolled and sealed the tomb with the stone, I left to tell Mary his mother of what I had seen."

"She didn't follow the body? That's odd isn't it?"

"They did everything so quickly. The sun—"

"Was going down. I got that. What happened next?"

"Nothing."

"Nothing happened? You didn't do anything else?"

She shook her head. "I spent the evening at Sabbath with Mary and others. Some of us decided to bring spices for the body after Sabbath."[1]

"What others?"

"Me. Mary and Salome. We wanted to further prepare the body."

"Jesus' mother came with you?"

"No. Mary the mother of James."

"Let me get this right. Jesus' mother is named Mary, your name is Mary, and there is a Mary the mother of James." I pinched the bridge of my nose.

"Do not forget Mary the mother of John Mark," Yoshua added.

"And Mary the sister of Lazarus and Martha."

I raised a hand. These names were killing me. "Okay, I get it." I didn't. "What next?"

"Do you keep Sabbath in your land, Brother Max?" Mary asked.

"Not as you do here." I thought that answer better than a straight no.

"We do not work on Sabbath. To carry spices to this place would not be lawful."

"And Sabbath ends at sunup, right?"

"No, it ends at sundown the next day. I had to wait for the sun to rise before I could come here. I waited all night to see the sun peek over the horizon. I left the moment it did. The other women followed behind. The garden was still in shadows." She looked at the open tomb. "The day the Master died, I saw them seal the tomb, but when I arrived, I saw it like it is now. Open. Horrible."

"Why horrible?"

"I thought they had taken his body. Stolen it. Defiled it."

"Who would do that? That's a little macabre."

Yoshua answered that question. "Max, you're dealing with people who hang others on crosses."

I got the point.

"I went to the tomb and looked in …"

"And?"

"On the stone ... on that stone sat an angel with white apparel. Light flashed from him like lightning.[2] He spoke to us."

This I had to hear. I encouraged her to go on. She didn't hesitate. "He said we should not be afraid, but I was. He then said that the Master who had been crucified was not in the tomb but had risen from the dead. He invited us to look into the tomb."[3]

"And did you?"

"Yes. Inside I saw an angel, a young man seated on the right side of the fore-room."[4]

"Another angel? In the first room, not where the body had been placed?"

"That is right, Brother Max. He was dressed in a white robe. None of us could speak."

"Did the angel say anything?"

I watched her eyes. Liars tended to blink more, break eye contact, and laugh at unusual times in their story. Mary gave no sign of lying.

"Oh, yes. He told us not to be amazed, but that Jesus of Nazareth—the crucified—had risen and was not in the tomb. He also said that the Master was going to Galilee and that we were to tell Cephas."

"Cephas. Peter?"

"Yes, Simon Peter, also called Cephas."

"And did you?"

"Yes, but first, two men in dazzling apparel appeared in the tomb with us.[5] We fell to the ground and bowed. I was so afraid. Never have I seen anything like these angels."

"Couldn't they have just been men?"

She looked at me like my brains had just poured out my ears. "No, Brother Max, these were not just men."

"I assume they also had a message."

"Yes, Brother Max. That's what angels do."

Silly me. "What did they say?"

"They asked why we were seeking the living among the dead and then reminded us that the Master taught us in Galilee that he would be delivered into the hands of sinful men, be crucified, and rise on the third day." She paused. "We left with the news in our hearts. I found Peter and John and told them of all I had seen."

"And they believed you?"

Mary lowered her head. "Men do not often believe the testimony of women.[6] They ran to the tomb to see for themselves."

"Tell the rest of it, Mary," Yoshua said.

"I followed Peter and John, but they ran ahead. I cannot run fast. They had been to the tomb and left. Later I learned that they went in and saw the wrappings."

"You said you saw Jesus?"

"I did. I would not lie about such a thing."

"No one is calling you a liar, Mary. I'm just trying to learn as much as I can. At what point did you see him?"

"When I first arrived. Well, shortly after I arrived."

"When you arrived with the other women." She shook her head and I could see that she was getting frustrated.

"I am not telling this right."

I had seen this many times. Stress squeezes the mind. Witnesses often recount what they saw then later add to it. They're not embellishing, just remembering items previously forgotten or believed already mentioned.

"The darkness grows," Yoshua said. "It is not wise to be on this side of the walls. We can hear the story as we walk."

We made the first hundred yards in silence, giving Mary time to think. "I arrived at the tomb first," she said. "As I told you, I left as soon as the sun edged over the horizon. The others were not comfortable leaving that soon. They did not think the sun high enough. I could not wait."

"So all of you came to the tomb, but you arrived alone."

"Yes. Exactly that. I saw the tomb open and began to weep. I knew someone had taken the body of the Master. When I first saw the tomb, I went and told Peter and John. That is when they came. By the time I had returned to the tomb, they were gone. Later I heard that they saw the wrappings."

She pushed away a tear from her cheek. "My heart was in pieces. I wept. I just knew they had stolen the body. I went to the door of the tomb and looked inside. Two angels sat where the body was supposed to be. One at the head and one at the foot."

"These are the angels you mentioned earlier?"

"No, those I saw after the other women arrived. These asked me why I was weeping. I told them that someone had taken the Lord's body. Then I heard something behind me. I turned and a man was standing there. I did not recognize him. I thought him to be the gardener. He said, 'Woman, why are you weeping? Whom are you seeking?'"

"Did you have an answer?"

She fell silent as a small group of men walked past. Once out of earshot, she continued. "I told him that if he had been the one to move the body to tell me and I would take responsibility for it. Then ... then ..."

I gave her a moment.

"Then he called my name. He called my name in the way he used to call it. 'Miriam.' Most people call me Mary. Then I knew. My eyes were opened and I saw him standing there. In joy I seized his feet and wept. I had no words."

"So much for ghosts?" I said.

"He was no spirit, Brother Max. I touched him, held him. Too much. He told me to cease my clinging.[7] Then he was gone."

"Just like that? Gone? Right before your eyes?"

"Yes. I know it makes no sense, but it is what happened."

I let that sink in some. "What about the other women?"

"They arrived with the spices just after he left. Before I could say anything, the angel on the stone appeared. The rest is as I told you."

One of the hardest things for a cop to do is to determine if someone is telling the truth. Early on we are taught to look for inconsistencies and challenge the person being interviewed. I was walking through twilight with a woman who was certain she had had a conversation with a resurrected dead man, yet nothing in her demeanor or words made me think she was anything but honest.

"Do you believe me, Brother Max? The other men didn't. They didn't believe the other women either."

"Wait. Are you saying the other women who came with the spices saw Jesus too? You said he had disappeared."

"He did, but after we left the tomb; after the angels gave us a message to deliver, the Rabbi met us on the road. On this very road."

"He just appeared?"

"Yes. Like me, they fell down and worshipped. He said we were to tell his brothers that he would meet them in Galilee."

"His brothers? The disciples?"

"Yes."

There was no forensic test I could run on Mary. I would either have to believe her or believe that her mind was not all it should be. It surprised me to realize that the latter seemed more far-fetched than the former.

As we approached the city, Mary fell back a few paces, still a product of her time.

chapter
17

I need corroboration, Yoshua. I need more than one eyewitness to a supposed resurrection."

The setting sun had painted slips of salmon across the sky, but the streets of Jerusalem remained abuzz. Dim lights poured from windows and washed the streets. I carried one kit and Yoshua toted the other in his left hand, the side least damaged during the beating.

"Is it so hard to believe?"

"You bet it is, pal. I've seen hundreds of corpses. Not one ever got off the medical examiner's table."

"We could speak to the other women."

"I don't want to sound like some male chauvinist here because I'm not, but Mary admitted that the disciples didn't believe her, and I'm guessing they didn't believe the other women. They know them better than I do. Maybe they have a reason for skepticism."

"Mary did not lie."

"I'm not saying she's a liar, but she could be confused. I wasn't there, and she didn't mention you being there either."

"You should eat and rest," he said.

"Not yet. If I lay down, my muscles will tighten and the pain will grow. I need to keep moving."

"I'm not sure that is wise."

"Wise or not, it's a fact." Truth was I didn't want to eat. I didn't want to sleep. If I closed my eyes, the images of Yohanan being scourged or nailed to a cross would come back, and no way did I want to relive that. Not now. Not ever again.

"Where do you plan to go?"

"That fortress place."

"The Antonia Fortress?" For the first time since I met him, Yoshua seemed stunned.

"Yeah, the Antonia Fortress. There are a couple of soldiers I want to talk to."

"Do you know how many soldiers there are in and around the Antonia Fortress?"

"Lots. I spent a few hours there, remember?"

"Yes, of course I remember. Do you recall that I came looking for you? I know a few things about that place, and one thing I know is that there are more men there than one man like you can interview, assuming they'd even talk to you."

"The right ones will be there."

"How do you know that?"

I stopped. "It hasn't escaped my attention, Yoshua, that

everywhere I go, evidence, witnesses, and people of interest are waiting. Strikes me as a little odd. It's as though all the evidence has been preserved just for me." I started walking again. "Those guards are there, or will be there, just like Malchus was in the garden of Gethsemane; just like Mary was hiding at the tomb; just like everyone important has been available to me."

Yoshua said nothing.

"They'll be there, pal. You'll see."

† † †

The long, steep steps up the raised fortress taxed my discipline and endurance. The first few rises hurt, the last few made me think my bones were separating from their joints. Any minute I'd drop to the ground like a 180-pound serving of pudding.

When I reached the wide landing, two soldiers greeted me with a brusque, "Stand where you are."

I didn't recognize them. There was no reason for me to do so. My first visit to this place revealed that hundreds of soldiers came and went from here. I reminded myself that six hundred or so soldiers came to help arrest Jesus. Yoshua was right. This was needle-in-haystack work.

"I'm looking for a couple of soldiers." I felt a slight relief that Lucius and his buddy weren't the ones talking to me. Hopefully, they were out keeping the streets safe from freedom.

"You found them," one of them said. "State your business." He looked at Yoshua with disdain. My relatively clean-shaven face earned me an ounce more respect. Still, it wasn't enough to keep this guy from shoving me down the stairs.

265

"I just did. I would like to speak to some soldiers about something that happened a few days ago."

"What happened a few days ago?"

"Aside!"

At the sound of the man's voice the soldiers stiffened and took a step to the side, opening a way for an older man with black eyebrows that needed mowing and skin that would intimidate a leather saddle. Some men develop features; his were chiseled into hard flesh. "What goes on here?"

The soldier to my left answered. "Centurion, this man says he seeks soldiers involved in an event from a few days ago."

The centurion examined me like a biologist hovering over some specimen. He took a step closer and it was all I could do to hold my ground. I doubted this man had ever laughed out loud. He then studied Yoshua for a few seconds. He seemed to dismiss him without a word, a man not worthy of time.

"What event?"

"A man was crucified and buried last …" I looked at Yoshua.

"Friday."

I doubted that was the word used by these people, but it is the word I heard.

"What of it?" The guy was no nonsense.

"He was buried in a tomb not far from the city walls. A tomb in a garden. Some of your men were assigned to watch the tomb."

That got a response. First the duty guards who had stopped my entrance shot a glance at each other and the centurion, then they immediately returned their attention to me. The officer frowned so deeply I half expected the corners of his mouth to touch his shoulders.

"Are you from the council?"

It took a second for the question to sink in but his tone and expression told me I had the right man. "The Sanhedrin? No … but I have a couple of friends there." I debated whether or not to mention Naqdimon and Yoseph. I chose not to. Let him wonder if my friends included the high priest and father-in-law.

"You can tell them their secret remains safe."

"A few answers are requested." Again, I let him assume that it was the high Jewish court that wanted the answers.

"I do not answer to Jews or to their court."

No yardage made with that play. Time for another approach. "It was your men who stood guard at the tomb?"

"Follow me." He pivoted on his heels and marched into the building. We followed. A few steps later we were in an inner, open court, surrounded by a colonnade that sheltered open rooms. Soldiers milled around, some played a game on the floor, rolling what looked to me like dice. The centurion ignored them. The soldiers, however, did not ignore the centurion. They cleared a path, stepping aside, yielding to the forward progress of the high-ranking man. Other, older soldiers—wearing the same distinctive cape and decorations on the armor I had seen on the centurion at Yohanan's execution—were the only ones who paid him no mind.

He moved as a man with purpose, each stride propelling him three feet farther. The others stared at us. Oddly enough, Yoshua drew more attention than I did despite my modern dress. A free-walking Jew in the Antonia Fortress must have been an unusual sight. Pilate's words came to mind, "Do you know they wouldn't even step inside this fortress to bring their charges? To step foot in this place would defile them. Defile them!"[1] I guessed a Jew willing to walk into this place was rare, indeed.

The centurion led us to a small corner room. Several soldiers, sans armor, passed their off hours swapping stories and drinking something from cups.

"Out," the centurion ordered. "Beer."

267

Ten seconds later we stood in an empty room. One minute after that, a man appeared with a pitcher and one cup. Apparently the centurion missed the class on how to be a good host. He took a long draw of the fluid, stepped to the window, and looked out. "Ask your questions, then leave."

I gave Yoshua an I-told-you-so look. He raised an eyebrow but kept silent.

"Were you at the tomb?"

"If you come from the council, then you know that I was. One centurion and three men."

"Does a man of your status normally pull guard duty?"

"A centurion stands at each crucifixion.[2] The day you speak of, the day when the King of the Jews was executed, it fell to me to oversee the process."

The process. What an absurd euphemism. At least he didn't laugh when he uttered King of the Jews. "You accompanied the body to the tomb?"

"Of course not. Why should I care what a Jew does with his dead? Two men of the Pharisees took charge of the body. Pilate gave them permission."

"Then how did you end up at the tomb?"

"Because of his people." He motioned to Yoshua with the cup. Dark beer slopped on the ground. "The chief priests and Pharisees came to Pilate and asked for the guards. I had supervised the execution and Pilate thought it right that I and some of my men be the ones to stand watch."

"I bet you thought it a waste of time."

"I do not question those in authority over me. I do what I am told and I do it well. If the procurator wishes to waste my time, then my time is his to waste."

"So you watched the crucifixion?"

"I said I did. Are you deaf?" He turned to the window. Why wasn't he facing me?

"You know, rumor has it, Jesus rose from the dead." I waited for the laughter. It never came.

"He died unlike any man I have ever seen." His words were softer and distant. "Three men died that day. My men gambled for the few paltry possessions the man had." He turned back to us. "Do you know what he said from the cross? I mean, while he hung above the ground? He asked his God to forgive us." He ran a hand across his chin, scratching against the day's growth. "I have been spat on from the cross, cursed, begged for mercy, but never, never has anyone forgiven me."

For a moment I thought I saw the beer cup shake in his grip. "The pain must have stripped his senses from him. He was half-dead from the scourging. Most men would have died. They worked him hard that day. More than I've seen before."

"How certain are you that he died?"

This time he looked stunned, as if I asked the world's dumbest questions. "I shoved my spear into his side—to the heart. He did not flinch. Water and blood flowed. I know dead men. He was dead."

I thought of Yohanan on the cross. There had been no doubt in my mind that the young man had died.

The centurion's eyes went soft. "The earth shook that day. The moment he died."[3]

"An earthquake?"

"The earth did quake." He looked into his cup and whispered, "Surely he was the Son of God." Then, as if he had made a social faux pas, he snapped his head up and grimaced. "You are not getting the money back."

That knocked me back on my heels. What money? "The money is yours to keep. Tell me what happened at the tomb."

"The story is no different than what I told before."

"I missed that meeting."

Donning his best you're-wasting-my-time face, he set the cup down. "There were four of us. Me and three of my men—good men, every one. Brave in battle. Quick to obey an order." He began to pace. "We could see the glow of the sun over the hills. We were thankful for it. The night had been cold." He bit his lower lip as he remembered.

"We were eager for our replacements. We had only an hour to wait. Not long. Then we would have warm quarters and food ..." He trailed off and I waited for him to continue, letting him choose his pace. "The ground shook again."

"An aftershock," I said.

"Call it what you will, but it shook with the same anger as the day of the crucifixion."

Aftershocks are usually less intense than the earthquake that spawns them. I dismissed the detail. In a day before seismometers, gauging intensity was nothing more than a judgment call. Then the story got weird.

"He came from the sky."[4] Again he bit his lip.

"Who came from the sky?"

He didn't look at me. The centurion was living in the past, seeing events that I'm willing to bet he had been trying to forget.

"A being. From out of the heavens. He descended, and the earth shook."

If he started telling me an ET abduction story, I was leaving and calling it a night. "You saw a man fly down from the heavens?"

"Not a man. He didn't fly. He ... just descended to the tomb. The light was so bright. His clothing so dazzling it hurt our eyes like the glint of the sun off a shield or sword." He fingered the cup. "I could barely stand to look at him."

"But you did."

"The being went to the stone and as the earth shook, he rolled it back."

"Wait just a second. I've seen that stone. I examined where it would rest once in place. No single man is going to push it back by himself. It would take two, maybe three men."

He threw the cup against the wall. "He moved it, I tell you! With these eyes I saw it. With this mind I perceived it. Did you come here to call me a liar?"

"No, Centurion," I said quickly. This man's ego was fragile. I would have to be careful how I continued.

"You say you've been to the tomb. Did you see the seal?"

"Yes, I did."

"A man breaks that seal under penalty of death." He clinched his fists. "I pulled my sword and started forward, my men by my side. I ... He ..."

Again I had to wait for him to gather his words from the gale of thoughts that blew in his mind.

"I shouted that the being should stop. He looked at us and the light around him grew like the sun. I don't know how or why, but the light felled us."

"Felled you? It knocked you down?"

"We lost consciousness, but before I fell under the spell, I saw him."

"The being? The angel?"

"I still saw him, but in the open doorway of the tomb he stood. The one called the King of the Jews. He looked at me. He looked through me. When we awoke, he was gone: the being and the one who had been dead. You already know what happened next."

"Pretend I don't."

That brought an icy stare. "What purpose is served by repeating it?"

271

Since he thought we were from the Sanhedrin, I took a guess. "It was the chief priests and others who asked for the guard, so you reported to them." He gave a reluctant nod. "Why not go to Pilate or some other superior?"

He didn't answer.

Yoshua spoke his first words since entering the fortress. "Failing at their duty can lead to great punishment for the soldiers of Rome. Even death."

"Is that true, Centurion?"

"It is."

"So you went to the council because you feared reprisal from your superiors?"

"Our work was Pilate's favor to the Jews to keep peace, so we told them of what we saw."

"And what did they do?"

"At first they met and discussed all we had said, then they thanked us with gifts and suggested we tell others that the dead man's disciples stole the body while we slept."

The buzzing of contradictory thoughts filled my head. "Let me get this straight. They gave you gifts to say that you fell asleep at your post while a handful of Jews snuck in, moved the sealed stone, and carted off the corpse of their Teacher. Is that correct?"

"It is."

"Those must have been some gifts. I'm guessing it wasn't season tickets to a dinner theater."

He looked puzzled but didn't answer.

"They gave you money, didn't they?"[5] Great. There were bad cops even in the first century.

"Not just money."

I gave that some thought. If severe punishment waited any

soldier who failed to carry out his duty, then why would they agree to take money to tell a story that made them look bad?

It hit me. "Protection. Not only did they offer you a bribe, they promised to protect you."[6]

He took a deep breath and his eyes narrowed.

"The Sanhedrin persuades Pilate to execute a man he believes is innocent, and he is willing to do so. Now they think they can protect you from him if he learns what happened."

"Do you have more questions?"

I doubted he would answer any more if I did. My welcome wore out with that last statement. I started to thank him but couldn't bring myself to do it. The guy helped crucify an innocent man, took a bribe, and spread a lie that would get him jailed for perjury if on trial in my time.

"I'm done."

"Good. It's time you left. You can tell the council that things remain as they were. Nothing will come of this tomb thing."

"I've got two thousands years of history that say you're wrong."

I walked from the room.

The centurion called for another beer.

Part of me couldn't blame him.

"Well," Yoshua said, "you asked for corroboration. Did that qualify?"

chapter
18

I ate out of deference to Yoshua who insisted that my strength had been taxed well beyond normal. Food would not ease the pain of my ribs, my back, my kidney, or my arms. I needed something stronger than watered wine, vegetables, bread, and lentil soup. I wished for a medicine cabinet bulging with Vicodin, or at the very least a large bottle of ibuprofen. My kits, which now seemed to weigh three times what they did when I brought them downstairs from the hotel room a few days ago—a couple of millennia from now—rested on the floor in the corner. A thin layer of dust covered them, and the aluminum casings bore dents and scars.

I felt like those cases. Still, I kept my complaints to myself. It didn't seem right to gripe when Yoshua sat hunched over the table, too battered to recline on one arm. Our day began an eon ago, and seeing the end of it came as a welcome relief.

Fingering a piece of bread I had used to sop up the last of the soup, I thought about what I had seen and been forced to see. Images of the beating endured by Yohanan, the cross, the sound of the spikes being pounded through his ankles, the screams of his pain, the wailing of his family played in an endless loop and left my heart in jagged shreds, a slowly beating piece of meat.

In between each image, I heard Mary Magdalene's voice, her sincere plea to be believed, the sadness she felt when describing her own experience at the foot of the cross, and the impossible-to-describe joy of having seen her Teacher alive once again.

I wanted to dismiss her tale. I wanted to dismiss her. Nonsense was nonsense no matter how genuine and noble the person who believed it. But the idea would not leave at my command. Yoshua certainly believed in the resurrection. Others had hinted at it. I had overheard bits and pieces of conversation muttered among friends but nothing spoken aloud.

Unbelievable, all of it. The mortar of my resolve began to crumble again. I felt as raw and unbalanced as when I lost my temper with Yoshua in the street, except this time it wasn't anger that haunted me. That remained, but like an overworked muscle, it had given in to exhaustion and been replaced by the stronger, heart-crushing, breath-stealing emotion of sadness.

I couldn't put a finger on the primary source of the ache. Surely it was stress from my beating and the psychological injury of what I had seen; scenes carved into the tender flesh of my memory.

Mark's family had taken their meal downstairs, leaving the

large upper room to us. Mary tended our facial wounds. Propriety kept her from examining our ribs. That fell to Hosah, who pushed on tender blue flesh. Yoshua's rib cage looked horrible. He said the pain wasn't bad, which made him a better man than me. The longer I sat, the worse I felt.

"Do not despair, Max," Yoshua said after a long silence. The door to the room had been shut and the window shuttered. Another cold night was expected, and neither of us needed to be shivering.

"I'm not despairing."

"Of course you are. Emotions are just as real when denied as when acknowledged."

I started to toss a quip his way but discovered my quiver had gone empty. The food settled a boiling caldron in my stomach, but the intangible thing inside every man bore injuries that didn't come from a beating in a Jerusalem street.

"I don't know how much more of this I can endure." The confession surprised me.

"You are a strong man, Max. One of the strongest I've met. I am proud to know you."

"I wish I could return the compliment, but I hold you responsible for all this." Saying the words wounded me even more. Yoshua had laid his own body over mine to spare me any more blows. The purple flesh of his ribs, his swollen mouth, the red marks on his face all reminded me that he probably saved my life.

"I know you do, Max. You're right. I am responsible."

"How could you do this to me? *Why* would you do this to me? None of what I've discovered is new. You knew where everything was and how it got there. Evidence that is days old looks fresh. That can't be by accident or coincidence."

I tossed the remains of the bread I held. "I can't do proper forensics work, and I think you've known that all along. Two field kits are not enough to deal with a crime scene that stretches over so much terrain. I have no lab. Any trace evidence I collect is meaningless. Sure, I can observe and draw some conclusions, but that's it. Crime-scene forensics isn't like what you see on television. Crimes aren't solved in an hour."

"Everything you say is true."

"So now you're being agreeable." I let slip a tiny laugh. Anything more would have made my ribs hurt. "So why the dog and pony show?"

"I can't answer that. Not yet."

"You mean you won't answer that."

He nodded. "That's precisely what I mean. I can tell you, Max, it has never been about *gathering* evidence, only about seeing it."

I rubbed my face. I was so tired even the bed pallet on the floor with the odd-smelling blankets looked inviting, almost irresistible. "Yoshua, I can't handle riddles tonight."

"That's what you do, Max. You handle riddles. And you're good at it. In most cases."

"What do you mean, 'in most cases'?"

He looked as weary as I felt. The pain he felt drew deep lines on his face and forehead. I noticed that he ate only half as much as usual. I worried for him.

"Will the dreams come tonight?"

"What dreams?" I knew what dreams he meant.

"They come most nights, don't they?"

"I don't want to talk about it." I rose from the bench, grimacing, and shuffled to my bed.

277

"And that, Max, is why the dreams come back."

"Thanks, Dr. Yoshua. I'll see if my insurance covers psychiatric bills."

"No need. The price has already been paid. Good night, Max."

I looked at the pallet and had two fears. First, I feared the pain I would feel lowering myself to the floor; then I feared the pain I'd feel trying to get up in the morning.

I had been right about the first fear. The short trip down to the floor was like taking the beating all over again. With careful moves and clenched teeth, I worked myself into as comfortable a position as possible.

"Yoshua, do you know what a cop's greatest fear is?"

"Tell me, Max."

"Some people think a cop fears being shot or shooting someone else. Those are real enough, but it's not what we fear the most." I paused as an unwanted voice piped up again. I stuffed it back into its hole. "Most of all, a cop fears being called to the scene of a violent crime and hearing the dispatcher give his address."

Yoshua said nothing, and that pleased me. That last statement was all the confessing I planned on doing.

A few minutes later I heard Yoshua grunt and groan as he fought his way into bed. After he settled, I said, "Yoshua, about what happened in the street today. I'm sorry I lost my temper."

"Give it no thought."

"And about … what happened after … with the soldiers … thanks."

"You're welcome, Max." I think he was sincere.

†Ť†

278   I knew the house. It was an older bungalow home in the Allied Gardens neighborhood of San Diego. Small, and typical of homes built the decade after World War II, it showed the love and care of homeowners who loved midcentury design. I also recognized

the home because it was mine. I had painted the pale green trim and the yellow siding myself. I had planted the six rose bushes that lined the wall, and I was responsible for the oil stain in the driveway, the result of a clumsy attempt to change the oil in my car.

I stood in my neighbor's yard across the street, ankle deep in unmowed lawn. He seldom cut his grass. The street wore a blanket of silence, and a thin white mist filled the air. The mist carried a vague, unpleasant odor to it. Something—a cat, a squirrel, or a rabbit—in the distance had died, and nature was claiming its own through putrefaction.

Twilight gave little resistance to coming night.

Things were missing. At this time of day the smells of dinner cooking and the sounds of television programs should be leaking out of nearby homes. The only sound, however, came from the maple tree in the front yard of my house. It creaked and groaned as if resisting a hurricane, but only a slight breeze blew.

I gazed at the house but made no motion toward it. For years it had been my home, the place I provided for my wife and daughter. It was here that I returned after every workday. Here we reared our daughter through childhood and teenage years. It was here—

The house moved as if recoiling from some unseen danger, its walls bulging out as if made of rubber and engorged with some vile thing seeking to break free.

Paralysis seeped up from the ground, freezing my feet in place. From within the house I heard an indistinct sound, then another, louder, coarser. The noise of something breaking.

279

A scream.

Pleas for help; appeals for release; petitions for mercy. Each one louder than the one that preceded it.

I knew the voice. I heard it countless times before; heard it as an infant cooing, as a toddler giggling, as a child asking end-less questions, as a teenager testing her parents' limits. Now those sweet tones had been sullied by terror, laced with petrify-ing horror.

I started forward. My feet refused to move. I tried again but I remained as unmovable as a park statue.

"Daaaa—"

The voice from my home grew louder. More breakage, the sounds of a struggle. A laugh.

"DAAAADDYYYY!"

I pulled at my legs. I tugged with all my might. I could feel muscles strain, tendons pull until on fire, but no steps came. I looked at my feet. The grass had grown around them, morphing into vines that clung to my ankles, rooting me in place.

The cries, the screams, the yells grew but no one came to help. No lights came on in the other houses. Where were the neighbors? The cries were so loud that surely someone else had heard. Someone had to hear and come to help.

"No. NO. DAAADDYYY!"

I pulled at the vines but they felt made of concrete, unyielding.

The laugh came again, and again.

I called out to my daughter, whom I could not see. I reached for her, stretching in a useless, futile effort to somehow touch her.

Silence came as loud as a sonic boom.

No more pleas for help. No more desperate cries from the daughter who was out of my sight, out of my reach.

I wept. I wept like I had so many times before. My insides had melted, leaving a useless shell of the man I had been. All my train-ing, all my experience, useless. I was useless, unworthy of a family, unworthy of life.

Raising my head, I looked at the house that had been home and that would never be home again.

Blood trickled from the corners of the windows.

†✝†

The image had been a dream but the tears were real. When I realized I no longer slept, I opened my eyes to the dark room. The pallet beneath me reminded me where I was, and *when* I was. A pair of arms encircled me, not squeezing but cradling. Strong arms. Familiar arms.

Yoshua said nothing. Offered no words. Gave no advice. Asked no questions. His embrace spoke too loudly for anything else to be heard.

The tears came riding on giant swells of sobs, and for the first time in two months I let them come, too tired, too beaten, too worn, too confused to mount any resistance.

The tears had won.

And despite the pain of his own broken body, there was Yoshua.

Holding me.

Supplying his strength where mine failed.

In the swirl of my agony, I had the sense that he was the only man on earth who had lost more than me.

chapter
19

Yoshua said nothing about the events of the previous night. The servant girl that had served our first meal in this place brought a breakfast of bread and fruit to the table. Hosah, Mary, and Mark made no appearance. Perhaps Yoshua, who rose before me, may have told them I needed some time. I wondered if Yoshua had slept at all. I had finally succumbed to emotional and physical exhaustion. When I awoke, Yoshua was up.

"Leave the kits," he finally said. "They'll be safe here."

"I won't object to that." The thought of carrying the cases made me hurt. "I take it you have plans for us today."

He gave the slightest of nods. Once again, he seemed weighed down, like a man who had to do some unpleasant task that only he could do. That didn't bode well for me.

Thirty minutes and a torturous walk through the bustling streets of Jerusalem later, we came upon a modest house with a wide courtyard. Unlike many of the courtyards, this one had no animals penned within its walls. A ceramic stove sat in the middle, and a catch basin for water was near the house. Several pots of water rested by the front door. As with all the houses I had seen, the window was covered with a lattice frame.

Several people sat on small, low-to-the-ground stools. All wore thick cloaks to fight off the chill of the morning air. Three women and one man talked softly as we approached. Once he sighted us, the man stood and greeted us. I recognized him and he me.

"Brother Yoshua, Brother Max, please come in," John ben Zebedee said. The three women rose and their gaze went to the ground. One woman was known to me, the youngest of the three. "Brother Max, I am proud for you to meet Mary of Magdala, my dear mother, Salome, and Imma Mary, blessed mother of the Master."

Imma? Wasn't that what Yohanan called his mother with his last breath? Stunned, it took a moment for me to comprehend the simple truth that I stood just four feet away from the mother of Jesus. She looked up but made no eye contact. Her face had as many lines as a road map. Gray hair peeked out from her head-covering and her eyes were a moist brown. Her shoulders were round and her posture slightly crooked. This was a woman who had seen much and knew more. A keen intelligence burned behind those dark eyes.

283

Salome looked to be a few years younger, but I couldn't tell. People aged faster here than in the twenty-first century. That much was clear.

"I'll bring wine," Salome said to her son.

"Perhaps we could visit inside," Yoshua said.

John looked puzzled, as if the request was somehow odd. I remembered Yoshua telling me that people lived in the courtyard and slept and stored provisions inside. It took a few seconds, but I guessed at what Yoshua planned. I was getting good at anticipating him.

"Of course, Brother Yoshua. As you wish." John led the way. I slipped my shoes off and the others did the same with their sandals. The women followed us, carrying the small stools.

The inside wasn't much to look at. The exterior walls marked off one large room with several half walls that defined two sleeping areas. There were no chairs, no tables. It reminded me of a monk's room. Salome busied herself with cups and wine, bringing one to the men and then to the women. As she did, I noticed Yoshua staring at Mary. He seemed hypnotized.

Once Salome had settled on a carpet, John said, "You bless this house with your presence."

"It is we who are blessed," Yoshua said.

With the niceties finished, John said, "Your injuries look worse than when we last met."

"There has been more trouble," Yoshua said and explained. When he finished, the small house fell silent as each person tried to absorb the account.

"HaShem be praised that your life is still yours," John said.

"HaShem be praised," Yoshua repeated. "Has Mary told of our meeting at the tomb?"

John said she had. "Do you have more questions, Brother Max?"

I struggled to pull everything together in my mind. In our previous meeting John had told me that Jesus assigned the care of his mother to him, and Yoshua had asked about her well-being. Now I sat within arm's reach of the most famous woman in history. She had yet to speak.

"Brother Max, are you well?" John's face showed his concern.

I came to. "I'm sorry. What did you ask?"

"I wondered if you are well. Are your injuries troubling you now?"

More than I can explain. "Thank you, I'll be fine." I looked at Mary … Imma. Yoshua had somehow silently given his seat to her and sat crossed-legged on the floor. I noticed that he had positioned himself closer than I expected a man would in this culture.

"Is it appropriate to call you Imma?" I asked the woman close to Yoshua.

"Some have taken to calling me Mother." Her voice came across soft but solid.

As I looked at her, an image came to mind. Years ago a photo appeared on the cover of *National Geographic*. The photographer—a Steve McCurry, I believe—had captured the face of a twelve-year-old Afghani girl. Her skin was dark and she wore a tattered red robe. Her eyes, however, had captured the attention of the world. Green as jade, they contrasted her dark and dirty skin. They were eyes that had seen too much pain and mistrusted everyone. But those eyes contained a story; a tale of sights not spoken, of events longed to be forgotten. At the tender age of twelve, when girls in my country argued with their parents about the right to wear makeup, she had seen death and destruction and the poverty of a relief camp in Pakistan.

Years later the photographer relocated the girl, now a woman, and ran a picture in the magazine. Less than twenty years had passed, but the woman looked as if she had aged forty years. Still her eyes were green as before and full of memories.

285

When I looked at Mary ... Imma, I saw the same thing. The eye color was different but the sense that this woman had seen twelve lifetimes of good and bad, joy and grief, was undeniable.

"Imma, some tell me your son has returned from the grave alive. Have you seen him?"

In slow, deliberate motions she shook her head.

"But you have heard the rumors?"

"I have. Mary has told me of his appearance. John tells me of the grave wrappings he saw in the tomb and of what the others are saying."

She wasn't forthcoming. I couldn't blame her. I was a stranger, dressed in odd clothing, beardless like a Roman, quizzing her about something painful. I've never been uncomfortable interviewing someone, but here I felt on edge.

"Mary mentioned angels. She said she saw several."

"She is blessed of HaShem. An angel brought me news of my conception. Four times an angel spoke to my dear husband, Joseph.[1] Angels announced the birth of the Messiah to shepherds. Why would HaShem not send his holy ones to announce the promised resurrection?"

How could I tell this first-century woman that such things were impossible?

"You doubt, do you, Brother Max?" She didn't look at me. Her mind, her thoughts, were rooted elsewhere. I couldn't shake the idea that this woman knew more than the sum total of any ten thousand men. I didn't have the sense that she possessed a high education. Her knowledge came from someplace else and in a manner I couldn't fathom. Those thoughts bothered me. I had only known her moments. How could I know such things?

"Yes, Imma. I do."

"You worry that your doubt will offend me?"

Spot on target. "Yes. I do not wish to add to your grief."

The slightest, smallest smile I have ever seen tugged at her mouth. She looked away, her sight in the past. "When I wore the virgin's veil, so many years gone now, the angel Gabriel appeared to me.[2] My parents and those of my dear husband-to-be had reached agreement and I was given in betrothal to Joseph, a carpenter and a kind man, faithful and true to the Most High.

"Gabriel told me the impossible. I, a woman who had known no man, was to conceive by the Holy Spirit the very Son of God. I asked how such a thing could be and he told me that nothing was impossible with God.[3] I believed him and all came true."

I had heard the story almost every Christmas, but hearing it from her made it come alive.

"My son came into this world, a child dependent on a maidservant like me. I, of all women, suckled the Son of God. I held his hands as he took his first steps. I watched him grow and learn the carpenter's trade from Joseph. Late in my son's twelfth year, Joseph died. Jesus became the man of our family, and he served us like none other could until his time came."

Pride and sorrow blended in her voice. She spoke with such certainty, such conviction that I felt like a candle in an oven.

"Imma." My voice dissolved into a croak. "Imma, do you really believe that your son is *the* Son of God?"

For the first time she looked at me. We had moved beyond social dictums. "I knew when the angel told me; I knew when my son filled my womb; I knew when I gave birth to him in a cave in Bethlehem; I knew when he turned water into wine in Cana; and I knew when they nailed him to the cross."

"You were at the cross?" I remember the terrified cries of Yohanan's mother.

Again she looked away. Tears began to fall. The other women lowered their heads and dabbed at their eyes.

My senses severed their moorings. I was back at the cross of Yohanan. The clank of hammer to nail filled my ears. The crack of bone as spike pierced ankle bounced in my brain. The screams, the pleas, reverberated through my empty, hollow soul. Imma Mary had watched her son brutalized and could do nothing about it. Nothing. No matter how much she might have wished it otherwise, nothing could stop what occurred.

I watched as she, without obvious thought, touched fingers to her cheek, and instinctively I knew she recalled blood splatter on her face—her son's blood.

I could ask no more questions of this woman. She outclassed me in every area of life. In all that she had seen, in the acid of memory that would dissolve the sanity of the most sturdy, she showed no bitterness.

Yoshua offered no words, didn't come to my rescue. His head hung, supported by one hand. John made no effort to hide his wet eyes. He, too, had been there.

More than anything, I wanted to flee.

"Brother Max?" Imma addressed me. No sense in trying to speak. My voice had left. Instead, I just locked eyes with her. "Have you ever lost a child?"

The knockout punch. My stomach dropped like an elevator with a broken cable. Every nightmare came back: every macabre image, every unforgettable sound, and every experience that branded my brain.

"I'm not sure how that matters.... It really isn't pertinent ... a daughter. I lost a daughter."

Her lips drew tight. "I'm sorry for your loss."

"It's all right." Three of the dumbest words I've ever spoken.

"It is never all right. It always hurts. It always will."

I considered excusing myself, just standing and walking out the door, and I might have done just that if it had been Yoshua making such a statement. What did he know of losing a loved one? But it was Mary the mother of Jesus who spoke to me. She knew. She understood. Her soul bore the same ragged holes that mine did. If anyone could understand how a painful memory could make it impossible to believe, then she was the one.

"What name did you give her?" Mary asked.

"Deborah."

"Deborah daughter of Max." Mary seemed pleased with the name. "In Hebrew the name means 'a bee.'"

That drew a smile on my face. Deborah moved through life like a bee, shifting interests like a bee changes flowers. Always looking, always asking, always searching.

"We called her Deb. She never liked Debbie or Deborah."

"Children seldom like what their parents name them." Her eyes softened. "It is time to lance the boil, Brother Max."

What? "I don't understand."

"You are filled with infection."

How did we round this corner? "I appreciate the concern, Imma, but I'm not here because of my loss."

"No? Why are you here?"

I looked at the others. They were seeing something I couldn't; knew something I didn't. None gave any hint of interrupting or correcting Mary.

"I'm here to ask you questions about your son and the crimes committed against him."

"Please then, Brother Max, ask. I am HaShem's maidservant. I will answer any questions you ask."

No viable questions came to mind, only stupid ones. "So tell me, what's it like to be the mother of the most famous person in history? Did you find it painful to watch Jesus die? So what are your plans now?" I could ask none of those, nor could I come up with a single investigative question. The gears of my mind shuddered to a rough stop.

"Why are you here?" she asked.

"Yoshua has been leading me to all the places your son visited before his execution."

"This is not one of those places." Her words were soft as a velvet pillow, but every syllable landed with the power of a body blow. "This is a rented house."

"Well, he's also introduced me to people like John and Mary Magdalene who were eyewitnesses to the events so that I could ask questions. He brought me here to ask questions."

"Did he?"

I looked at Yoshua who kept his gaze on the ground in front of him.

"Yoshua?" I prompted.

He didn't acknowledge me or my words. I shook my head. I didn't want to talk about it. The shrinks tried to get me to open up and failed, what could these back-century people do?

"A bee. I never knew that," I said.

"Deborah is a good name," Mary said, "strong and beautiful."

"Just like her."

"Her father is handsome; I am certain she was pretty."

I nodded as my eyes burned. "Very pretty. I worried about her, I worried for her."

"That makes you a good parent," Mary said.

I wished the others would say something. This was becoming a dialogue shared by two, but the others remained still and silent.

"Not good enough, Imma. Not good enough."

"She died without you?"

How could she know this? "No. I was at work. At a scene of a crime. Ironic isn't it?"

"She died at the hand of a violent man?"

I couldn't say the word so I just nodded. Fire kindled in my belly. Anger coursed through me like a wild beast trapped in my body. "She was home alone. She chose to go to school in San Diego. I think she made that choice so she could stay with me and her mother."

"Your women go to school?" John asked the question. Mary shifted her eyes to him and he lowered his head as if he had just been slapped.

"Things are different where I live," I said. "She came home. As I said, I was working a scene. My wife, Deb's mother, was out of town visiting her parents. They are both ill and well along in years. She's been driving to Phoenix every few weeks to help out. I suppose I should be thankful that she wasn't home as well. Then again, maybe if she was ..."

"Your wife still lives?"

"Yes. After the funeral, her father was hospitalized. She's been with them for a month. I think part of it is so she can be away from me."

"Why would a woman not want to be with her husband?"

Why am I talking about this? This is none of their business. None of it. Something seemed to be controlling me. I wanted to end the discussion but I kept on talking. "I'm not an easy man to live with, especially recently."

"The man of violence killed your daughter in your home?"   291

When an earthen dam grows weak, too stressed to hold the great load of water behind it, it gives way with a small crack. Once the fault appears and the water begins to run, there is no reversing it. A small fissure grows until chunks of the dam give way. Within seconds it is impossible to tell a dam had once been there.

My dam gave way. Images of what I saw when I returned home late that evening slammed into my consciousness. The blood, the splatter ... and my darling daughter lying in an ocean of her own blood. For the briefest of moments I looked at it as just another crime scene, but that next second all my training evaporated—and so did my life.

"The man who did this. Has justice been served?"

"He's still free. We haven't caught him."

"So you have never seen him?"

I wish I could. For one moment; for just one minute alone with him ... "No."

"Yesterday, I saw one of the soldiers who nailed my son to the cross. He walked down this very street."

"What did you do?"

"What *could* I do?"

I had no answer. The thought that this quiet but capable woman might have to see her son's killers from time to time stunned me. "Life is unfair."

"Yes, Brother Max, it is. It has always been so."

"Imma, how do you live with what you know, with all that you have seen?" Tears ran down my cheeks. "Every night I dream of my daughter. Every night I see horrible things."

"I, too, dream, Brother Max."

"Of the cross."

"Of the cross; of the scourging; of the hatred of the religious leaders who taunted my son as he died for them; of the soldiers casting lots for my son's garments while his blood dripped from his feet. I dream of the spear thrust in his side."

"How do you keep from going insane?"

"Every day HaShem grants me the strength for that day."

I snapped. All the fury that I had stuffed in the back of my head broke free. "Well, that's the problem isn't it? I've received nothing from God, but he sure didn't mind taking my child from me. And that's not all. Deb was a Christian. That's right. She was one of you. The year before her death she started attending a local church. It became the core of her being. She read her Bible every day. She prayed. She tried to convert her mother and me. She was in church every time the doors were opened. What did it get her? WHAT DID IT GET HER?

"I'll tell you what it got her," I ranted. "Absolutely nothing. Some punk hood broke into my house and put a bullet in her chest. Where was HaShem then? Where was the glorious, mighty God as she suffered alone and bled to death while her killer still walks around sucking in air he has no right to?"

I sprang to my feet. So did John.

"Brother Max, please do not speak to Imma in that tone."

"Shut up, John. Just shut that stupid mouth of yours."

He took a step toward me. "Brother Max, you are in my home—"

I seized him by his cloak, spun him, and pressed his back into the wall. "I said shut up. You know nothing. *Nothing.* You don't know what goes on in my mind, in my heart. As far as I know, you're not even real." The small part of my brain not yet poisoned by weeks of unvented fury, of acid-laced sorrow that ate a new layer of my life away every day, told me that I had rounded the bend, that these people were friends, and if not that, then at least they weren't the enemy.

293

I could no longer control myself. For the last few days I had done my best to keep my mind and actions civil, but every day I lost a little more. I lost it with the guards of Annas, with Yoshua when I shoved him to the ground, and with the Roman soldiers who beat Yoshua and me.

Too long I had been told to wait, to be patient, to try to relax. Such things were beyond me. The gunman that killed my daughter murdered the reasoning part of me.

A hand touched my arm. Yoshua. It had to be Yoshua. This time I'd give him more than a shove.

I spun. I raised a fist. I located my target and saw that it was Mary who touched me. I fell into those eyes.

I released John and my legs gave way, and I dropped to my knees and into the tender arms of a woman who understood my grief.

Sob rolled over sob. Weeks of pain that polluted my mind and soul poured from me. All my anger, all my fury, all my hatred for others and myself emptied in a soul-shaking catharsis.

I hated life.

I hated myself.

But then something soft touched my head. Mary stroked my hair and wept with me.

They all did.

Despite their tenderness, my eggshell existence finally crushed.

I would never be the same. I could never be happy.

Life had no meaning.

I prayed that God would do me a favor. *Kill me now. Send me to hell if you want. It can't be worse than this.*

chapter
20

My long-pending nervous breakdown had come, and an hour later had gone, much to my surprise. For eternally long moments I knew that my mind would never be the same, but as minute gave way to minute, I grew more stable. First the uncontrolled weeping stopped, next the unreasoning anger settled, then the overpowering sadness took a hiatus. When images of my daughter came to mind, I still felt the hot knife of remorse in my gut, but it didn't disable me.

The others had gone back to visiting in the sun-drenched courtyard. The sound of those passing by tossing greetings back and forth made its way through the window and into the dim room.

I had dropped to my knees and then later to the floor where I remained for what must have been the better part of an hour. Later I sat on the floor in the corner of the room, trying to pull myself together. Only Mary the mother of Jesus stayed inside with me. That surprised me, considering my violent outburst. John did sit close to the door, and I could see that his head was turned so that his ear faced the room. No doubt he was listening carefully. Jesus had given him responsibility for his mother, and John seemed to take that very seriously.

Mary remained the same unflappable person I had met when I first arrived at this house. She sat on a stool near the opposite wall sewing a patch on a garment.

We talked, first as victims of a murdered child, then as two adults who shared a common wound. She spoke of Jesus' early years, of his work as a craftsman, cutting and shaping wood. "He liked making wheels for carts," she said. "I never understood why, but he always found joy in making something round."

"Completion." It was a suggestion. "Maybe he liked the idea of things coming full circle."

"Perhaps." She told me of how he stayed behind in Jerusalem to teach the teachers when he was only twelve,[1] and how she and the rest of the family traveled off without him. "It was the last time we made the trip with my husband, Joseph." I saw the sadness in her eyes, but it lingered only a moment.

She also told me of how she pressed him into working a miracle at a wedding in the town of Cana.[2] She smiled when she told that story. "He told me it was not his time yet. I told the servants to do whatever he told them to do. It obligated him to act. Such things a mother can get away with."

I shared stories from Deb's years of growing up. Each one hurt like a stab wound, but also brought something new, a sense of joy.

Time stood still for me but not for the others. John poked his head in. "Imma, it is time to go. Will you be joining us, Brother Max?"

"I don't know."

"Of course he will," Mary said.

I rose, and the great woman waited for me to exit first. Once outside the courtyard, Yoshua led us through the streets. The women walked several steps behind us. It felt wrong. All three women had been at the foot of the cross, as had John. Two women named Mary had a special relationship with Jesus. I couldn't shake the nagging feeling that I should be walking behind them.

Jerusalem is such a small city that it took only a few moments for me to realize that we were headed back to Mark's house. "We're going back to the upper room?" I asked Yoshua.

"Yes, Max. There will be others there."

"Who?"

"You will see. Much has happened over the last few days. Some of the disciples have seen the Lord."

I looked at John. "Yes, Brother Max. I, too, have seen the Lord in the flesh."

"Why didn't you say something when we were at the house?"

"I did not have the opportunity. I believed you came to ask questions. I assumed you would ask about what I and the others had seen. Imma Mary mentioned it."

Again, I felt manipulated. I knew evidence had been preserved for me to see, although I didn't know how that was done. At times I felt as if events over a longer period had been compressed for me.

The room was packed with people. More than I expected, and the addition of three women and three men made it all the more 297 crowded. The table had been moved to the side, and the servant girl had placed platters of fruit, vegetables, bread, and wine for any who wanted it. Then she left.

The women settled into one side of the room, the men to the other. A couple of men argued. Yoshua and I were at the back of the room. He leaned in my direction and whispered, "Do you see the man with the reddish beard? That is Thomas the Twin, called Didymus in Greek. The barrel-chested man next to him is Peter. Of course, you know John."

"Thomas seems a little hot under the collar."

"He is. Several disciples claim to have seen Jesus alive, but he refuses to believe. He wants proof."

"Sounds like my kind of man."

"You have things in common."

I tilted an ear toward the discussion and picked up shreds of the conversation.

"You do not believe us? We who have been your companions while the Master taught?" For some reason I had imagined Peter to be bigger than all the rest, but he stood the same height as John, although he wore an additional twenty or even thirty pounds.

"Not until I see with my own eyes the nail marks in his hands and the spear wound in his side will I believe that he has risen from the grave."[3]

I smiled at Yoshua. "I like him."

"Figures," Yoshua said.

"How come the door is closed and locked?" The window remained open and a man stood near it, his eyes never leaving the street below.

"All the close disciples are here. It is a dangerous time. Some fear the religious leaders or even the Romans will come and arrest them."

"It's a lousy state of affairs when a man can't trust his leaders."

"It only gets worse," Yoshua said. He gave me a strange look, one of slight sadness.

A gasp rippled through the crowd, and those who had been sitting shot to their feet. Some moved forward, others moved back.

No words were spoken. I struggled to stand, fighting off the pain from the beating that still haunted me.

Someone stood near the door. At first I thought everyone's fears had come true, that temple guards or Roman soldiers had gained entrance, but there was no panic, no indication of a struggle.

From my place at the back wall I could see very little. Too many men blocked my view.

"Sit. Everyone sit." It sounded like the voice of the man Yoshua identified as Peter.

Slowly the people complied, and soon we were all seated on the floor.

Only two remained standing. Thomas the Twin and a man I hadn't seen before.

"Peace be with you." The stranger's voice came across strong, filling the room. He wished the crowd peace, but not one of them looked at peace. Especially Thomas. He smiled. "Thomas, here are my hands, reach your finger. Here is my side, reach here your hand and put it into my side. Do not be of unbelief, but of belief."[4]

Even from the back of the room I could see Thomas shake. His shoulders heaved uncontrollably. I knew the feeling. "My own Lord, my own God!" He dropped to his knees.

The man laid a hand on Thomas's head. "Is it because you have now seen me that you have come to believe? Happy are those who have not seen yet arrive at belief."

I leaned over. "Yoshua ... Yoshua, is that who I think it is? Is that ... Yoshua?"

I turned. Yoshua was missing.

I wish I could explain how what happened, happened, but I can't. I don't think anyone can.

Time stopped.

The noise of the excited gathering went mute. Heads no longer moved. People didn't shift their bodies. Yet, *I* could move.

I stood, and the man at the front looked at me. My insides melted like wax. He approached, stepping carefully between the seated disciples and friends.

His garments were white, as pure a white as I have ever seen. His head was covered with a thin hood. I could see dark-brown eyes moist with joy. Dark-olive skin looked brand new as if he had been born a full-grown man just this morning.

This was ... It couldn't be. I had seen the evidence, knew of the beating, and interviewed those who watched him die. I had not only been to his tomb, I had been *in it*.

I had seen pictures of Jesus, paintings done by artists who lived centuries later. None of them resembled this man. Those paintings made Jesus over in the image of the artist. Anglo painters created an Anglo Jesus. The man before me was as Jewish as those I saw around Jerusalem. His untrimmed beard hung to the bottom of his neck, his nose angular and sharp. His—

It took a moment for me to see them: Small holes, like greatly enlarged pores, ran in a ragged line across his forehead. What had Pilate said? Something about his guards weaving a crown of thorns and forcing it down on Jesus' head, even beating it down with rods of wood.

He raised his hands and pushed back the thin white hood that covered his head. Short dark hair covered his scalp. I let my eyes follow the marks that extended from his forehead, along his temples, and along the tops of his ears.

As he lowered his hands, I reached forward and took his wrists. The action came with no thought. It came from an undeniable, irresistible impulse.

He did not pull back.

He let me touch him.

I turned his wrists out so that his palms were visible to me. Holes. I could see where a sharp object had been forced through the center of the palm. I thought of the nails driven through Yohanan's hands. Slowly, without a word, I pushed the sleeves of his outer garment back. Ugly bands of scars that looked like severe rope contusions marred his wrists.

My heart fluttered as I turned his wrists again, this time to view the backs of his hands. They were there, scars indicating a large puncture. As if stricken with a sudden neurological disease, my hands began to shake.

I looked down at his bare feet. As if reading my mind, he pulled his tunic up a few inches. The remains of puncture marks marred the tops of his feet, positioned between the long metatarsals. The spike would have passed between the bones in the feet. These wounds were different from what I saw inflicted upon Yohanan who had been pierced through the ankle. Yoshua had said that the Romans crucified in various ways.

Yoshua?

I looked to the side where he had been sitting moments before and saw again the empty place that he had occupied. Then I looked into the face of Jesus and saw the same eyes as Yoshua, the same smile, the same cheekbones, the same lips.

"Yoshua?"

"Yes, although most prefer Yeshua."

The shaking in my hands invaded the rest of my body. "All this time ... these days ... it has been you. I mean you are ... him."

He nodded. "Hold still, Brother Max."

Yoshua ... Yeshua ... Jesus raised scarred hands and cupped my head. Something warm, like bathwater, ran through my body.

301

The pain in my head ceased. The sharp burning in my ribs dissolved until I could feel nothing of the injuries. I felt bruises disappear, damaged lips returned to normal. In a second every wound and injury I had received at the hands of Jewish guards, a high priest, and Roman soldiers was gone.

What does a man say in a moment like that? Words had fled, leaving only raw emotion. For seconds I could not speak. I wondered if I was dreaming.

"No, Max, you're not dreaming."

I had to ask. Maybe I had been felled by a stroke; maybe my mind had detached from its moorings, but I had to ask. This moment was real to me. If I failed to ask, I would forever hate myself. "Can you bring her back? Please bring her back."

Tears immediately flooded his eyes as he gazed at me. He shook his head. "No, Max, I will not bring your daughter back."

"What kind of Savior are you that would let that happen to her?"

"The kind that let it happen to himself." Again he raised a hand, this time setting it on my shoulder. "Max, I feel every ounce of your pain, and I felt every bit of hers. She is happy now, never to be alone or in danger again. She longs to see you."

I convulsed into sobs. He let me cry for a while then said, "You need to forgive, Max."

"What? Who? Forgive the man that killed my daughter?"

"You. Max, you need to forgive yourself. You could have done nothing. You are not at fault. Evil killed your daughter. Not you."

"I should have been there. I'm her father. It's my job to protect her."

"Until I return, there will be evil. You have seen it here, and you have seen it in your time."

"So evil will always win?"

"No. When I return, things will be very different. Until then, the battle is fought by men and women of faith."

"How do we win?"

"One soul at a time, Max."

I no longer fought the tears, no longer tried to keep the over-whelming sorrow at bay. "Why me? Why bring me here to see all of this? Did you do all this just for me?"

"For you and thousands of others. This story will be told, and it will be told in your voice."

"I'm no preacher."

"That doesn't matter, Max. What you now know to be true does. You'll know what to do and when to do it. Do you trust me?"

What little strength I had gave way. What shred of bitter resolve that I had cultivated for so long, liquefied.

I collapsed to my knees.

"My own Lord, my own God."

"Blessed are you, Max Odom. Blessed of God."

From my knees I watched as the man who had been known to me as Yoshua stepped away, moved through the frozen-in-place to the woman people had started calling Imma. He gazed down at the seated woman who had reached into me and reshuffled my soul. He bent and set his forehead on hers. When he straightened, rivers of moisture ran from his eyes. He took a deep breath and returned to the front of the room. He raised both scarred hands and then stopped. He made eye contact with me.

"I'm proud to call you friend, Max, and proud to call you brother. Do not forget what you have seen."

"I won't."

A smile crossed his face. "Thank you ... pal."

303

The room twisted. The walls seemed made of rubber. A hum filled my ears. Before I could speak—

White.

chapter
21

The phone rang, reaching deep into my sleep-sheltered mind. It confused me. There are no phones in the first century.

I leaped from bed and spun on my heels, taking in my surroundings. The hotel room looked the same as when I left it ... how long ago was that?

Riiiiing.

The phone on the nightstand sounded again. I snapped it up. "What?"

"Mr. Odom? This is the front desk. I'm calling to inform you that your driver is here to pick you up."

"My driver?"

"Yes, sir. You are expecting a driver, yes?"

"Um, yes. I'll be there in a minute." I hung up and rubbed my face.

A dream? No. It couldn't be a dream. But how? When? How long?

"Settle down," I told myself. "Focus. Think one thought at a time."

I forced myself to take several deep breaths and calm my mind. My heart bubbled with conflicting emotions: joy to be back; sad to be back. How could that be?

Sitting on the bed, I tried to sort out what had happened. I recalled showering and lying down for a quick nap. Pulling the pillow to me, I touched the material. Wet. I fingered my hair. Still wet from the shower. I couldn't have been out for long.

A profound sadness washed over me. The whole time I wanted nothing more than to wake up in this room, and now that I had, I felt robbed.

So it had all been a hyper-real dream after all. I rose, looked in the mirror, and saw the same man looking back that I had seen when I first entered this place. In my dream I had been in first-century Jerusalem for several days, but my clean-shaven chin said that nothing more than minutes had passed.

I pulled a suit coat from the garment bag and exited the bedroom of the suite. Time to get back to work, to get back to reality. I had no stomach for it, but I had traveled this far on someone else's nickel; I needed to make good my commitment.

The living-room area of the suite looked as it did a few minutes ago. My kits rested on the floor ...

Something was wrong with my kits. I lifted one. I had brought two new aluminum cases packed with field evidence tools. This kit showed signs of rough treatment. Scratches marred the surface and two of the bottom corners had been dented. An image from the dream returned. When I lost my temper with Yoshua, I had dropped my kits. They had been exposed to rough treatment other times as well. But the kits I had shipped here had never been in the field.

I set one of the kits on the table and opened it, forcing my mind to recall what I had gathered in the dream. I found an evidence envelope like the one I used to hold the fiber found at the garden of Gethsemane. It had been sealed. I opened it and found nothing but a thin layer of dust. Next, I dug out the premoistened swabs I had used to test for blood at the garden and at the tree where Judas hanged himself. Where the blood had been on the cotton tip remained a dark powder. Everything I had gathered had dissolved into dust. It was useless.

No, not useless. It told me the truth. Despite how things appeared in this room, I had not been dreaming.

It had all been real. I didn't know how, but I held no doubts.

† † †

The elevator made four stops before disgorging its contents of six people into the wide hall off the lobby. I let the others exit first then lugged my cases with me into the bustling community of tourists who chatted loudly about all they had seen. Through the expansive lobby windows, I could see three tour buses, a line of taxis, and a stream of cars on the street.

Weary but excited tourists made the lobby a beehive, and I had to move slowly through the coagulation of humanity. Finally, I pressed through to the concierge, a man with droopy brown eyes, gave my name, and told him I was looking for my driver.

He nodded and pointed toward one of the windows just to the left of the door.

"The short man. The one standing at the window. He gave his name as Joseph."

I thanked the employee and started to the front of the lobby. I felt like a salmon swimming upstream. Reluctantly, the gibbering mass of travelers parted before me and I forced my way to within a few feet of the driver.

He had his back to me but I could tell that he was short, slim, and well proportioned. His hair was a dark shade of brown and trimmed close to the scalp. He wore a button-down blue shirt, black pants, and black dress shoes. He seemed untroubled by the noise, the hubbub, or the rapidly filling lobby.

"Joseph?"

He turned and smiled. The grin seemed genuine, as if he had been looking forward to this moment. I judged him to be in his midthirties. His skin was a shade darker than the bellhop and his eyes were chocolate brown. He wore no beard.

"Yes. Are you Mr. Maxwell Odom?"

"I am."

"I've been asked to drive you to the conference center. Are you ready?"

He seemed a nice enough man, but I missed Yoshua. "Yes, we can leave anytime." Someone caught my eye. "Do you mind waiting a minute?"

Joseph said he didn't.

I pushed back through the crowds until I reached the bellhop who had helped with my bags. "Hey, pal," I said.

He turned. "Mr. Odom. Is everything all right?"

"Everything is good ... great ... wonderful. Listen. I think you're right. I should see some of the sights of Jerusalem." I set my kits down and reached for my wallet. "Will you arrange for a guide?" I pulled two twenties from my billfold.

"I will see that it's done."

"Great. This is for your trouble. I'll pay the guide when I meet him. I have some time tomorrow afternoon. Think you can arrange it by then?"

"Yes, sir. Tomorrow is my day off, but I'll make sure your guide is here."

"Day off? You want to go with me?"

"I could." He seemed puzzled. Rightly so. I had given him trouble a short time ago for touching my kits.

"Great. I'll count on it. My treat. I have a story to tell you. You're not going to believe it."

"Um, yes, sir." I started to leave. "Mr. Odom?"

"Yeah?"

"If I'm not being impolite, what happened to your beautiful cases? They're damaged."

I looked down at the battered aluminum. "Beautiful, aren't they?"

Knowing the bellhop must be thinking that I had lost my mind, I pushed back through the crowd, met up with Joseph, my driver, and exited the lobby.

Outside, pedestrians, cars, and belching buses greeted me. I stopped and turned to face the hotel, all twenty-four stories of it.

"Is there something wrong, Mr. Odom?"

"No. Everything is fine."

I couldn't help feeling a little sad.

E-mail

To: Alton Gansky < alton@altongansky.com >
From: Max Odom < withheld >

Greetings Al,

Once again, I want to thank you for helping me tell my story. I'm much better at gathering evidence than at putting words on a page.

In your last e-mail you asked a few questions. What follows is my response.

1. Yes, I am well. As you know I took six months leave of absence from the department to get a few things settled. I spent the time in Phoenix with my wife. God has been good. Our relationship continues to heal, despite all I had done to injure it. Her father passed away last month, but she is dealing with that loss as well as one can expect. Losing both a daughter and her father in the same year has taken its toll, but her new faith is seeing her through it all.

2. I did return to San Diego for the trial. Homicide detectives made an arrest in Deb's murder while I was in Jerusalem. The evidence proved overwhelming, and the defense plea-bargained a life sentence to avoid execution. I'm okay with that. It wouldn't change anything if I wasn't.

3. While in San Diego I put the house up for sale. I don't think we can live there and with my father-in-law's passing we've decided to relocate to Arizona for a while and keep an eye on Mom. I'm consulting and teaching field forensics now. I like it.

4. You ask if I think anyone will believe my story. I've ceased worrying about it. Whether or not they believe what happened

to me is true is less important than that the readers believe the truth of the message. My one desire is that every reader take away the simple fact that Jesus is real and died for them just as he died for me. The evidence is overwhelming for any who will look. I came to Christ the most difficult way possible. Thankfully, most people don't have to endure what I did. Perhaps if I had been more open to the truth, I could have avoided some of what I experienced. That being said, I wouldn't change a second of my time in first-century Jerusalem. Some of what I saw still haunts me, and if I'm lucky will haunt me until the day I die.

Do me a favor, Al. Make sure the readers know that the same strength and comfort I've received from Jesus can be theirs also. Pain is pain, sorrow is sorrow, and none of us is spared that. Still, I find life not only livable but worth living since I uttered those words that Thomas did so long ago: "My own Lord, my own God."

One of the things I've learned is that Jesus is not a two-thousand-years-ago Savior. He is a today Savior, and a personal one, too. I've seen a lot of crime in my day, but the greatest crime would be for me to turn my back on the One who faced so much for me.

Stay well, Al.

In Christ,
Max Odom

Note from the Author

This is a work of fiction wrapped around historical events. I used the Bible as my guide but also had to rely on some traditional information and make certain reasoned speculations. All the events that happened to Christ accurately reflect the biblical revelation. At times I created characters to better convey the idea and tell the story. In some cases it became necessary for me to assign names to people whose names are lost to time. Hosah, Mark's father, is one example.

The ancient Jewish mind did not always think chronologically as the contemporary Western mind does. This is especially true in the biblical accounts of the life, teachings, and actions of Jesus Christ where the importance of teaching takes precedence over chronology. Trying, for example, to perfect a timeline for the resurrection appearances of Christ is daunting. The facts remain the facts, however.

In an effort to instill a sense of realism, Bible verses in this work are not direct quotes based on modern translations. Many sources were used to formulate and translate the original languages into English.

May this book help you find the truth that Max Odom found in his unique adventure.

Blessings,
Alton Gansky

Notes

Chapter 2

1. Based on *PC Study Bible, Complete Reference Library 4.0* (Interlinear Transliterated Bible). Copyright © 1994, 2003 by Biblesoft.
2. Based on Exodus 13:9.
3. Psalm 25:2–3. Based on the *PC Study Bible*.
4. Based on Psalm 25:4–6.

Chapter 3

1. Based on Mark 14:14.
2. Mark 14:13.
3. Mark 14:51.

Chapter 4

1. John F. Walvoord, Roy B. Zuck, and Dallas Theological Seminary

Faculty, *The Bible Knowledge Commentary, New Testament: An Exposition of the Scriptures* (Wheaton, IL: Victor Books, 1983).
2. 587 BC by Nebuchadnezzar.
3. 19 BC.
4. AD 65.
5. Speculation.
6. Based on Matthew 26:36–37.
7. James S. Jeffers, *Greco-Roman World of the New Testament Era* (Downers Grove, IL: InterVarsity Press, 1999), 43.
8. Matthew 26:36–37; Mark 14:32–33.
9. Based on Matthew 26:38–39.
10. Based on Mark 14:35.
11. www.crimelibrary.com/criminal_mind/forensics/serology/3.html?sect=21.
12. Based on Luke 22:44.
13. www.ncbi.nlm.nih.gov/entrez/query.fcgi?cmd=Retrieve&db=pubmed&dopt=Abstract&list_uids=8982961.
14. Mark 14:41.

Chapter 5
1. Based on John 18:1.
2. Based on John 18:1.
3. Matthew 26:49.
4. Based on Luke 22:48.
5. Matthew 26:52–54.
6. *Malchus* means "king" or "reigning" (D. R. W. Wood, et al., *New Bible Dictionary*, 3rd ed. [Downers Grove, IL: InterVarsity Press, 1996]). His name is mentioned only in John. His healing is mentioned only in Luke. Only John and Luke mention that it is his right ear that is severed. This was Jesus' last miracle before the cross.

Chapter 6
1. No biblical evidence for Mark's father's name.
2. H. L. Willmington, *Willmington's Book of Bible Lists* (Wheaton, IL: Tyndale House Publishers, 1987).

313

3. Based on Isaiah 55:8–9.

Chapter 7
1. Based on Matthew 27:5.
2. Based on Acts 1:18–19.
3. Based on Matthew 16:16.
4. John 11:27.
5. D. R. W. Wood, et al., *New Bible Dictionary,* 3rd ed. (Downers Grove, IL: InterVarsity Press, 1996).
6. Matthew 26:6–13.
7. John 12:1–8.
8. Matthew 26:14–16.
9. Matthew 5:39.
10. Matthew 5:41.

Chapter 8
1. Matthew 21:9; Mark 11:9–10; Luke 19:37–38; John 12:13.
2. Matthew 21:12–13.
3. Matthew 21:14.
4. John 18:20.
5. John 18:22.

Chapter 9
1. John 19:26–27.
2. Matthew 26:45–46.

Chapter 10
1. Flavius Josephus, *Antiquities* 20.200, in *The Works of Josephus,* trans. William Whiston (Peabody, MA: Hendrickson Publishers, 1987).
2. Numbers 11:16–24.
3. Based on John 15:13.
4. Some research shows the council chamber on the north wall.
5. Based on Hebrews 11:1.
6. Naqdimon ben Gorion is mentioned in the Talmud (Ketuboth 65a,

66b). Some suspect that he is the Nicodemus of the Bible; however, a direct proof cannot be made.

7. John 11:50.
8. John 3:1–21.
9. Based on John 3:2.
10. Based on John 3:5–6.
11. Based on John 3:14–15.
12. Based on John 3:16–18.
13. Luke 22:63.
14. Based on Mark 14:58.
15. Mark 14:61.
16. Based on Daniel 7:13–14.
17. Based on Psalm 110:1.
18. Luke 22:66.

Chapter 11
1. Luke 8:3.
2. Luke 8:1–3.

Chapter 12
1. John 19:31.
2. John 19:10.
3. John 18:28.
4. John 18:30.
5. Luke 23:12.
6. Matthew 27:19. Tradition names her Claudia Procula (sometimes Procla). In one tradition she becomes a believer.
7. Matthew 27:24.
8. Matthew 27:19.

Chapter 14
1. Luke 23:28.

Chapter 15
1. Matthew 27:57.

2. Matthew 27:58; Luke 23:52ff; John 19:38.

3. John 19:39.

Chapter 16

1. Mark 16:1–2.

2. Matthew 28:2–3.

3. Matthew 28:5–7.

4. Mark 16:5–7.

5. Luke 24:4.

6. Luke 24:11.

7. John 20:11–18.

Chapter 17

1. John 18:28.

2. Matthew 27:54.

3. Matthew 27:54.

4. Matthew 28:2-4.

5. Matthew 28:12.

6. Matthew 28:14.

Chapter 19

1. Matthew 1:20; 2:13; 2:19; 2:22.

2. Luke 1:26ff.

3. Luke 1:37.

Chapter 20

1. Luke 2:42ff.

2. John 2:1ff.

3. Based on John 20:25.

4. Based on John 20:27ff.

Bibliography

Jeffers, James S. *Greco-Roman World of the New Testament Era.* Downers Grove, IL: InterVarsity Press, 1999.

Josephus, Flavius. *Antiquities.*

PC Study Bible, Complete Reference Library 4.0 (Interlinear Transliterated Bible). Copyright © 1994, 2003 by Biblesoft.

Walvoord, John F., Roy B. Zuck, and Dallas Theological Seminary Faculty. *The Bible Knowledge Commentary, New Testament: An Exposition of the Scriptures.* Wheaton, IL: Victor Books, 1983.

Willmington, H. L. *Willmington's Book of Bible Lists.* Wheaton, IL: Tyndale House Publishers, 1987.

Wood, D. R. W., et al. *New Bible Dictionary,* 3rd ed. Downers Grove, IL: InterVarsity Press, 1996.

About the Author

Alton Gansky is a full-time writer living in Southern California. The author of over twenty-five books, he specializes in novels and biblical nonfiction. He holds two earned degrees in biblical studies and served as senior pastor in three Baptist churches during the last twenty-two years. He is a frequent speaker at writer's conferences and churches. Readers can learn more about Alton at www.altongansky.com.